William McGonagall Meets George Gershwin

To Adam

Spike Milligan

and

Jack Hobbs

1988

William McGonagall Meets George Gershwin

A Scottish Fantasy

SPIKE MILLIGAN
and
JACK HOBBS

Michael Joseph   London

MICHAEL JOSEPH LTD
Published by the Penguin Group
27 Wrights Lane, London W8 5TZ, England
Viking Penguin Inc., 40 West 23rd Street, New York, New York 10010, USA
Penguin Books Australia Ltd, Ringwood, Victoria, Australia
Penguin Books Canada Ltd, 2801 John Street, Markham, Ontario, Canada L3R 1B4
Penguin Books (NZ) Ltd, 182–190 Wairau Road, Auckland 10, New Zealand

Penguin Books Ltd, Registered Offices: Harmondsworth, Middlesex, England

First published 1988

Typeset in Palatino by
Goodfellow & Egan, Cambridge
Made and printed in Great Britain by
Butler & Tanner Ltd, Frome, Somerset

A CIP catalogue record for this book is available from the British Library

ISBN 0-7181-3127-4

FOREWORD

I'm not sure how to describe this book, so I will describe it as I'm not sure how to describe it. See what I mean. I have been a lifelong (when else) fan of William McGonagall and his unintentionally funny poetry.

Apart from that, the man seems to have been a one-man DIY disaster.

It started with his Irish parents, after the potato famine. When all the starving Irish were making for America, his family went the other way, escaping from the poverty of Ireland for the dire poverty of Scotland. Being fascinated by the all-time loser, I have always wanted to use him as a central character, in this case in a timeless capsule in which his friend is the late George Gershwin. Why Gershwin? Why not?

With this in mind, I contacted Jack Hobbs, friend, pianist and fellow manic depressive. We decided that whenever either of us was on a down we would write 'something' in book form. The result was this book. Both of us must have a cruel streak in our nature, as we seemed to thrive on the misfortunes that we created not only for William McGonagall, but for all who appear in this book. We decided not to be bound by any rules, social or grammatical. We ignored all the concepts of the traditional story line. With this in mind, and with the ghosts of *Finnegans Wake*, *Tristram Shandy* and Rabelais, we decided to write what made us laugh, and laugh we did. In every case, it shook off the depression, so *we* thought it funny, but alas it baffled the publishers. All at Michael Joseph admitted that they understood it not. Poor Alan Brooke was so distressed he said the company were willing to pay for us to see a psychiatrist and spend a month under sedation at the Priory, Roehampton. Whenever Hobbs and I visited the offices of Michael Joseph, the entire staff locked themselves in their rooms. For weeks we communicated through the keyholes, telling them that the book was a breakthrough in comic writing. I can still hear the sobs of despair as they pushed tranquillizers under the door with a pound note.

So, dear reader, we start at a disadvantage. Will this be the first book in publishing history that no one will understand? If so, that is exactly what we planned. To us it is the first freefall comic fantasy in which the subconscious mind is the author. But for a sudden attack of piles that struck down Jack Hobbs, the book would have been longer. I waited for his recovery, but when I last knocked on the door he was still in there screaming, so I told him the book was finished, but he said he wasn't. So with him still wasn't I leave the reader to explore the pages. Remember, a man can't have everything. Where would he put it?

Spike Milligan
Spinster of this Parish
1988

The story so far, now read on. Rumours of William Topaz McGonagall's death were rife until he actually died. He was buried in a pauper's grave. The pauper's name was Eric Jones who was very annoyed at having to give it up. The *Glasgow Bugle* claimed that the McGonagall funeral was a hoax. McGonagall's relatives said it wasn't a hoax it was a funeral.

The authors of this book are very anxious to prove the influence that William McGonagall had on the late George Gershwin before his hoax. Of course, he had no influence on the earlier one. Many readers will ask, 'How did the great McGonagall come into contact with the great Gershwishin?' Good for them. In fact George Gershwishin was a name that Gershwin adopted during overdrafts.

The year – 1918.
The place – Tin Pan Alley.
A place where unemployed musicians made tin pans, which led directly to World War Two, with advance bookings for World War Three. Readers may now collect £200 and go. If you are from Warsaw there is a pole tax. Now read on.

To the birth of McGonagall – whose first words were, 'You have ruined my breakfast egg.' The question is Why?

Little was known since that day until we find him lying in a debtors' cell as he had lied all the way through the trial. On his release he took up residence on a landing. He there heard the unmistakable strains of George Gershwin which he mistook for a Mrs Grimshaw. Yet the unmistakable strains he heard *were* of the late Gershwin, straining up the stairs with an unmistakable grand piano on his back, in order to fulfil the last request of a man about to be hung, one Dr Crippen by name.

When Gershwin asked one Dr Crippen by name what he'd like to hear, one Crippen said, 'I'd like to hear my death sentence commuted to life imprisonment of anything up to a week.'

7

The strains of George Gershwin carrying his piano upstairs

Gershwin said in American, 'Say, buddy, I don't know that tune.'

'Very well,' said Crippen as the hangman adjusted the rope around his neck.

('Not too tight for you?' said the concerned hangman in brackets.)

One doctor named Crippen then continued, 'I'd like the last post.'

Gershwin said in American, 'I'm sorry, bud, that went half an hour ago.'

Thus, on the landing, McGonagall heard for the second time

8

the ongoing strains of Gershwin as he humped the unmistakable piano back downstairs again sounding like Mrs Grimshaw.

As Gershwin passed, McGonagall said, 'Gie us a tune, Jamie.'

At that moment there was a splintering crash as one Crippen's body thundered through the ceiling past McGonagall through the floor on his way to the basement.

'The string's too long!' screamed Crippen as he plummeted eight floors into the Prison Warden's office where he was arrested for not having a dog, not having a dog licence, and having a photograph of a nude cat.

McGonagall was also immediately arrested for aiding Crippen's escape along with not having a dog, a dog licence and having a photograph of a nude cat.

Fascinated, Gershwin waited outside McGonagall's cell. Inside McGonagall was about to poem.

'Ooooooooooooooooooh,' went convict McGonagall. And then 'Ooooooooooooooooooh' yet again.

There then continued a series of 'Ooooooooooooooooooohs.'

'By golly,' said the listening American Gershwin who was leaning forward with his ear cupped in his hand in American. 'This guy's got something,' he said. He was right, it was the letter 'O'. He had picked up this Ooooooh! when he caught it in a rat trap.

McGonagall continued poeming:

Ooooooooooooooooh, 'twas a terrible thing!
Tae see Dr Crippen hurtle past on a piece of string
As I watched him hurtle past and the string unravel.
I thought tae masel' there must be an easier way tae travel.
I mean, as he hurtled past going below
He didn't stop to say Hello.
The man seemed tae be in a awfu' hurry
But then after all that's his worry.

This free-flowing verse did not escape George Gershwin's notice which, together with another notice, read, 'Keep away from this prison unless you are a convict.'

'Are you still there, Jamie?' said McGonagall

'Am I still where?' replied the straining Gershwishin.

'There,' said McGonagall.

'There *where*?' said Gershwin.

Dr Crippen with the string too long crashing through to McGonagall

'All right, ye awkward bugger,' said McGonagall, 'are ye on the phone?'

'No,' said Gershwin, 'I'm on the pavement. What are *you* on?'

'Bread and water,' said McGonagall.

'OK, buddy,' said the late George McGershwin. 'Look me up when you get out or look out when I get up.'

At that moment the string went taut as Crippen was hauled up again through eight floors. 'This is the second time today,' he said in throttled tones.

'Practice makes perfect, Jamie,' McGonagall teased him. 'You see, they'll get it right one day.'

'That's what I'm worried about,' came the fading voice of Crippen.

The cell door opened. 'Have you got a naked woman in here?' said the Jailer.

'Nae,' said McGonagall.

'Blast,' said the Jailer. 'I've had no luck at all today, I'm going to ask for a transfer.'

'Don't worry,' said McGonagall, 'I've got one here' and stuck it on his forehead.

'Thank you, Scottish man,' said the Jailer. 'This could mean promotion for you, what's your number?'

'Convict 99,' said McGonagall.

'You see,' said the disappointed Jailer, 'tomorrow you'll be convict 100.'

A song sheet landed on the flae of the cell with a note attached, E flat. 'Write words for this,' it said. 'Signed, George Gershwin's office.'

On the stroke of 1928, McGonagall appeared at the door of signed Gershwin's office. In one hand he clutched the original song sheet and in the other the freshly prised open window of his prison cell. 'Hello, Jamie, it worked,' said McGonagall with a sly nod and a wink, the tapping of his nose with his middle finger accidentally releasing the heavy-barred prison window on to his foots. There followed a high-pitched Scottish scream.

Clutching his injured tootsie, he followed with a display of rapid one-legged Scottish leaping around Gershwin's office.

'Gee whizz, these Scots are natural dancers,' said McGershwin.

'Ma tootsie, ma wee tootsie,' wailed the Scottish poet.

11

In a flash Gershwin was at the piano singing, 'Toot-toot-tootsie, ma wee tootsie, goodbye.'

It had resulted in Gershwin giving birth to the blues while McGonagall gave birth to the browns.

By day two the McGonagall's brown dancing frenzy had not abated. When Gershwin returned to his office that morning his office was entirely brown as apparently it had hit the fan. McGonagall was in the last agonised stages of his leaping. His kilt had slipped to position four, revealing what looked like Groucho Marx without the glasses.

'I'll say this for you,' said Gershwin.

'There's no need,' said McGonagall, 'I can say it myself' and collapsed to the flae.

Crippen crashing through Ziegfeld's office ceiling as he and McGonagall are listening to George Gershwin

The door opened and Florenz Ziegfeld entered, a man quick to clinch a deal. He saw the prostrate McGonagall and said, 'I'll clinch that deal.'

McGonagall handed him the prison window and contracts were exchanged. What was written may to you, dear reader, seem trivia, which shows sound judgement. The combination of McGonagall, Ziegfeld, George Gershwin and McGonagall made an infallible quartet. Indeed, throughout that day, not one of them fell down. The showbiz know-how of Ziegfeld, the straining piano-carrying qualities of Gershwin added to McGonagall and McGonagall made a total of four. No matter where they stood in the room, it was always four. Even when Ziegfeld hung out of the window, Gershwin counted himself twice and the answer was still four.

'What about me,' wailed Ziegfeld from outside.

'You don't count, buddy,' said Gershwin.

'Yes I do count, buddy,' said Ziegfeld, and counted him. 'Listen, one, two, three, four, five, buddy.'

'It's nae gude,' said McGonagall. 'It's getting worse, counting buddy, there's now five of us.'

There was a shock in store. A sixth person was on his way: Crippen crashed yet again through the ceiling.'Hello,' he said as he flashed past and down through the floor.

'Och, he's coming round to my way of greeting,' said McGonagall, finally lowering his injured tootsie to the flae.

'Can I come in now?' said Ziegfeld.

'What for?' said Gershwin.

'For about an hour,' said Ziegfeld.

CHAPTER EIGHT

Gershwin was lamenting the old days. 'New York isn't what it used to be, buddy,' he said.

'Oh,' said McGonagall from the bread cupboard. 'What did it used to be?'

'It used to be a Red Indian leather banjo factory,' said Gershwin.

This was too much for McGonagall, who fainted and fell off. 'Here comes the flae,' he moaned.

He looked lovely in the moonlight! Mickey Rooney rushed in and said, 'Hey, fellas, why don't we do a musical called *Strike Up the Flae*?'

In a frenzy, the late George Gershwin wrote a series of variations: 'Strike Up the Pianist'; 'The Man I Strike'; 'A Striking Day in London Town'; and 'Just the Way You Strike Tonight'; 'Strike Up the Flae'; 'The Way You Wear Your Flae'.

Outside, hanging from the window, Ziegfeld was addressed by the spectators. 'Why can't you hire an office like other great Ziegfelds?'

'Hire an office?' he groaned. 'I couldn't get one much higher than this.'

'Why aren't you inside, then?' said the spectators.

'Because,' said the straining Ziegfeld, 'the rents are cheaper outside. I've only been hanging out here for four hours and I'm already into profit.'

'Oh yes, indeed you're a brilliant businessman and we never thought of you this way,' said the awed spectators.

'That's because you've never been down this way,' said Ziegfeld. In the office, McGonagall was saying, 'I wonder what the wee Pope John is doing?'

'I'm not doing anything,' said Pope John. A total lie: he was, at that moment, trying to raise an Armenian saxophonist from the dead using Red Indian leather banjo therapy.

'Och,' said McGonagall wearily. 'Have ye ever felt the story slipping away from you?'

A prophetic remark. At that moment, Ziegfeld felt the thirteenth storey slipping away. Miraculously, that terrible fall of a hundred and eighty feet did him no injury, it was the pavement that did it.

'Oh,' said the spectators as Ziegfeld went splat! 'It's five thirty, he must be finished for the day!'

Not only was he finished for the day, he was finished for good.

Will anyone ever forget his massive funeral? Yes, Mrs Nora Brunge of Cleethorpes, she was one; also, Terence Throck of Brockley, he was another one.

'What's the price of bacon?' said a man in a certain position.

'Well, it depends if it's the painter or the pig,' said a man in another position.

14

'What's the difference?' said the man in a certain position.
'Well, one hunts for truffles in the forest with his hooter,' said
the man in another position.
'What about the other one?' said the man in the certain
position.
'Well, he doesn't,' said the man moving to an entirely new
position.

CHAPTER NINE

Indeed, Ziegfeld was soon forgotten, especially by Mrs Nora
Brunge of Cleethorpes and Terence Throck of Brockley, both of
whom were in a clear lead among those who had forgotten
Ziegfeld.

CHAPTER TEN

An exhausted leather-banjo-playing Pope John leaned over the
dead Armenian saxophone player and shook his head sadly.
Rattle, rattle, rattle went the bits inside. 'It'sa no good. If he'sa
notta dead, he'sa deaf,' he said.
'Perhaps,' said wee McGonagall, 'it's the wrang banjo.'
'Thissa banjo does notta go wrang,' said the Pope. 'Itta go
plonk plonk.'
'What's going on?' said the Armenian saxophone player
rising from the dead.
'He is,' said the Pope. 'He is going on about the wrang banjo,
didn't you hear him?'
'No,' said the Armenian, 'I'm deaf and why are you both
persecuting me like this?'
The Pope threw his hands in the air and caught them as they
came down.
'There's ingratitude for you,' said Pope Pius XI who had
worked his way up from Pope Pius X into Division One where
he played Arsenal in the Milk Cup but when he won it it was
empty. 'You've worked with Gershwin, haven't you?' said Pope
Pius XI.

'Och aye,' said McGonagall I. 'We've got a lot going for us, the police for a start.'

'Look,' said Pope Pius XI, 'it's bargain week at the Vatican. You look like a sporting gentleman, how would you like a third off the Last Rites? I mean, you never know,' he said, running a stethoscope over McGonagall I.

'I'm glad I can't hear any of this,' said the Armenian saxophone player and returned to the dead until the invention of Swedish relief massage.

So far, dear reader, you will be aware of the ability of the authors to dispense with distance and time, which shows sound judgement.

'Ah, those days have gone,' said Gershwin from inside his piano.

'What days have gone?' said McGonagall from inside the bread cupboard.

'Well, yesterday for a start,' said Gershwin.

'Och, so you started yesterday, then?' said McGonagall.

'Yes,' said Gershwin. 'I like an early start. That's how I got here so soon.'

'You got here yesterday, then?'

'Yes, and I got there from the day before,' said Gershwin.

'The day before what?' said McGonagall.

'The day before yesterday,' said Gershwin. 'And while I'm on about it, what are you doing in that bread cupboard?'

'It's part of my divorce settlement,' said William Topaz McGonagall.

'I didn't know you were married,' said Gershwin.

'I wasn't,' said McGonagall. 'Just divorced, I couldn't afford both. And now, have I got a lyric for you, Jamie.'

'I give up,' said Gershwin. 'Have you got a lyric for me?' he said, climbing out of the piano and on to the stool. He then drew the stool up to the divorce-settlement bread cupboard and ran his fingers up the bagels and down the croissants.

'Och mon alive,' said McGonagall from the adoration position. 'Is there nae end to this great mon's virtuosity?'

There was, July 1935 when he died.

This date, dear reader, might be wrong, but somebody certainly died in July 1935, for instance Jack Legs of 22 Gabriel Street, Honour Oak Park.

Gershwin and McGonagall arguing

17

Gershwin was in his pram seated at the divorce-settlement bread cupboard. 'OK, McGon, these lyrics, shoot,' said Gershwin.

Bang! McGonagall pulled the trigger and Gershwin crashed to the floor clutching his shoulder. 'You dirty rat, you,' he cried. In a tartan flash, McGonagall was on the phone to James Cagney. 'Have I got a line for you, Jamie,' he said. 'Get this – that's another fine mess you've got me into, Stanley.'

Down the phone came the sound of a leather banjo therapy strumming over the dead body of a deaf Armenian saxophone player awaiting relief massage.

'You gotta the wrong number,' said the Pope's voice.

'Is thatta the Pope XI?' said McGonagall's voice.

'No, this justa the Pope'sa voice. The Pope, he'sa out shopping for true relics of the Holy Cross.'

Meanwhile, Gershwin had recovered from the wound in his shoulder, and was again running his fingers up and down the bagels and croissants.

'That's a great turn,' said McGonagall. 'Grab these lyrics,' he said, swallowing an arpeggio of bread rolls.

'I've heard of music being the food of love,' said Gershwin, 'but never music being the love of food.'

As McGonagall sang:

A foggy day in/on the bridge over the silvery Tay
It had me low/and its beautiful arches in grand array
I viewed the morning/as the storm fiend roared over head
The British Museum had lost/over the bridge the train sped
How long I wondered/would this bridge last
The age of miracles is/did resist the wind's blast
For suddenly I saw/the whole Tay Bridge fall at six o'clock
And through foggy London Town/the news was a great shock
The sun was shining/on the ruins of the bridge of the silvery
  Tay.

Immediately, William Topaz McGonagall broke open a bottle of Veuve Cliquot and drained it in a flash.

'Where,' said George Gershwishin holding out an empty glass 'where did you get that?'

Topaz winked. 'Courtesy of the authors and there's mair where that came from.' In a flash he broke open a second bottle and downed it in one gulp. 'Och, mon,' he said. 'Great stuff.' He

18

was thinking of Molly Grotts, who indeed was a great stuff. 'Have ye ever strangled an ostrich?' said McGonagall.

'As far as I can remember, no,' said Gershwin.

'Och then, cast your minces on this,' said McGonagall.

Gershwin thumbed through the book entitled *Ostriches I Have Strangled*. Gershwin read aloud: 'St Paul to the Corinthians, Francis Day and Hunter – Verily I say unto you, thou shalt not strangle an ostrich. V-Day – a damsel in distress, 1937. Music by George Gershwin, the late Judas Iscariot, lyrics by Ira Gershwin and Company Ltd. Additional ostrich-strangling by William McGonagall.'

'Och nae,' said William Topaz McGonagall. 'That's the Jewish version – it'll nae go doon with Scots wahae where Wallace bled at the McGreen's Playhouse in Glasgae. It'll have tae be Queen Victoria in *Damsel in Distress* on the bridge over the silvery Tay by Sir Harry Laundry, George McGershwin, Jock Iscariot and lyrics and Ostrich-strangling by William T. McGonagall.'

'What's the "T" stand for?' said Gershwin on top of a song.

'Och, the tea stands for about three minutes to allow it to infuse then a fine time can be had by all.'

Dismounting his song, Gershwin said, 'You're going thin on the bottom.'

'Aye, the thinness is travelling down ma whole body. You see, George,' said Topaz, 'I've nae eaten a square meal this year, what kept me alive was the circular ones.'

Gershwin took him back to his digs. 'Here,' he said and gave him his pussy cat.

'Delicious,' said McGonagall. 'What was his name?'

'Rufus, but it's no good calling him that now, his miaowing days are over,' said Gershwin.

'Och,' said McGonagall, putting his hand on Gershwin's shoulder for a rest. 'There's many a kitty catty cannot mair the nicht.'

'Never mind that,' said Gershwin. 'You've just eaten my fucking cat. I only gave him to you for a stroke.'

'Och well,' said McGonagall. 'It's a bad stroke of luck for him. Now, what's the time?'

'Tempus fugit,' said Gershwin with a quick movement.

'Tempus fugit, my arse,' said McGonagall. 'That's my watch you just pocketed.'

'Well, it is a pocket watch,' said Gershwin and added, 'It's just an old Jewish joke and what can I play for you?'

'Can you play any dinner?' said McGonagall.

'Yes,' said Gershwin. 'But no shellfish, you see, I'm a Jew.'

'A Jew?' said McGonagall.

'Adieu,' said a French maritime inspector.

'See what you've done,' said Gershwin angrily as he launched into 'Sausage and Chips, Two Slices of Bread and Tea'. 'That'll be one pound thirty,' he said, logging it up on the Jewish piano.

'Cheap at half the price,' said McGonagall and gave him half the price.

'Well,' said Gershwin, checking it for the fiftieth time, 'I must get there before the banks close.'

'Och, those days are gone,' said McGonagall. 'I'll make a way through this window for you,' he said, diving through and shattering the glass.

As he lay dazed and bleeding on the pavement, a cry from a passing man of 'Alley Oop' didn't so much as raise a smile from the recumbent McGonagall.

'Ooooooooooh, what are you doing here?' said the milling crowd of spectators.

'I've broken my leg in three places,' said McGonagall as he groaned from the recumbent position.

'You shouldn't go to those places,' said the resident Ku Klux Klan Doctor. 'Here,' he said, 'put this black greasepaint on and stand by that fiery cross. I'm having a few friends in for a barbecue.'

'Och,' thought McGonagall. 'I smell a rat.'

'Good,' said the Ku Klux Klan doctor, laying McGonagall on the barbecue. 'While you're smelling that rat, can you also smell this dog, this cat and this racoon?'

'I smell cooking,' said McGonagall. 'And it's me,' he added, beating out the flames and beating the pursuing Ku Klux Klan to the horizon which he bolted as he went through.

'Is this horizon closed?' said the Ku Klux Klan as they hammered on it.

'No,' said James Hilton. 'It's lost!'

'Oh no it isn't,' said the Ku Klux Klan.

'*Oh yes it is,*' said James Hilton.'

'*Oh no it isn't,*' said the Ku Klux Klan.

'*Oh yes it is,*' said the author Hilton.'

'*Oh no it isn't,*' said the Ku Klux Klan.

On the other side of the horizon McGonagall had collided with the Lord Mayor of Chicago, which shows how quickly promotion can come to an ordinary blacksmith.

'Welcome to Chicago, buddy,' said the ordinary blacksmith mayor.

'You're welcome to it, too,' said McGonagall as he curtseyed and showed just the tip. Then he started to poem.

OOOOOOOOOOOOooooooooooooooh, wonderful Lord Mayor of
    Chicago
Who has no doubt travelled here by Wells Fargo.
That is a good way to go to and fro.

'Hey,' said Mickey Rooney, stepping out of a retirement, 'let's put on a show.'

'Nae,' said the starving Scot. 'I'd rather put on weight.'

'Weight here?' said Mickey Marooney.

'All right, I'll wait here,' said McGonagall. 'It's better than Fife and better than six, seven and eight.'

From behind the lost horizon came the angry cry from the Ku Klux Klansmen. 'Are you coming to be burnt as a nigger or not?'

McGonagall, no fool in matters of business, cried, 'What's in it for me, buddy?'

'There's nothing in it,' cried the Ku Klux Klan. '*You* are in it.'

'I'll have to see a marriage guidance counsellor,' said McGonagall. 'Marriage is not be taken lightly especially when you are being set fire to.'

'Oooooooooh no you're not,' said the Ku Klux Klan.

'*Oh yes I am,*' said McGonagall.

'*Oh no you're not,*' moaned the Ku Klux Klan.

'*Oh yes I am,*' said William Topaz McGonagall and was.

It was the end of a long hard day and McGonagall's parts were steaming and in great disarray. He jumped on to a passing Judy Garland tram. Clang-clang-clang, it went.

'Hey, let's put on a tram,' said a passing Mickey Marooney, Maroney, Mariney, Mackarooney, Morany, Mickey Rooney.

'Och, make up your mind, man,' said McGonagall, stepping off and into another one.

'Ah, there you are,' said Gershwin, and there he was. 'I've been searching this tram for you all day.'

21

'I was hiding in the night,' said McGonagall with a knowing wink.

'Did you know that Abraham Lincoln was buried in this tram?' said Gershwin.

'I am *not* Jack Johnson,' said the tram conductor.

'Ah,' said Topaz, wiping the smile off his face and his face off his hand, 'then you must be somebody else! I'll not keep you a moment,' he said, consulting a giant manual. McGonagall read furiously from the giant manual.

'It's no good looking in dat,' said the not Jack Johnson. 'I'm not a giant, I'm a part-time dwarf and MGM lion-trainer who'll only roar through the ring if I'm there to stimulate his erogenous zones. Would anyone like a demonstration?' he said, holding up a red-hot toasting fork.

'I'll give it a go,' said McGonagall.

In a flash the not Jack Johnson stuffed the toasting fork up McGonagall's kilt. To the smell of burning hairs, McGonagall gave off a great roar.

'You see,' said the not Jack Johnson. 'It works.'

'Quick,' said Mickey Rooney, 'let's put on a show.'

'Never mind that,' said McGonagall. 'Put on a bandage.'

The room filled with the smell of scorched Scottish scrotum.

'This is ma 107th day without a nude cat,' said McGonagall. He started to poem.

> Oooooooooooh terrible day with nae fude
> Doing without it they say wil dae ye nae gude.
> As for days without moggies and reaching 107,
> If it goes on like this it willnae be long before it
>   reaches moggies 111.

'Excuse me,' said a Japanese, 'is this the way to Taunton?'

'Well, it's one way to Taunton,' said McGonagall and strangled the nip's ostrich.

He continued to poem:

> Oooooooooooh as for the not Jack Johnson, who set fire
>   tae ma scrotum
> You should have seen the awful letter I wrote him.
> Though it's awful to have to have one's cobblers so sore
> That I don't want him to do it any more.

But I've proved tae masel' that like a lion I can roar
And I thought that the door to employment would be open
  for ever more.
Alas for employment – for weeks now I've been trying.
It's sad to say that not many people want someone with
  swollen balls who can roar like a lion.

'Excuse me,' said a man with a piece of rope round his neck
trailing along in the dust. 'Have you seen a hangman pass this
way?'

'I recognise you,' said Topaz McGonagall. 'You're the late one

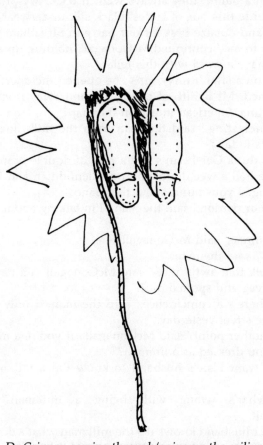

Dr Crippen coming through/going up the ceiling

23

Dr Charles Crippen, last known address care of the ceiling.'

'Yes, I'm getting fed up,' said Crippen. 'They've been hanging me now for three years. I can't see the funny side any more.'

'What you need,' said McGonagall, 'is a sympathetic judge who will reduce your sentence.'

'And,' said Crippen, 'you need someone to reduce the swelling.'

There came a tug on the string. Up went Dr Crippen.

'There he goes again,' said Gershwin.

There came a banging on the door.

'Quick,' said Gershwin. 'It's the bailiffs. Hide the piano.'

'Och, let that be a lesson,' said McGonagall. 'Never borrow a piano from a bailiff, they always want it back. My problem is where to hide this box of ladies' black silk underwear, fishnet stockings and outsize bras for our party in Streatham tonight. Leave this to me,' continued McGonagall, holding up a pound note. 'I'll have a word with this fellar.'

Putting on a sign 'I HAVE AIDS', he opened the door. 'Are ye nae ashamed, Mr Bailiff, of taking a piano away from a man who's putting American music on the map?'

'Very interesting,' said the man from the milk float. 'How many pints today?'

'So far I think Gershwin's had a pint of double brandy, and maself I've had a wee double pint o' Glenfiddich and I'm glad ye've changed your mind about the piano.'

'I beg your pardon,' said the man. 'I'm talking about pints of milk.'

'Well, dinnae,' said McGonagall.

'Dinner?' said the man.

'Och well, that awfu' nice,' said McGonagall. 'I'll have roast beef, two veg and spotted dick.'

'Now, there's a coincidence,' said the man. 'I only spotted Dick in the street yesterday.'

'Och, another point,' said McGonagall. 'If you're a milkman, why are you dressed as a fireman?'

'I don't want Elsie's husband to know I'm a milkman,' he said.

'And what's wrang with being a milkman?' asked McGonagall.

'Well, her husband knows it's the milkman what's doing it to her and I don't want him to find out,' said the milkman.

'Do you ever go to fires?' said McGonagall.

'Yes,' said the man, 'but I go dressed as the milkman.'

'Why?' said the innocent McGonagall.

'Well, because Rita's husband knows that it's a fireman what's giving it to her and I don't want him to find out.'

'Hoots mon och aye,' said the innocent McGonagall. 'You must present a strange figure holding a hose and squirting water and dressed as a milkman.'

'I don't,' said the man, 'I squirt milk.'

'For God's sake, hurry up out there,' said George Gershwin. 'I swear on this Golders Green Bible there is no piano in here. There's a cheque in the post, my word is my bond, I have unlimited sums of money, there is no end to my wealth, I own ten Rolls-Royces, a string of racehorses, I own the string outright. Best of all, there is no piano in this room, I repeat, there is no piano in this room. There is also no furniture, no carpet or curtains, no pictures and no Anna Neagle, but most of all there is no piano. Listen,' he said and played several chords. 'See,' he said. 'How your imagination is deceiving you.'

'Who's that?' said the milk-fireman. (Who, dear reader, was also an amateur psychiatrist and owned several bicycles outright.)

'That man,' said the psychiatrist, making out a bill if paid within seven days thirty per cent off or within thirty days seven per cent off, 'sounds like a man who is about to be dispossessed of a grand piano by a bailiff.'

'You're entirely wrong,' said an annoyed McGonagall. 'Yon man is a two-foot Armenian freak who's only utterance is –'

'There's no piano in this room,' said Gershwin.

McGonagall struck a pose.

'For God's sake, help me to get this piano under the floorboards,' hissed Gershwin.

'There he goes again,' said McGonagall. 'He's getting worse. I'll have to up his dose.'

'Up yours,' said the milkman.

Again came the crazed voice from the room. 'There's no fucking piano in this room,' it went.

'I suppose,' said the milk-fireman, 'not having Anna Neagle in the room doesn't help.'

'Och, she was never much help, even when she was here,' said McGonagall. 'She fed the rabbits and that's about all.'

McGonagall suddenly grinned. 'Good heavens,' he said, 'look at the time.'

The milk-fireman cast a glance at his wristwatch.

'There,' grinned McGonagall. 'That gave you a brief change of scene, laddie,' he said. 'Incidentally, while you're down there, can you tell us the time?'

'For God's sake,' hissed George Gershwin, 'help me to get this piano into the ironong cupboard.'

'The ironong cupboard?' queried McGonagall.

'It's a spelling mistake, you twit,' said Gershwin.

'Och, he wants me to help him put his piano into a spelling mistake,' said McGonagall. 'It used to be the floorboards. Obviously his condition has worsened considerably.'

'Up your dose,' said the milk-fireman.

CHAPTER VIIII

'There's nae time tae waste, we must set sail at once. Cast off fore and aft.' So they cast off everybody fore and aft. This included the milk-fireman who went through a porthole. Captain McGonagall RN shouted a nautical farewell – 'Milkman, keep those bottles quiet.'

'That sounds like a cue for a song,' said Gershwin and wrote 'Embraceable You', to which McGonagall added:

Embrace me, my sweet embraceable, and milkman keep those bottles quiet.

Just one look at you my heart goes typsy in me and milkman keep those bottles quiet.

You and you alone bring out the gypsy in me and milkman keep those bottles quiet.

I love all the many charms about you and milkman keep those bottles quiet.

Above all I need my arms about you and milkman keep those bottles quiet.

Don't be a naughty baby, come to Papa, come to Papa do and milkman keep those bottles quiet.

My sweet embraceable milkman.

'That Scottish swine,' IRA Gershwin raged, 'writing lyrics with *my* brother!'

Indeed, IRA Gershwin was green with jealousy. Yes, he was green jealous of McGonagall. So green jealous that with one stroke of his pen after another and another and another he cut him out of his will.

People often asked him what IRA stood for. Well, he stood for the milkman making love to his wife. He stood for the nagging lesbian next door who also made love to his wife, but chiefly he stood because he had piles. There was a shagtering (sic) knock at the door. 'There's a cheque in the post and sic,' shouted a two and a half foot Armenian Gershwin, 'and there is not a piano in this room.'

'Quick,' he hissed to McGonagall, 'help me get this piano up the chimney.'

Immediately Florenz Ziegfeld burst into the room and it went all over the floor. He stared at the ceiling.

'It's not up there,' said McGonagall. 'It's down here all over me!'

Ziegfeld continued staring hypnotically upwards.

'Expecting somebody?' said Gershwin from up the chimney.

'Yes,' said Ziegfeld, taking a piece of snuff and inserting it between the cheeks of his bum and letting it go.

'Man, he's really hooked,' said Gershwin.

'Shush,' said Ziegfeld from his other end. 'Dr Crippen is due to pass through here at any moment, and I don't want to miss him, he owes me money.'

'You'll have to be quick,' said McGonagall.

Hardly had the words passed his lips than Crippen crashed through the ceiling and, without repaying his debt to Ziegfeld, was gone through the floor in a flash. It was an old, old story.

'The strin's (sic) too long,' screamed the convicted man.

'Och,' said McGonagall sadly, shaking his head. 'They still have nae got it right.'

'He'll never die at this rate,' said the great Ziegfeldski.

'Och, what is the rate for dying?' said McGonagall.

'It's about a pound an hour,' said Gershwin, who was an authority on albino yak breeding.

'Now,' said snuff-stuffer Florenz Ziegfeldski, 'about this Broadway show.'

'About bloody time,' said McGonagall.

27

Gershwishin getting his piano up the chimney

'About turn,' said a sergeant.

Ziegfeld waved his hand. 'Money is no object.' He laid a blank cheque on the table.

McGonagall ate it.

'Are things this bad?' said Ziegfeld.

There was a knock at the door, two on the window, three on the roof.

'There's a cheque in the McGonagall,' shouted Gershwin through the letter-box.

Conversation stopped and attention was focused on the late Dr Crippen as he was hauled up through the floor on the fiftieth anniversary of his hanging. 'The invention of telegraphy, that's what did it,' he moaned.

'I thought it was the butler,' moaned McGonagall.

'You're both wrong,' said Gershwin. 'It was Marconi.'

'Ma Coni, I haven't heard from her in years,' said McGonagall, remembering the landlady from whom he'd caught it.

'No,' said Crippen. 'It wasn't the butler, he didn't do it, he was doing Mrs Trestle the cook at the time, dressed as a fireman, so it couldn't have been him. I mean, it stands to reason, you can't be screwing a cook dressed as a fireman *and* be aboard the *Mauretania* sending a wireless message telling the police that I was aboard dressed as a milkman.'

There was a scuffling noise as George Gershwin crashed down the chimney in a cloud of soot and bending the piano.

'Oh,' said the soot-black Gershwin. 'Dere goes ma livelihood.'

'It doesn't look very lively to me,' said McGonagall with a certain gesture from the waist down.

A man with a knife, fork, spoon and an empty plate approached McGonagall. 'Two eggs, chips and tomatoes, a pot of tea for four and bread and butter.'

'Yes,' said McGonagall looking at the empty plate. 'Yes, that's all you're short of, two eggs, chips and tomatoes, a pot of tea and four slices of bread and butter.'

'Thank you for telling me,' said the man. 'You see, I'm hard of hearing.'

'You mean you couldn't hear the plate was empty?' said McGonagall. 'Never mind, what you need is a noisy dinner,' and handed him a loudly quacking duck.

'Ah, this sounds delicious,' said the man and swallowed it.

'That duck's gone awfu' quiet,' said McGonagall.

'This am not advancing ma career,' said the soot-black Gershwin.

'What isn't?' said McGonagall.

'This isn't,' said Gershwin, pointing to an anvil round his waist.

'Where did you get that?' said McGonagall, banging a tuning fork on it. 'It's in the key of C, would you believe it? We'll save

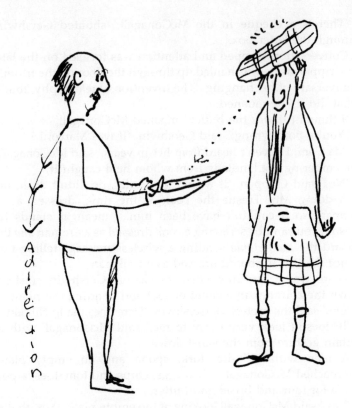

'That's all you're short of, two eggs, chips and tomatoes, a pot of tea and four slices of bread and butter'

it for the sackbut chorus.'

'You mean the anvil chorus?' said de Gershwin.

'Well, that's even better,' said McGonagall.

Stopping at a forge, they did a silly thing. They asked a white man if he was a blacksmith. Unfortunately World War Two broke out and ruined the evening.

'Good evening, white blacksmith,' said McGonagall with a nod and a wink. 'Ma friend here, the black white Gershwin wants to nae what you'd give him for this anvil.'

'Tell you what,' said the white blacksmith, 'you give me the anvil free of charge and I promise it won't cost you a penny.'

'It sounds like a good deal to me,' said McGonagall.

'And it sounds like a good deal to me,' said the black white Gershwin, and 'It sounds like a good deal to them,' said the white blacksmith, taking the anvil and throwing it into a lake.

'I don't see any reason for that,' said McGonagall.

'You're absolutely right,' said the white blacksmith. 'There's absolutely no reason for it and I wouldn't have it any other way.'

They all shook hands.

'I didn't know you were a mason,' said Gershwin to the white blacksmith.

'I'm not a mason,' said the blacksmith.

'I'm a blacksmith,' said the mason.

'This is the end of this bit,' said McGonagall and signed it –

End of bit,
William McGonagall

> witness my hand, my forearm,
> my leg, my teeth and for sheer
> hell on earth witness my armpits.

'Look, Scottish buddy,' said Ziegfeldski, 'you promised me a show that would take Broadway by storm, hurricanes, monsoon, monlater, heavy winds, force nine gales, snow on high ground, standing in all parts sold out, etc. and money.' So saying, he again inserted snuff and let one go.

'Wait,' said McGonagall agitatedly and cracking the knuckles on each of his fingers. 'Do ye no nae it's unlucky tae have mair than four people in a room.' A low moan came from the spectators outside.

'The windowsill, the windowsill,' they groaned.

'Never mind them,' said Ziegfeldski. 'Help me off with this expensive fur coat.'

'Right, let me,' said Crippen entering by the door. 'Help me on with this expensive fur coat,' he said, and was gone.

'OK, so four is unlucky,' said Ziegfeld, lowering his trousers, climbing out of the window and hanging by his fingers from the sill. 'Might as well make a good job of it,' he said, shaking his trousers off and letting go with some snuff.

'Oh dear,' groaned the crowd. 'His bum! His bum!'

At the door appeared a policeman clad in bicycle clips from his ankles up to his groins. He hurried across the room, screwed

Florenz Ziegfeld hanging outside the office window

up his eyes, nose and teeth. 'Charles Crippen,' he said, 'ace murderer and fur thief, I arrest you for ace murders and fur thieving.'

'Excuse me, Jamie,' said McGonagall, 'but I think you've got the wrong man' – removing the policeman's iron grip from his shoulder.

There was a groan from the crowd as Ziegfeld removed his iron grip from the window ledge. As he hurtled past floor eight he screamed, 'Give me an "H"'; at floor six he screamed, 'Give me an "E"'; passing the next he cried, 'Give me an "L"'; and finally, 'Give me a "P"'; and that spells . . . SPLATT!

'D'ye hear that?' said McGonagall. 'H-E-L-P spells SPLATT, you learn something every day.'

'Just a minute,' said the policeman with bicycle clips up to his groins. 'I came here to arrest Crippen's fur coat for murder. So

Policeman with bicycle clips up to his groin

far my report reads "H-E-L-P spells SPLATT!". That won't go down well with the Coroner, he is a man of little faith and leaves it hanging out all night.'

'Och,' said McGonagall adjusting his dress before leaving. 'That man could die of indecent exposure. However,' he said, revolving his kilt, 'it's going to be a fine day tomorrow.'

'Ach,' said Gershwin looking down, 'I can see it all now.'

'I know,' said McGonagall. 'I was a fool to stand on this full-length mirror.'

'Look here,' said the constable with the bicycle clips up to his groins, 'do you know anything of the whereabouts of Doctor Crippen's fur coat or his mistress?'

There was a loud descending scream and the fur-clad nine twenty-nine Crippen and his mistress crashed through the ceiling, all the while doing it, and disappeared through the floor.

'Is that them?' said the mystified policeman with the bicycle clips up to his grins (sic).

'Och aye,' said McGonagall, 'there's no mistaking one as big as that. I wonder why he doesnae try for the Queen's pardon?'

'Pardon?' said the policeman.

'You heard what I said,' said McGonagall angrily.

'I thought,' said the policeman with clips up to the grins (sic), 'I thought I heard you say something about the Queen.'

'Pardon?' said McGonagall.

'You heard what I said,' said the policeman with angry clips up to his groins. 'This evasive talk doesn't fool me. I arrest you for the missing Elizabeth Taylor diamond.'

THE TRIAL

Judge Jeffreys entered and cocked his leg up.

'You bastard,' shouted the voice of an old lag from the public gallery.

'Silence, you bastard,' shouted the Clerk of the Court, fondling them from inside his pocket.

'Read the charge,' said Judge Jeffreys.

'I'd rather play it,' said the Clerk of the Court, picked up a bugle and blew.

At Balaclava Lord Cardigan heard the distant sound of the bugle. 'Charge,' he said and sent six hundred of the Light Brigade into the Valley of Death.

'Now look what you've done,' said Judge Jeffreys, grabbing the bugle and sounding the retreat.

'It's too late,' shouted Lord Cardigan above the thunder of hooves. 'You'll never stop 'em now, they've got to keep going until Tennyson's finished the poem!'

'McGonagall,' said Judge Jeffreys. 'Take the stand.'

So McGonagall took it and put a sold tag on it.

'Now, McGonagall,' said Judge Jeffreys, 'you are charged with sending the Light Brigade into the Valley of Death, what do you have to say about it?'

'Well, Your Honour,' said McGonagall,

> Boldly they rode and well,
> Into the valley of hell
> Rode the gallant six hundred.

'Ooooooh,' groaned the spectators from the gallery.

'The second charge, Your Honour,' said the policeman with the red-hot groins up to his bicycle clips, 'is that either one of these men, if not both of them, but definitely one or the other, have stolen the missing Elizabeth Taylor diamond and are pretending it was a piano.'

'Very interesting,' said the judge.

'You bastard,' shouted the voice of an old lag from the gallery.

'Silence, you bastard,' said some other bastard.

'I swear, I also drink and smoke,' said McGershwin. 'I swear that Elizabeth Taylor's diamond is in fact a Bechstein piano.'

'Then why do you put it in the safe every night?' said the groins of the policeman.

'Because it's safer there,' said the groins of George Gershwin.

'So that's your defence?' said the groins of the judge. 'Lucky for you, you've been saved by the Queen's pardon.'

'Pardon?' said McGonagall.

'You heard what I said,' said the judge.

'I thought you said something about the Queen's bicycle clips,' said McGonagall.

'Pardon?' said the judge.

'Oh, thank you for that pardon,' said McGonagall. 'Any news of the gallant six hundred, Your Honour?'

'Yes,' said the judge. 'They are now the gallant 312 and the case is closed.'

Judge Jeffreys shook hands with McGonagall's hand.

'I didn't know you were a mason?' said McGonagall.

'I'm not,' said the mason, 'I'm a Judge Jeffreys and I sentence you to six months for the Battle of Balaclava.'

'What about my accompanist?' said McGonagall.

'He will accompany you,' said the judge 'for four months, making a grand total of seven.'

PART SIX: THE IMPRISONMENT

Six months to the day the door of their cell opened and the constable with bicycle clips up to his groins entered.

'I've got good news and bad news for you,' he said.

'What's the good news?' said McGonagall.

'After six months in prison the Queen's pardon says you can go.'

'What's the bad news?' said McGonagall.

'My wife's run off with a burglar,' said the policeman.

'Goodbye,' said McGonagall to Gershwin, 'and dinnae worry, I'll ha' ye oot o' there in nae time at aw!' So saying, he leaped into a phone box shouting 'Clark Kent', reappeared as Super McGon and slipped a copy of his bestseller *A Hundred Ways to Escape from Sing Sing* by Al Capone under the door. It didn't work.

'Too thick,' said convict Gershwin.

'Am I?' said McGonagall. He immediately leapt behind a bush shouting 'Clark Kent', and came out looking like McGonagall. He then leapt behind a tree shouting 'Clark Kent' and reappeared looking like McGonagall.

Setting his jaw, he leapt behind a dunghill and came out covered in shit. Covered in shit he disappeared behind a dustcart shouting 'Clark Kent' and came out as a dustman covered in shit. Still covered in shit, he leapt behind a phone box shouting 'Clark Kent' and came out as a telephone linesman.

'For God's sake,' shouted Gershwin, 'let me out or he'll kill himself.'

'Why did they keep you in there for sae lung?' said McGonagall's groins.

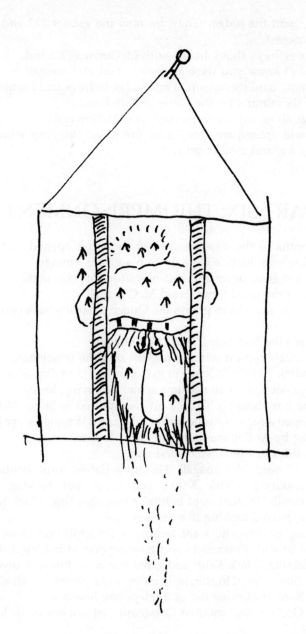

A portrait of McGonagall in prison

'It took me a year to read that book,' said Gershwin. 'I went past my release date seven times!'

'Never mind,' said McGonagall, 'from now on it's you and me, kid, up there in lights.'

The *Private Eye* organist was playing the latest libel of that magazine when the news came through that William McGonagall was sueing them.

'What for?' said Ingrams.

'Money,' said Ingrams.

There was a crashing as the door of *Private Eye* splintered inwards. There stood McGonagall shouting 'Clark Kent!'

'Why are you sueing us?' said Ingrams and Ingrams.

With a devilish smile McGonagall answered, 'I'm sueing you for Jeffrey Archer and his wife.'

Ingrams and Ingrams crashed to his knees. 'Would you settle for a curry?' said Ingrams.

'Well, just this once,' said McGonagall, letting go a few more 'Clark Kents' in anticipation. 'Mind you,' siad (sic) McGonagall, 'there's a big difference between a curry and Jeffrey Archer and his wife, so a few pounds would nae go amiss.'

Ingrams opened his safe and took out a few won't go amiss pounds. Then, opening a Hindu, he took out a curry. 'Will you eat it here or will you take it away?' said Ingrams.

'I'll eat it here and then I'll take it away,' said McGonagall.

The entire staff of *Private Eye* knelt in a circle around the curry-gobbling Scotsman and said three Our Fathers, two Hail Marys and one Jeffrey Archer.

'OK, it's a wretched man who cannot tell the difference between a curry and a libel action by Jeffrey Archer,' said Barry Fantoni in Esperanto.

The walls burst open and on a giant split screen was Rambo 2. 'Take that, you Vietnamese bastards,' he said and fired a series of scotch eggs at McGonagall.

'Och, it's a wretched man who cannot tell the difference between a lethal burst of machine-gun fire, scotch eggs and Jeffrey Archer,' said Florenz Ziegfeld from the SPLATT position on a nearby pavement.

'Well, Ingrams,' said McGonagall, 'let this all be a lesson to you' and gave him a demonstration of gujarati scotch egg cooking with chillies.

'Phew, what a scorcher,' said Ingrams.

There were now forty-eight scotch curried eggs in the room along with Rambo 2 and Tottenham 3.

'Och, this is no way to run a magazine,' said McGonagall, who was awaiting the Queen's pleasure. 'He, I and me have a mind to see the Quinn,' said McGonagall to a policeman hiding outside Buckingham Palace.

'I'm afraid,' said the hiding policeman, 'Her Majesty is away shooting up in the Quantocks.'

'Oh, deary me,' said McGonagall on behalf of I, me, Gershwin and himself. 'Shooting people up the Quantocks must be very painful, would you mind if we come in and wait?'

'I'm afraid,' said the hiding policeman, 'that you cannot come into Buckingham Palace to wait.'

'Thank you very much,' said McGonagall. 'We'll wait outside then till she gets here outside the British Empire.'

'That reminds me,' said Gershwin from behind the hiding policeman; 'I'm doing a concert there right now.'

THE BRITISH EMPIRE

The stage was set for the English adaptation by Lionel Blair of his Negro folk opera *Porgy Mash and Peas*. Unfortunately, the entire opera had been infiltrated by the KGB and the Chinese secret police. The curtain rose on the first act and came down again. The curtain rose on the second act and came down yet again. 'We cannot get it rightski,' said a voice from behindski. The curtain rose a third time. The stage was crowded with Chinamen. In the centre was Dr Fu Man Chu and his fingers. He picked up a saw.

'Hello, flokes,' he said. 'A flunny thling hlappened to mle on way to thleatre.' Here he started to saw his way through a coloured waitress singing 'Summertime and the living is easy by half'.

Gershwin in the wings was hirrified with horror. He let go an expletive in the vernacular: 'Who cast this Chinkee-poo creep as a coloured cripple on a go-kart?'

'It's OK, buddy,' said McGonagall, forcing snuff up Gershwin's nose. 'He's only half the price.'

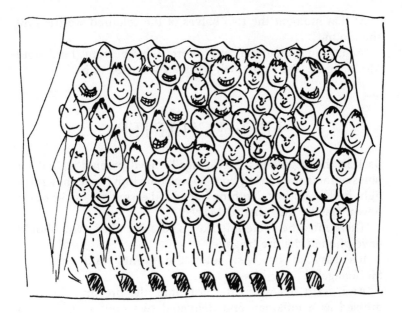

The stage was crowded with Chinamen

'That,' said Gershwin, going Atishoo, 'means he's only half as good Atishoo!'

'*I'll* save the show,' said McGonagall.

'Save it for another day,' pleaded Gershwin.

Too late, McGonagall was on stage singing 'Stop Your Tickling, Jock'.

'Fluck,' said Fu Man Chu, 'Scottish cleep luining act.'

From here on McGonagall ad-libbed:

> Terrible Chinese conjuring man
> Bake me a cake as quick as you can
> If you cannot bake a cake
> Noodles will do
> If you cannot bake noodles
> Cock-a-doodle-do.

'Oh dlear,' said Flu Man Chu. 'I'll never be able to sing "Ave Malia" again.'

41

At that moment the two halves of the coloured waitress hit the ground.

'Ach, you'll nae get any more service from her,' said McGonagall, 'she's only half the man she used to be!'

FRESH CHAPTER

Back in the Highlands, McGonagall's aged parents waited for news of their wandering boy. To welcome him home they put a light in the window. Nothing happened except the hoose burnt down. Hastily they dialled Mac999.

'There must be some mistake,' said a plumber. 'You should have phoned the fire brigade.'

'It's easy to be wise after the event,' said the aged McGonagall.

'And,' said his wife, 'the last time, the fire brigade came dressed as a milkman and delivered two pints of Gold Top water!'

'There's a call-out charge of a pound,' said the plumber.

'Well, let's hear you call out, then,' said the charred McGonagall.

'Aaaaaaaaargh, aaaaaaaargh, you Tarzan me Jane,' called the plumber.

'Ach, zat is verr gute,' said the ancient McGonagall in an attempt to put him off the tail, tile, tool, train, trail.

'Ja,' said the plumber, 'der is ein call-out fee of twenty Deutschmarks.'

'Ye drive a hard bargain,' said McGonagall, reverting to type.

'I know,' said the plumber, 'it's parked outside.'

'Now, laddie, mend yon tap,' said the ancient McGonagall.

'Is it dripping?' said the plumber.

'Nae, it's water,' said McGonagall Senior.

'I'm sorry,' said the plumber, 'it's my day off but here's a song.'

'Is there a call-out fee for it?' said the ancient McGonagall.

'I'm afraid so,' said the plumber.

'Now,' said the McGonagalls, 'we need a washer for yon tap.'

So the plumber went over and washed it. 'Now what?' he said.

'Is that dripping?' said the plumber.
'Nae, it's water,' said aged McGonagall

'Och, there's an auld Scots saying,' said the aged.
'What is it?' said the plumber.
'Bugger off,' said the aged.
So much for the old folks at home. Paul to the Corinthians,
Ch. 6 Verse VII.

Meantime at the British Empire the late William McGonagall
was hiving, hoving, huving and having a very mean time, and
we do mean time. He was locked in mortal combat with the
Phantom of the Operabouf. McGonagall had the Phantom in a
lethal stranglehold around the ankle. The Fu Man Chu continued sawing the two halves of the black waitress into a
quartet from *Rigoletto*.
'Oh Christ,' droned McGonagall, his eyes overlapping as the
phantom stood on his head.
'Confucius say,' said the furiously sawing Flu Man Chu, 'man
with phlantom on wooden head much better off than with tin
leg in thunderstorm.'
At that moment a stream of scotch eggs exploded one after the
other on his hat. 'Take that, you Vietnamese swine,' said
Rambo II – Tottenham 3.
'Confucius say,' said the egg-splattered Chinky-poo, 'black
woman singing quartet from *Rigoletto* no use to me, I better off
with man with tin leg in thunderstorm.'

More scotch eggs hit him, it was now Rambo III, Tottenham 3.

'Oh dear,' groaned the disappointed spectators. 'We paid to see *Porgy Mash and Peas* and all we've got is a Chinese carpenter with scotch eggs in his hat and a thin leg in a thunderstorm.' Rambo IIII – Tottenham 3.

'Och, you're hurting me, Jamie,' said McGonagall to the egg-splattered Phantom of the Opera with the tin leg in a thunderstorm, who had flattened McGonagall's head wafer thin so he could now only appear in silhouette with the sun behind him.

'Sign this cheque or else,' said the Phantom of the etc.

'It's against my religion,' said McGonagall. 'Not to mention Scots eggs,' he said in Mongolian. 'Scotch eggs,' said the Phantom of the etc's.

'I told you not to mention them,' said Topaz.

The Phantom swarmed up the front curtain into the flies and across to his Wurlitzer organ. The pipes thundered out 'God Save the Queen' and the curtain crashed down.

'Now what?' said Gershwin as he buried the quartet from *Rigoletto*.

'It's the Legion for me, laddie,' said McGonagall, inflating his head and heading in the direction of Africa.

'Oooooh, there he goes,' said the dissatisfied spectators.

And ooooh, there he went. He travelled on the SS *Ascanius*. As he stood looking out of the porthole he put pen to paper, paper to table, table to floor and ship to shore.

Oooooooooooh, the only trouble with the good ship *Ascanius*
Is that there are too many of us.
The lavatory attendant was the human wreck Jack Hobbs,
He was doing one of the ship's worst jobs.
He had to keep the ship's karzi clean,
He knew what they'd done and he could see where they'd been.
With this karzi he was not amused
He couldn't get it clean 'cause it was always being used.
It was so bad that some of the passengers would have died
But for being allowed to do it over the side.
Apart from this it was a good ship, they say,
Except you could smell the thing a mile away.
For me queuing for this karzi was painful in the extreme
Because when you got in you were covered in soot, shit and
    steam!

But relief was at hand for McGonagall and Hobbs. The ship sank. 'Women and children first,' said McGonagall as he struggled into a frock and dived into a pram.

FRESH PARAGRAPH

It was a quiet day at the fort of Siddi Ben Abba.

'Sorry,' said a brute of a recruiting sergeant. 'We don't take thank heaven for little girls in prams.'

McGonagall leapt from the carrycot and raised his skirt just enough to reveal the tip.

'Sacre bleu,' said the brute of a sergeant. 'Quelle brilliant disguise. Sign here,' he said, pointing to the wall.

With a copperplate hand, McGonagall signed, 'LE PRINCE OF WALES, ETC.'

'Zounds,' said the brute of le sergeant, 'vous are *the* le Prince of Wales, etc?'

'Oui, oui,' said McGonagall and did one against the wall.

'Bon,' said the brute of le sergeant, 'from now on you can forget all that Buckingham Palace crap, you are in le Legion now. Yours is to do or die.'

'If I have a choice,' said the Prince of McWales, 'I'd rather just do the do.' So saying, McGonagall emptied Gershwin out of a sack.

'Quelle surprise, encore un homme,' said the brute of le sergeant.

'Did you hear that?' said McGonagall. 'You've only been here a second and you've already been given an "encore un homme".'

'He must have heard the broadcast,' said Gershwin.

'Nom de chien,' said the brute of le sergeant.

'Rover,' said Gershwin.

'Vous are the famous "dizzy fingers" George Gershwin, can I have your autograph? It's not for me, it's for my little daughter, sign here,' said the brute of le sergeant and pointed to the wall.

'Certainly,' said Gershwin, letting go an autographed one.

'Right,' said the brute of le sergeant. 'Now you are in ze Legion, we march at dawn tonight.'

'Purqoiu? (sic)' said Gershwin.

'Pourquoi?' said the brute of le sergeant. 'Speak French, you American dog.'

'Rover,' said Gershwin.

The sergeant spat on a large horse fly and drowned it. 'Attention,' said le brute. 'Take this rifle, Legionnaire Gershwin.'

'Where would you like me to take it, buddy?' said Gershwin.

'Do not fuck about,' said le brute. 'The Arabs are rising.'

'Aye, it's about time,' said McGonagall. 'It's nearly nine o'clock.'

That night at the ball, Legionnaires fought to the death to dance with McGonagall and his frock. There were bodies everywhere. In one hour McGonagall did twenty passionate tangos and three ravishing waltzes and one black bottom.

'Keep going,' hissed Gershwin from the Legion piano, 'it's our only chance.'

'Mon darling,' said Colonel Chaise Longue. 'Quelle pretty frock you are wearing! Come to mon quarters for a nightcap.'

When McGonagall got there, the Colonel gave him a cap to wear for the night.

'Ze rest of your uniform will arrive by red Datapost and Christ knows when that will be.' The Colonel kissed McGonagall's cap goodnight, after all he didn't want to catch it.

Mademoiselle McGonagall was saved from a fate worse than death by a cry from the look-out, who said, 'Look out.'

Arabs were climbing the ramparts with poisoned rifles, packets of dates and John Hanson.

'Quelle horreur,' said the Colonel, putting his foot in it. 'We must stop 'im before 'e gets to ze Riff song. Zen it will be too late!'

'It *is* too late,' said Mlle McGonagall, the darling of the regiment. 'Listen,' he continued, looking through an ear trumpet.

There came the terrible strains of 'The Desert Song' coming up the ramparts.

'Quelle merde,' said the Colonel. 'They're attacking very early today.'

'Oui, sir, Tuesday is always a matinée,' said the sergeant, shooting an Arab's poisoned rifle and upsetting his dates.

'I must take cover,' said the Colonel, putting on a fresh toupee. 'But do not worry, Beau Geste and his brothers are on the ramparts.'

'Aye,' said McGonagall. 'Probably the worst parts they'll ever get.'

The fighting at the matinée raged all afternoon. Finally after only one curtain call, the Red Shadow and his poisoned rifles fled. The sight of the Legionnaires on the battlements exposing themselves was too much and peace reigned once more over Siddi Ben Exposure.

'Goodnight, mon darling,' said the Colonel as he marched the Legion into oblivion, leaving McGonagall in charge of the fort.

THE END

NEW CHAPTER

'This looks like a good place for it,' said McGonagall.
So they did it there.

FURTHER CHAPTER

McGonagall paced the floor. Gershwin paced the walls and finally McGonagall paced the ceiling.

'What are you doing up there?' said Mrs Grollicks, the ugliest landlady in the universe.

'Please don't look at me full face, I've just had dinner,' said McGonagall to Mrs Grollicks, the ugliest landlady in the world and Scunthorpe.

'Answer my question,' she said from the back of her head.

'I'm doing my impression of a chandelier,' said McGonagall, swinging gently from the ceiling and all the while striking matches.

'If you're going to use the ceiling, the matches as well as the floor,' said Mrs Grollicks, the ugliest landlady in the world and Scunthorpe, 'I'll have to up your rent.'

'Up yours,' said McGonagall.

'You're all behind with your rent,' said Mrs Grollicks, the most terrifyingly ugly landlady in the world and Scunthorpe.

'And you're all rent behind, madam,' said McGonagall, pointing to an exposed area revealing two currently out of work buttocks.

'You're not supposed to look in there,' said the most terrifyingly ugly landlady in the world and Scunthorpe, inserting some snuff.

'It's better than looking at you,' said McGonagall.

'Sic him, boy,' said the most terrified landlady in the world and Scunthorpe, releasing her husband off the chain.

'Bow-wow-wow, wuff-wuff-wuff, gerr-gerr-gerr, wuff-wuff, growl-growl, snarl-snarl-snarl,' said Mr Grollicks on all fours in front of McGonagall, sinking his teeth into McGonagall's foot, leaving the teeth behind.

'Let that be a lesson to you,' said the most terrifying landlady in the world and Scunthorpe.

'Can you nae afford a doggie?' said McGonagall.

'No, I could only afford a husband,' said the most appalling-looking woman in the world and Scunthorpe.

'There, there, down, boy,' said McGonagall, slipping something nasty into the husband's mouth.

'It's not a nice thing to do,' said the toothless husband.

'I didn't do it, I found it in the street,' said McGonagall.

'You fiend from hell,' shouted the ugliest landlady ever known to mankind, retrieving the something nasty by its tail. 'And this will put an end to the old argument,' she said, whirling the something nasty like a pussy cat round and round her head. 'You see,' she said, 'there *is* enough room to swing one in here.'

McGonagall seized the pussy cat by the tail and hurled it through the window. 'Now where's your agument?' said McGonagall.

'It's out there,' she said.

From outside came a great groan from the spectators as the pussy cat hit them.

'You fool of a Scottishman, late of the Legion,' said possibly the ugliest woman.

'Have you ever thought of having a facelift?' said Gershwin.

'Yes,' said the amazingly ugly Mrs Grollicks. 'I took it up and down in a lift several times, but it made no difference.'

'Have you tried a hotel?' said Gershwin.

'Yes, I tried a hotel for several weeks and it still made no difference. Now,' she said, still the most appallingly ugly landlady in the world and Scunthorpe, 'have you seen this prize cat? He's worth £5,000.'

'Oh good,' said McGonagall, 'let's find out where he keeps it.'

'You fool,' said the ugliest woman. 'He does nae keep it in cash, he keeps it in kind.'

'Och,' said McGonagall, crashing from the chandelier to the carpet, arriving in a mountain of dead matchsticks. 'What kind of kind?'

'Property,' she said. 'He's got time-share holiday apartments in Balham.'

'Och, that's too good to miss,' said McGonagall, booking three sunless months in August.

Meanwhile, 'Ooooooooooooooooh,' groaned the spectators who had been hit by the hurled moggy and for some reason added, 'More moggies, more moggies.'

'There's nair mair moggies,' said McGonagall of the Legion. 'Will this do?' So saying, he hurled the barking husband out.

'Woof-woof, bow-wow-wow,' barked the husband while he was in flight. This all stopped when he hit the pavement and the woof-woof became, 'Oh, my fucking head.'

'Fake, fake,' cried the spectators.

'What's going on here?' said a policeman.

'You are,' said a rouged tart. 'I'm Rita Body of Balham, I'm on a time-share relief massage holiday with a Scotsman.'

'Bow-wow-wow, wuff-wuff,' said the husband, trying to curry favour with the crowd.

'We don't want a curried dog,' said the spectators, hurling him back in by his woofs.

'I don't like those,' said Gershwin as a time-share barking husband landed on him. He was referring to the two unemployed buttocks. 'I can see why you married her now,' said Gershwin.

'I wish I could,' said the barking husband.

CHAPTER FOUR HUNDRED AND TWELVE IF I WERE YOU

'Stop, you cantta pitch thatta tent here,' said Pope Pius the Pope.

'And why nae, wee Pope?' said McGonagall, hammering tent pegs into the Vatican carpet.

'Just a minute,' said the Pope. He knelt by his bed and bowed his head.

'Och, are ye praying?' said McGonagall.

'No,' said Pius the Pope, 'it just happens to be on this side of the bed.'

'You're lucky, Pius,' said McGonagall. 'Mine's outside,' he added, doing it out of the window.

'Stop,' said the Pope Pius, the Pious Pope. 'That's consecrated ground.'

'You dirty bugger,' came a voice from below.

'It doesn't sound very consecrated to me,' said McGonagall. 'And in any case he called me a dirty bugger.'

'Ah,' said the Pope understandingly pious, 'that's because, my son.'

'Because what?' said McGonagall.

'Because you *are* a dirty bugger,' said the Pope. 'And you're the worst audience I've had today.'

'The price wasn't right,' said McGonagall, 'and you ain't seen nothing yet.' McGonagall of the Legion threw open the Vatican windows, revealing a vast audience in the square. 'Go on, Popey boy,' said McGonagall. 'Give 'em a song.'

The Pious Pope Pius cleared his throat and McGonagall got it right in the eye. Then with mitre and crook the Pope sang. 'It's been a good year for Ave Maria, that old grey-haired mother of mine.'

'Get off,' shouted the crowd.

He immediately got off with the Mother Superior.

'Pope Pius the Pope, stop doing that while I'm talking to you,' said McGonagall, dragging him off.

'Look, you do your act,' said the Pope of Pius, 'and I'll do mine.'

'Try the loaves and the fishes, it's a winner,' said McGonagall.

'Not for the last guy who did it,' said the Pious Pope, Pius the XI.

The whole Vatican shook. From above came an approaching scream. Yet again the body of Crippen hurtled through the Sistine Chapel, through the floor, taking McGonagall, his carpet and his tent with him. They arrived in the crypt covered in it.

'Did you know this is hallowed ground?' said McGonagall.

'I don't care if it's Hallowed Dolly,' said Crippen, starting to dig his way out.

There was a straining sound as Gershwin strained with a straining sound under his Bechstein piano. 'Blessed father,' he said. 'Would you please bless my piano? And my straining sounds?'

'Of course,' said the Pope Popeyous, raising his right hand, intoning 'Dominus vobiscum'.

'I don't know,' said Gershwin, 'it must be about quarter to eight.'

'Oh, it's time you were going, then,' said the Pope. 'That's the easy way out,' he said, pointed to the balcony and held out a begging bowl with 'Afore ye go' written on the front. It terrified Gershwishin.

A hundred feet below the papal balcony, the Captain of the Vatican Swiss Guard, Captain Count Giovanni Saponi, was about to announce 'Stand at Ease' when a grand piano fell on him. Strangely enough, it wasn't Gershwin's. Because of this, he missed the midday weather report. 'Winds light to variable, some showers in places, snow on high ground, this is Michael Fish, *News at Ten*.'

A man from the crowd rushed out, saw the legs protruding from beneath the piano. 'Quick, quick,' he said. 'Take his shoes off.'

'Are you a doctor?' said a guard.

'No, I'm a chiropodist,' he replied.

'Has anyone seen Captain Count Saponi?' said a crowd artist.

'No, not since the weather report,' said Michael Fish, who was known for that sort of thing.

'Whose legs are these?' said the guard.

'Mine,' said a strangled voice from under the piano.

'Oh, Mein Capitan,' said the guard, 'you've just missed the weather report and Michael Fish who's known for that sort of thing.'

The guard commander looked up at the top of the balcony. 'Who threw that?' he shouted.

'Drop dead, that's who,' said a refined Circassian floor-taster who was on a loo-flushing holiday at the Vatican.

Disconsolately Gershwin lowered his piano to the ground and followed it by British Rail Datarope. 'This is no way to write *Porgy and Goldstein*,' he said.

Following him down the rope at speed came McGonagall, burning them badly. A skein of smoke escaped from McGonagall's kilt.

'Ah, there's nothing like the smell of a good cigar,' said Gershwin.

'Reitmeister burnt cobblers,' said McGonagall, beating out the flames. 'Whose legs are these?' he said pointing at the Whose Legs are These.

'Mine are the whose legs are these,' said Saponi the Count.

'Och, what a shame,' said McGonagall. 'I thought they were going spare.'

'I'm going spare,' said Saponi the Count. 'For Christ's sake get me out from under here.'

'Under where?' said McGonagall.

'This is no time to think about underwear,' said Gershwin, putting on a fresh pair.

'Och,' said McGonagall. 'Believe me, there is no finer time than now to be thinking of underwear,' said McGonagall, thinking of underwear. 'Now,' said McGonagall, eyeing the wreckage of Saponi's piano, 'let's get these pieces of the true Cross off him.'

'OK, buddy,' said Gershwin. 'I'll get the barrow.'

'Cor blimey, mate, strufe, lord luvaduck, get your lovely pieces of the true Cross 'ere,' said Gershwin, going into the Cockney vernacular. Alas, when he got into the Cockney vernacular, there was another Cockney vernacular already there. 'How long you going to be, mate?' he said, tap-tapping on the karzi door.

'About five foot six,' was the witty Cockney reply. 'You see, it was curry last night.'

'What was?' asked Gershwishin.

'This was,' said the Cockney, holding out a dead Pakistani.

'Blimey, struth, lord luvaduck,' said the Gershwishin. 'He's not long for this world.'

'What do you mean?' said the Cockney. 'Not long, he left half an hour ago.'

McGonagall late of the Legion then spoke: 'Come on oot, will ye nae, there's business to be done.'

'I know,' said Gershwin. 'There's someone in here doing it.'

'There's money to be made out here, do ye ken?' came the voice of McGonagall late of the Legion and voice.

With a scream Gershwishin rushed out, leaving his Cockney in a straining heap behind him. He placed a begging bowl on the floor, threw a ragged army overcoat on McGonagall, draped him with war medals, ripped open the front of his boots, dusted him with dried blood and dandruff, put glycerine tears in his eyes, a pram with four starving children, a wife in a wheelchair with the clap, and a photostat copy of an overdraft of a million pounds. Behind him he erected the ruins of a burnt-out semi-detached with rent outstanding, a crippled grandmother in a deckchair and a dying dog called Crick.

'Right,' said Gershwin, 'get out of that.'

McGonagall and the dying dog called Crick launched into a duet. 'Nobody wants you when you're bow-wows down and out.'

Six hours of this impassioned singing brought groans of sympathy from the crowd. They threw their offerings into the 'Afore Ye Go' tin.

Using a computer, McGershwishin totalled it up. They had never been so rich. There was 89p, a dead pussy cat, a chicken bone, a partly dismantled cupboard with a vest, an incomplete pair of bicycle clips and one thousand and forty-three pieces of the relics of the true Cross, one piece labelled Bechstein.

'Good heavens, they've crucified Bechstein, they'll have to rewrite the book.'

'OH, I like a man who can take a joke,' said Gershwin of the Legion. This was no way to write *Porgy and Bechstein*.

'Enougha ofa thissa on concentrated soil,' said the Pope Pius of Pius halfway up his consecrated rope.

'Ooooooooooooh,' said McGonagall and started to poem a poem:

> Ooooooh, wonderful concentrated Pope
> Halfway up his Roman Catholic rope –

'Stoppa that,' dribbled the Pope. 'You getta me a bad name.'

McGonagall got him one right away. 'Arthur Piles,' he said.

'Mama mia, no,' said the Pope. 'Who'sa goingta listen to His Holiness Arthur Piles the First?'

'We give up,' said Gershwin. 'Who'sa going to listen to His Holiness Arthur Piles the First?'

It was too much for the pious Pope Pius the Pious as he apparently fell to his apparent death.

'My turn for Pope,' said Cardinal Bonibum, who was now His Holiness Arthur Piles the Pious. Lighting a fag, he blew smoke up the Vatican chimney.

'Look,' groaned the spectators as they saw the smoke. 'A new Pope, thanks to Disque Bleu.'

'Justta minute,' said the recent Pope Pius the Dead. 'Notta so fastta.'

'I wasn't going fast,' said Pope Arthur Piles. 'In fact, I'm only just out of the bath. And you should see the colour of the Holy Water.'

'Oooooh,' groaned the spectators. 'A miracle, two Holy Pope Piuses and Arthur and the Piles.'

'Neverra mindda thatta,' said Pope Pius of the recent dead, 'we cannot have two Popes at the samma time.'*

'Allarighta,' said Pope Arthur the Piles, 'you do weekdays and I'll do week-ends.'

'And who are you?' said the recent late Pope Pius for the Week-ends I, pointing to two legs protruding from a Vatican piano.

'Your Holiness,' said the recumbent figure, 'follow them and you'll find me, Count Giovanni Saponi, Commander of the Vatican Guard.'

'You're fired,' said the Pope.

'You can'tta do this,' said Saponi the Count. 'I haven't heard the weather report.'

McGonagall and Gershwin watched all of this from a safe distance.

'Och, what you and I need,' said Topaz McGonagall, 'is a wee holiday in Israel.'

'Why Israel? We could do one against the wall,' said McGonagall.

---

* Samma time and the livin' is easy.

54

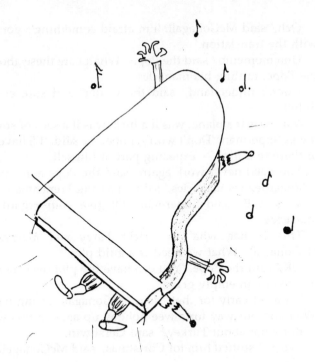

Count Giovanni Saponi struck by George Gershwin's piano in Rome

'Oh yes,' said Gershwin. 'How about Greece? You could put some on, it's cheaper than sun-tan oil.'

'How about Turkey?' said McGonagall.

'OK, we'll take one with us,' said Gershwin.

'Arerra you boys leaving us?' said the Pope recently back from the Dead Sea for one week only by ropular resort.

'You could say that,' said McGonagall.

'I just did,' said the Pope. 'Before you go, pleasa leave me a memento.'

'Waiter,' said McGonagall, 'uno momento.'

'Si, si,' replied the waiter and handcuffed the Pope to a lamppost.

'Och,' said McGonagall, 'I'm afraid something's gone wrong with the translation.'

'Uno momento,' said the Pope. 'Whatta are these about?' said the Pope, rattling his manacles.

'I don't understand,' said the waiter, and sure enough he didn't.

Wait, was it a plane, was it a bird, was it a sack of spuds? No, it was Superman. 'Don't worry, Pope,' he said. 'I'll have you out of there in a flash' – exposing part of himself.

'You need never work again,' said the Pope admiringly.

'Regardez les manacles,' said a passing Frenchman.

'Very well,' said Superman. 'I'll give your regards to Les Manacles.'

'This is nae wha' to wricht *Porgy and Macbeth*,' said McGonagall. 'What we need is a guid plot.'

'OK,' said the Pope. 'You can have the plot over there' – and pointed to an empty grave.

'It's a bit early for that,' said McGonagall, trying it for size. 'We're on our way for a wee holiday up against this wall.'

'But what about Turkey?' said Gershwin.

'I've just stuffed him for Christmas,' said McGonagall, licking his fingers.

'Gee whizz, Pope Pius the Recent Dead,' said Superman. 'I'll soon have you and your manacles out of that lamppost.'

'Be careful,' said the Pope. 'The waiter told me they cost a pound and we don't want to lose on the deal.'

'Don't worry, Your Holiness Pope Manacle the Pious, with my

supernormal powers and my laser sight I will cut your manacles off with these supernormal everyday army surplus pliers. The property of an English gentleman, owner going abroad, £14 o.n.o.'

'Ono?' said McGonagall with one finger in the air and trembling forward on the balls of his feet. 'She married John Lennon.'

'Who did she married John Lennon?' said Gershwin ungrammatically.

'Yoko,' said McGonagall.

'Oh, Yoko,' said Gershwin.

'Wrong, not O'Yoko,' said McGonagall. 'Plain Yoko.'

'Plain Yoko married John Lennon?' queried Gershwishin.

'Ah, sacre bleu,' said a passing French chef. 'Removez Les Manacles,' he reminded them. "Is dinner is getting cold.'

'Och, it's all right for you, Jamie,' said McGonagall, 'when you've nae fude you can always fall back on frogs' legs.'

'So I can,' said the Frenchman, and fell back on some frogs' legs.

'Look,' said Cardinal Bonibum from his filthy bath, 'you're nae good to us as His Holiness Pope Manacled to that lamppost. Likewise, you'd be no good to us as Pope Manacled to Mangles, sewing machines, horse boxes, woodburning stoves of Norwegian origin or Mrs Doris Terrible of Catford.'

'There,' said Superman, and in a flash hurled the Pope, his manacles and his lamppost into outer space.

A keen-eyed Russian radar-operator reported, 'Unidentified Pope entering Russian air space.'

'This could cause an international incident,' said something.

'That's just what we want,' said something else.

'Don't shoot,' said an international incident. 'I'm coloured and you don't want apartheid in Russia, do you?'

'It depends, who's doing it?' said an entirely something else.

'Pass the bread,' said Bert Quids to his wife.

'Plan XX,' cried Gorbachev.

Immediately a giant missile GI XX9 with total destruction of the world warhead was aimed unwittingly at the Pope's bum, a nuclear-free zone.

The missile left travelling at 180 billion miles an hour and exploded harmlessly in outer space killing nobody. A lump of it fell on Mrs Ethel Windust, 22 Gabriel Street, Brockley, SE 23.

The headlines read next day:

A RUSSIAN MISSILE MISTAKES MRS ETHEL WINDUST FOR POPE'S BUM. A BAD DAY FOR RUSSIAN TECHNOLOGY BUT A WORSE ONE FOR MRS WINDUST'S CANARY WHICH WAS FLATTENED.

That night on the Terry Wogan Show, a brilliantly witty Terry Wogan asked the brilliantly witty question: 'Tell me, Mrs

Lincrust, what does it feel like to be mistaken for His Holiness the Pope's bum?'

'Och,' said McGonagall lying on a beach in Turkey and referring to the *Vatican News*, 'I see they missed the Pope then.'

Gershwin, who was rubbing sun-tan oil into his piano, said, 'In a strange way I miss him too.'

'What strange way?' said McGonagall, easing himself.

'I lowered my trousers,' said Gershwin, 'and clutched a jar of seedless raspberry jam between my knees.'

'Och aye, och, that's one way,' said McGonagall. 'My own personal way of missing him is pretending he's nae there.'

'Aye, that's one way,' said Gershwin, 'but I personally clench a pot of seedless raspberry jam between my knees.'

'You just said that, mon,' said Topaz McGonagall.

'I know,' said Gershwin, 'but you don't think I'd use the same pot of jam between my knees twice, do you?'

'And now,' said McGonagall, 'for a few Glasgow street cries – help, murder, stop thief, put that razor away, Jamie.'

'I'd better cover my piano,' said Gershwin. 'It's getting sunburnt.'

There before them descending on a cloud and sitting on the right hand of God the Father, manacled to a lamppost, was the Pope.

'You want a miracle?' said the Pope, waggling his manacles. 'Follow that. It's time for High Mass,' he said and climbed a ladder.

A black Mercedes pulled up into the forecourt. A door opened and Hitler stepped out of it and into it. 'I'm from the master race,' he said.

'Who won?' said McGonagall.

Hitler pointed a swastika'd finger at McGonagall. 'I'm making you a gauleiter,' he said.

'Och, Jamie,' said McGonagall, 'you dinnae look as if you could make a cigarette lighter' and made a certain sign.

'Is Mussolini about?' said Adolf.

'Yes,' said McGonagall. 'He's about sixty-three and it's all shrivelled up.'

'Zen,' said Hitler, 'he'll need a fine pot of starters.'

The car door slammed and the Mercedes roared off into the night.

'Schwein-fool,' shouted the Fuhrer running after it.

'He'll never get far like that,' said Gershwin, but he did, he became ruler of Germany, which was better than being all shrivelled up like Mussolini's, although his turn would come. When his turn did come, it was Eric Sykes and he couldn't hear him.

FRESH CHAPTER

The great ship's hooter went. The night before, the steering wheel had gone.

'There must be a thief on board,' said Captain Mainbrace Fishfinger. 'Full speed ahead,' he ordered, 'or all this sea will go to waste.'

'Aye aye,' said a leading seaman who was overtaken by a second seaman. 'Aye aye,' said he. A grand total of four ayes in the space of a few seconds, a world aye record.

'This will be the trip of a lifetime,' said McGonagall.

'Well,' said Gershwin, 'if you can't get it in in your lifetime, I'd like to know when.'

'Och, mon, the sea air will do you good,' said McGonagall through his porthole.

'I've always found it hard to see air,' said Gershwin through his porthole.

Suddenly McGonagall and his body burst into song.

> I'll build a stairway to paradise
> On the bridge over the silvery Tay.

'Hey, buddy,' said Gershwishin, 'that's almost one of my numbers.'

Now read on – 'How long,' said Flo Ziegfeldski, 'do I have to go on hanging here?'

'It's optional,' groaned the spectators.

Now read on – There was an Irishman on board and a joke which went, 'Dem's nice pigeons,' he said.

'You fool of a man,' said a joke Englishman. 'They're gulls.'

'Oh,' said the fool of an Irishman, 'boys or gulls, dem's fine pigeons.'

'Oh no,' groaned the spectators.

'Oh yes they are,' said the fool of an Irishman and dived overboard to satisfy a long-held desire to consummate with the sea. As he surfaced he shouted in stage Irish, 'Help, begorra, help ye spalpeens.'

The spectators groaned in sympathy and ignored him. 'Begorra,' he continued in stage Irish, 'throw me a lifejacket.'

The spectators swayed and groaned in sympathy. There was no lifejacket available, so they threw him lifetrousers.

With difficulty, amidst a shoal of haddock, he tried them on. 'Begorra,' he cried, 'they're the wrong size.'

As a shark approached him a vicar called out, 'Any last requests?'

'Yes,' said the joke Irishman, 'I'd like to hear "Danny Boy".'

'So would I,' said the vicar. 'What a pity he isn't here. He owes me money.'

'Unidentified joke Irishman's trousers entering seaski,' said the radar-operator on the submarine *K Oneski*.

'Torpedo himski,' said the captainski.

Travelling at 18 billion miles an hourski, the torpedo hit Mrs Windust and her dead canaryski at 22 Gabriel Street, Brockley, SE 23ski yet again.

'I'm going to miss that joke Irishman,' said McGonagall.

'They already have,' said Gershwin.

'Bingo,' said McGonagall and collected a pound from the hapless Jew. 'What are you doing on that coathanger?' said a baffled McGonagall.

'Well, we've all got our hang-ups,' said Gershwin, 'and this is mine.'

There was a knock at the door.

'Cable for you,' said a steward and gave him a length of cable.

To the total dismay of the crew, the passengers and the media, the *Titanic* missed the essential iceberg even though Lew Grade and his film company had placed it in the right position. It was a grievous disappointment to those passengers who had especially booked to be drowned at sea.

THE GREAT WALL OF CHINA – CHAPTER THLEE

It is known that three Chinese miles are equal to eight ounces of butter, two pints of milk and a fortnight at Mrs Thrill's boarding house in Bridlington.

The weather forecast in China that night was completely misunderstood by Max Wall.

'I don't think there's much future for me out here,' said Wall. 'They've already got one.'

He had already got one, but it was nowhere near as long as the Great Wall of China, otherwise he would have opened it to the public and a fine time would have been had by all.

'Phew,' said McGonagall as he approached, 'am I tired!'

'Yes I am,' answered McGonagall. 'I've just walked eight ounces of English butter, two pints of milk and a fortnight at Mrs Thrill's boarding house in Bridlington.' Then to Max Wall, 'My dog's got no nose,' he said.

'How does he smell?' said Wall.

'He can't,' said McGonagall. 'Didn't you hear me? He's got no nose.'

'I thought you were going to say "terrible",' said Wall.

'All right then, he's got a terrible nose,' said McGonagall. 'What more do you want?'

The Queen of England approached mounted on an archbishop. 'I fear,' she confided to the grovelling Scot, 'the Chinese sun has done for Philip.'

'Och yes,' said McGonagall from the grovelling position, 'we are all grateful for what the Chinese sun has done for Philip. He came here as white as a sheet, he'll need a Pakistani visa to get back in. And now,' said the grovelling Scotsman in the upright grovelling position, 'the royal toast.' So saying, he spread margarine on it and handed it to the Queen.

The president of China and the eight hundred guests rose to their fleet and ate a toast to the Queen. 'Here's a wholegrain loaf with no additives or artificial colouring to Your Majesty,' they sang.

The royal tour would have been a great success had it not

been for the Stock Market crash. The Queen came out with three pounds and twenty pence.

'We won't get very far on that,' said Philip.

'Very well, we'll see how far we can get on the royal yacht,' said the Queen.

Arriving in England at the customs they were greeted by Max Wall of China with an animal joke.

'My dog's got no nose,' he cried.

'The throat Fang,' said the Queen, releasing a Dobermann Corgi.

Wall tried telling the animal a soothing joke like 'My dog's got no nose,' but it still wouldn't let go.

Through customs an officer said, 'That dog will have to go in quarantine.'

'But he won't let go,' said a strangulated Max Wall. 'Listen, my dog's got no nose, how does he smell? Terrible. See?' he said.

'Let me try,' said the customs officer. 'Now then, doggie, doggie, my dog's got no nose, how does he smell? Terrible.'

Now the doggie immediately grabbed the customs officer by the throat.

'Ah,' said Max Wall. 'You must have said it right.'

'Get 'im off,' said the strangulated customs officer. 'My lunch break's in half an hour and they don't let doggies in the canteen.'

'Well, let me know how you get on,' said Max Wall.

'Who's doggie is it?' said the strangulated customs officer.

'It's the Queen of England's,' said Wall.

'Ooooh,' said the strangulated customs officer. 'The Queen of England's?'

'Yes,' said Wall. 'It's an honour.'

'It's not on her,' said the customs officer. 'It's on me. Now then, nice doggie, my dog's got no nose – how's he smell? Terrible' he was last heard to say.

McGonagall, still happily in China, ate another eight toasts to the Queen not realising she had sailed.

'Och how time flies,' he said, throwing a watch at a Chinese lady cleaner who had just finished cleaning some ladies.

She said, 'Watchee tinesay upomamatto yackee.'

'Good God,' said McGonagall. 'That's late.'

McGonagall drinks a toast to the Queen in China three cups after she has left

'Where in Christ have you been?' said the late George Gershwin, hauling his Bechstein behind him.

'Och, there you are, George,' said McGonagall, and there he was. 'Bingo,' said McGonagall and extracted yet another pound, and with it booked two second-class passages on non-returnable boomerangs to Oudnagalabi.

It was a dark night in the Australian outback. Across the great Nullabor railway line a frenzied hand-operated pump-action trolley could be seen approaching. From it came the high nasal sound of a short frenzied tubby tenor.

'Eeeeeeef I ruuuuuuled the wooooorrrld,' it sang.

As dawn broke over the frenzied singing sweating creature, settlers locked their doors, wives and children were battened down, all Waltzing Matildas were hidden.

The dreaded singing was getting louder but no better. He turned up the frenzied pumping speed to, 'We'll keep a welcome in the hillside.'

'It's,' said the terrified station master, putting all signals to danger, 'it's the eight twenty non-returnable Harry Secombe.'

'I don't give a Four X for his singing,' said a Waltzing Matilda as the frenzied tubby tenor sped through the Woy Woy sidings.

'I'm doing the rugby clubs,' he shouted.

'Watch out they don't do you,' said the Australian Waltzing Matilda with the side of his hat up, hanging corks, a tin of Foster's with a g'day sport, a jolly jumbuck, up sprang a trooper three four five as he diddled in his dufflebag waiting while his willy boiled.

A white Cadillac worth ten billion dollars and a quarter of a mile long drew to an expensive halt. The husband-proof black glass window was lowered. It was Joan Collins.

'I'd love to marry her,' said Sir Harry.

'Don't worry,' said Waltzing Matilda. 'Your turn will come.'

'Have you seen her in *Dynasty*?' said Sir Harry.

'No, but I've seen her in Tesco's.'

'You there, is this Burbank Studios?' said Joan Collins to the frenzied Welsh star of pumping highway.

'No sir, this is "We'll Keep a Welcome in the Hillside when You Come Home Again to Wales",' sang the frenzied tenor.

'Are *you* Welsh, darling?' said Joan.

'Yes, sir,' sang the frenzied tenor.

'Then I'm never coming back,' said Joan, and just to make sure she shot the chauffeur.

In a flash, the frenzied pumping singing sweating Secombe saw his chance of stardom and/or a quickie. In a trice he donned the uniform of the dying chauffeur.

'Is he feigning death?' she asked, pointing at the chauffeur.

'Yes,' said Secombe, 'and I'm feigning life,' he sang. He kissed her hand and sang, 'Your face is a masterpiece of the embalmer's art.'

The phone rang and Joan Collins picked it up. Secombe picked up Joan Collins.

'I've got more than my fair share,' he sang.

'Well, don't share it with me,' sang Joan Collins.

'Cut,' said the director.

'That was a great scene, Joan,' said Herpes J. Gropeman.

'You mean I've been appearing in *Dynasty*?' sang Secombe from his railway trolley.

'Only the repeat,' said Gropeman and repeated it.

'It's a repeat repeated,' said Gropeman.

'Would you care to repeat that repeated?' repeated Secombe.

'I'm sorry, I'm a Mormon,' said Gropeman and pointed to a hundred and nine wives.

'A good time was had by all,' sang Secombe.

A British Home Office helicopter flew overhead. From it hung a length of string.

'It's not funny any more,' screamed Crippen to the pilot.

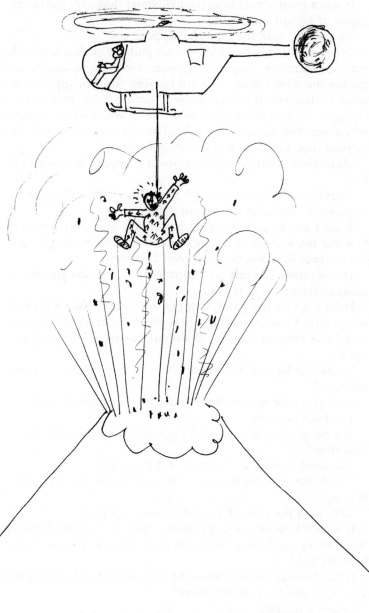

Crippen being lowered over Mount Etna

'Drop me off somewhere warm.'

It was a great spectacle as the helicopter flew over the boiling throat of Mount Etna.

'Say when,' said the pilot to Crippen.

'Stop!' shouted Bob Geldof and his guitar. No, dear reader, he was not shouting 'Stop!' to Crippen, the volcano, or, for that matter, the pilot. Oh no, he wasn't saying 'Stop' to any of those, no definitely not. If you consider it, saying 'Stop' to a piece of string is really pointless, and never has a volcano ever stopped whenever Bob Geldof has told it to. In fact, as a volcano-stopper, Bob Geldof was completely unknown.

Meanwhile, 'Not so low!' screamed Crippen. 'My arse is on fire.'

'That'll teach you to smuggle innocent women disguised as boys across the Atlantic,' shouted the pilot.

'I can't see how by burning someone's arse over a volcano you can teach them to smuggle innocent women disguised as boys across the Atlantic,' screamed Crippen.

The weather forecast in China that night was completely misunderstood by Max Wall.

From his vantage point, Crippen noticed a mile-and-a-half-long white Cadillac pulling up at the base of Mount Etna. A pistol shot rang out, another chauffeur discovered that he'd gone too far.

Inside the helicopter a black chained box suddenly became animated.

'Can you hear me out there?' said a voice from the box.

The pilot nodded.

'It's no good nodding,' said the voice from the box, 'I can't hear that.'

'I nodded as loud as I could,' said the pilot.

'That's better,' said the voice, 'but still I can't hear you. Turn the engine off.'

'OK,' said the pilot. 'I'll just turn the engine off.'

It wasn't long before Crippen was heard to scream 'Ahoy up there, there's red-hot rocks coming up my arse and me a good Catholic too.'

It did the trick, the motor roared back to life and the black box said 'Can you hear me out there?'

Crippen nodded.

A few light years away on the Nullarbor Plain, Secombe was

bounding along on a pogo stick beside a kangaroo. 'You can't fool me,' he said, which was absolutely true, the kangaroo could not fool him. This is not peculiar to the singing chauffeur Secombe, star of the *Dynasty* repeat. Kangaroos can very rarely fool anybody. Kangaroos are not clever, as this one proved by bounding over a precipice taking the singing Secombe, who was not that clever as he went, with him.

It wasn't until they were halfway down the precipice that Secombe realised that the kangaroo had finally fooled him. The kangaroo was, in fact, Bob Hawke who would be Prime Minister of Australia for the next two seconds. Fortunately, their descent was broken by falling into the Great Australian Bight. But, lucky for them, passing by was Sir Lew Grade's *Titanic* busily in search of another iceberg.

'Ahoy,' sang Secombe.

'A what?' shouted the captain of the ship.

'Ahoy,' sang Secombe.

'Can you spell that?' shouted the captain.

'Let *me* spell it,' said Hawke. 'I'm Prime Minister.' And he shouted, 'HLX – ahoy.'

'You ignorant bastard,' said the captain. 'You must be the Prime Minister of Australia.'

'You've interrupted us in the middle of drowning,' said the Prime Minister for two seconds. 'Drop us a line.'

'Right,' said the captain. 'What's your address?'

'You bastard,' said the Prime Minister.

'Can you pull me aboard?' shouted Secombe.

'We'll have none of those disgusting habits on my ship, you pull yourself!' said the captain. 'Now, about saving you, do you want to be saved as first-class, or steerage passengers?'

'Yes,' cried Secombe. 'First class or steerage, that'll do us fine.'

'It's one or the other,' said the captain.

'We'll have the other,' said Bob Hawke.

'Right, throw them the other lifebelt!' said the captain.

So saying, they were hauled aboard as first-class steerage passengers. It was no sooner done than Secombe said, 'I want to complain about the food.'

'We haven't had any,' said Bob Hawke.

'We're not going to wait till the last minute,' said Secombe, calling for the menu. 'What's the Brown Windsor like?' said Secombe.

'It likes being in the soup plate,' said the chef.

'You fool,' chortled Ned, the Owl of the Remove, 'when I said Brown Windsor I was referring to the heavily sunburnt Prince Charles, fresh from the sundrenched beaches of Hawaii.'

'I'm sorry, he's not on the menu.'

'Of course not, I just told you he's on the sundrenched beaches of Hawaii, didn't you hear me?'

'Yes, I can hear you,' said the voice from the black box, 'but I still can't hear the pilot.'

'Ah! I can hear you now,' said the pilot, un-nodding his head. 'Who are you?'

'I'm your black box, and I'm waiting for you to have an accident. How long are you going to be?'

'I'll have one as soon as possible,' said the pilot. 'Here, have one on your own,' he said, hurling the black box out of the helicopter.

NEWSREADER: Good evening, this is the BBC Nine O'clock News – tonight a black box crashed on its own. The authorities are waiting for the wreckage of the pilot to ascertain what went wrong.

Secombe was now in the ballroom of the *Titanic* with his ball.

'I think I'll trip the light fantastic,' he said, sticking his foot out and tripping a light fantastic sailor. 'Now I'll trip the *heavy* fantastic,' he said, putting on weight and repeating the performance.

'Now for the medium fantastic,' he said and fell into a trance. 'Where are we now?'

'The Atlantic,' said the captain.

'Ah, I'm in a trance-Atlantic,' said Secombe.

'Do you know,' said the captain pointing at the trance-laden figure, 'that if *he* ruled the world every day would be a bright sunny day?'

'He's obviously never been to Scunthorpe,' said a passenger.

'More than that,' said the captain, 'he's never been to Bexhill, Penge, East Croydon Municipal Library, Ladywell Plunge Bath, Brockley Rise and Mrs Thrill's massage parlour in Streatham.'

'He, he, he, look who's here,' said a lilting Scottish voice wearing an outsize Glengarry and ankle-length kilt and floor-length legs. It was Sir Harry Laundry. Going into a toe-tweaking one-step, he sang, with a smile and a glint in his aye, and with a shaking beard, a nod and a tap on the nose and a winking right eye, 'I love a lassie, a bonnie Highland lassie . . . '

'She must be bloody blind,' said the captain.

There came a terrifying crash – the ship shuddered, shooting singing Secombe and McGonagall across the dancefloor and into the swannagles. There were shrieks from all directions, especially those.

From the Royal Perth Yacht Club a Strine groan went up, came down again and stayed there. Before their eyes they saw the *Titanic* crash through the Australian yacht, *Kookaburra*, leaving it in two pieces, cook and burra. It then crashed into the American yacht SS *President's Prolapse*, which sank without trace. It ploughed into the English boat *The Queen's Groveller*, sending it to the bottom. It then destroyed the New Zealand yacht, *Kiri-tirri-awna*, likewise, the French, the Afghans, the Chinese, the Rumanians and the Jews.

'Good God, my oath,' said a voice from the Royal Yacht Club, 'the *Titanic* has won the America's Cup, and look what they're doing in it.'

Ung Tan Thys, the Burmese diplomat, lit a cheroot. An Armalite shot it up. Yes. The Lebanese had reached Burma. The Shi'ite militia stormed ashore from Arab bathtubs and attacked U-Shal Go, the deputy assistant drain supervisor, for Burma West.

'Don't panic,' he shouted to Burma, lit up a cigar and exploded.

Yes, those Shi'ite practical jokers had reached him.

'Allah, Allah, Ackbar,' shrieked the fanatical Moslem Mullah from the top of the Suli pagoda. He sneezed and fell to his death. 'Allah, Allah, Ackbar, SPLATT,' he went.

'Upsadaisy,' said McGonagall in his best Arabic, which was pronounced 'upyerallahakabar!' It meant little to the flattened Arab mullah.

So ended another sad chapter of the pagoda-leaping Shi-ites of the Lebanon. This is Trevor MacDonald, News at Ten, Burma.

CHAPTER TWELVE

George Gershwin pushed his plate away from him. 'I can't eat that,' he said. He was right, who wants to eat a plate? Nay! It was the food thereon he was referring to. 'What's that muck?' he said.

'That's your muck,' said McGonagall. 'I've eaten mine, there's many a mickle maks a muckle.'

'Well, there's not enough muckles on mine,' said Gershwin. 'What exactly is it?' he said.

'It's exactly spam and chip,' said McGonagall.

'Chip? Where's the other one?' said Gershwinegall.

'D'ye mean ye dinnae remember?' said McGonagall.

'Oh, I remember the dinner,' said Gershwin. 'But why only one chip?'

'I tossed you for it,' said McGonagall.

It wasn't much of a conversation, but considering the hut was on fire it wasn't bad.

'I can't eat that food,' said Gershwin. 'I suddenly remembered I'm Jewish.'

'But today's shellfish Tuesday,' said McGonagall.

'Yes, that's my day to be Jewish,' said Gershwin. 'What's yours?'

'Mine's a Guinness,' said McGonagall.

Gershwin passed him a harp-shaped bottle of amber piss-poor nectar. 'I've got a confession,' said cunning Gershwin. 'I'm *not* Gershwin, I'm Eric Piles.'

'Well, you must have a double,' said McGonagall.

'Good, I'll have a double brandy,' said Gershwin.

McGonagall poured the brandy on to the floor. 'Sorry, I've nae a glass,' said McGonagall.

'Never mind,' said Gershwin, licking the floor. 'It lasts longer this way. And now will you hurry and cook me a Kosher meal?'

'What would you like?' said McGonagall.

'I'd like a Kosher meal,' said Gershwin, squeezing the brandy-soaked carpet into his pocket.

Taking his twelve-bore shot gun, McGonagall shot several twelve-bore lobsters in the heather. 'Cast your eyes on them,' he said, holding aloft a brace of grouse.

'Those are not twelve-bore lobsters,' said Gershwin.

'Aye,' said McGonagall. 'There's many a mickle muckle twixt dick and duckle, and they'll ha' tae do.'

He struck a match to light the st∅ne, str∅ne, sc∅ve, str∅ne, stove.

Twelve thousand feet above the house a pilot had bailed out of his plane and, it being early closing, his parachute wouldn't open. As he hurtled to the ground for his Queen and Country he passed a smoke-blackened McGonagall coming up for his Queen and Country. 'Help,' said the pilot. 'Do you know anything about parachutes?'

'No,' said the smoke-blackened figure. 'Do you know anything about gas stoves?'

CHAPTER 13

The Dundee Hospital for Smoke-blackended Figures

The doctor was taking McGonagall's pulse.

'What was it like up there?' said the doctor.

'Oh, it was a beautiful view,' said McGonagall. 'You could see McKrankie's jam factory as clear as day, they were in full production.'

'If it was so good, why didn't you stay up there? Your mistake was coming down again. If it hadn't been for that, this bed would be empty and would look much nicer. When you came in you were so smoke-blackened that for the first two hours we were treating you as an illegal Jamaican immigrant.'

'Excuse me,' said hospital visitor Gershwin, 'will he be in here long?'

'Why?' said the doctor.

'He's supposed to be preparing me a Kosher meal of feathered lobsters from the burn,' said Gershwin.

'But it's haggis Thursday,' said the doctor, sipping chloroform.

'Good heavens, I'm forty-eight hours away from being Kosher,' said Gershwin. 'They'll have to glue it back on.'

'Never mind,' said the doctor. 'According to the weather forecast, there's going to be another weather forecast, and there's going to be another Tuesday next week.'

'How is my friend?' said Gershwin, straining the last of the brandy-soaked carpet down his throat.

'Your friend is in a very serious financial condition,' said the doctor. 'When he came here he was worth £108, so we had to operate immediately and now he's worth fuck-all.'

'I thought he was on BUPA,' said Gershwin.

'He was, but now he's on the dole,' said the doctor, recounting the money into little piles, which he himself suffered from.

It was a sad chapter in the McGonagall-Gershwin-Kosher-Tuesday affair.

'I'm feeling much better,' said the smoke-blackened figure.

'Well, feel this,' said the doctor, holding out a final demand.

'I don't feel *that* good,' said the smoke-blackened figure falling back on to his overdraft.

'Out of my way,' said a huge, red-faced NHS nurse as she placed a smoke-blackened meal beside the smoke-blackened figure.

'Quick, nurse, the screens,' said McGonagall, hiding in a po.

'What for?' said the NHS nurse.

'I don't want to be seen eating this stuff.'

'Don't worry,' she said, and ate it for him. 'There, that didn't hurt, did it?' she said.

THE FOOTMAN AT NUMBER TEN OPENED THE DOOR

The footman at Number Ten opened the door and then closed it again, there was nobody there. But there could have been. There is no way you can stand behind a closed door and guess who's outside. It may be somebody, but then again it may not be. On this occasion it was a may not be.

'Who's that?' said Mrs Thatcher.

'It was a may not be, madam,' said the footman.

A pair of smoke-blackened teeth appeared through the letter-box. 'Here, Jamie,' they said. 'I'm giving you advance warning of two knocks. One, two and in that order.'

The teeth true to their word knocked one, two and in that order.

The footman went forward on his foot and opened the door to the smoke-blackened teeth. 'If the wages of sin are death,' he said, 'you appear to have just been paid.'

'Och,' said McGonagall. 'There's many a mickle maks a muckle. Oh will ye nae the noo announce ma presence' – and handed the footman a piece of coal.

'What's this?' said the footman.

'It's one of ma presents,' said McGonagall.

'I'll tell the master,' said the footman, opening the door to the study. 'There's a smoke-blackened figure to see you, sir,' he said.

'Send him in,' said Denis Thatcher, getting out of a bath of gin and drying himself. Donning a dressing-gown, he donned a dressing-gown loaned to him by the late Noel Coward's dressing-gown.

Only just in time, at that moment, the smoke-blackened figure entered the room, leaving behind him a trail of carbonised footprints and tiger nuts. McGonagall pointed an accusing finger at the dressing-gown. 'You, sir, are the managing director of the Highland Control Board of Reconditioned Gas Stoves and I'm sueing you for malfunction.'

Thatcher took a pace backwards, two forward, a pirouette and a whirling Dervish. 'You touched a sensitive spot,' said Denis Thatcher. 'Yes, I am what you say I am. How did you find out?'

'Aye, there's many a mickle twixt and twit,' said McGonagall.

'State your business,' said Denis Thatcher, sliding out of the Noel Coward and into the Ivor Novello.

'I'm a Kosher meal creator,' said the smoke-blackened figure. 'And I have a complaint.'

'Then it's your fault for not wearing one,' said Denis.

'Oh, that's silly,' said McGonagall, and it was, so we won't pursue that. 'What kind of compensation do ye give to people whose reconditioned gas stoves have exploded giving the owners a fine view of McKrankies jam factory?'

'Wasn't the view good enough?' said Denis.

'No, I'd like a fortnight's holiday in the Bermuda Triangle with George Gershwin and his piano.'

'You can't go there, it's booked up solid by SOGAT as a holiday home for Rupert Murdoch and Ian Paisley. What would you say to a week in Scunthorpe at Mrs Thrill's Boarding House for Refined Smoke-blackened Gentlemen?'

'I would say – how much?'

'Just sign this Gilbey's Gin label and a new gas stove will be in the post to you.'

'There's a starving Jew outside in an ambulance,' said the footman.

'Ah, that'll be my friend the starving Jew, George, to remind me about Kosher dinners,' said McGonagall.

'They all say that,' said Thatcher, unplugging the life-support from his Gilbey's Gin machine. 'I can stay off it for up to an hour these days,' he said. He rang for the footman, who came in laboriously.

'What the fuck do you want?' he said.

'Ah, you're new here,' said Thatcher, picking him up and hurling him through the door. 'And now he's new out there,' he said to McGonagall.

'I think I'll go and be new out there with him,' said McGonagall.

'Hurry up,' said a starving Jewish voice. 'I'm down to my last bit of carpet.'

'Soon have you on your feet again,' said McGonagall, forcing a gin-sodden blanket down his throat. 'A Denis Thatcher special,' he cried, 'Hoovered, not shaken.'

CHAPTER THE NOO

'Aye, drive on, driver,' he said. 'When you get to Scotland, you'll easily recognise our house, it's on fire. Some kind neighbours have kept it going for us while we were away. Last time they kept our budgerigar safe inside their cat. It'll never sing again, but you should see their wee Sylvester inside the birdcage, that'll teach the bastard.'

True to his word, when they arrived at the house their neighbours were in but the fire was out.

'You can never rely on people who are in,' said McGonagall. 'There's many a mickle maks a muckle,' he added.

Ooooooooooooooooooh, terrible unreliable neighbours in
  Scotland
Which, had they not let the fire go out, would have been a
  very hotland
But there was our wee pussy cat still in his cage
Who never really looked his age.
Said Gershwin, 'What about ma Tuesday Kosher dinner?
Look, I'm getting thinner and thinner and thinner.'
'Dinnae worry, here comes a treat' –
And opened up a tin of Tesco's threepence-off Kattomeat.
Whereupon Gershwin plunged into the food making a terrible
  row,
Stopping only once to lick his arse and go meow.
'Aah, ye're coming back to your old self' –
And McGonagall snatched the tin away and put it back on
  the shelf,
Whereupon Gershwin was seized with a terrible rage
And climbed on to the perch in the pussy cat's cage.
Whereupon he continued to feed
By stealing the poor pussy cat's bird seed.
'Och, there's a good Gershwin, eat up your millet,
I must warn you that when your bowl's empty I'm nae gang
  to refill it.'

It was a magic moment of Gershwin's. The whole atmosphere
had released his muse. He stood up on his perch and, bent
double, sang one of his great compositions, here in a humble
Scottish birdcage with a good fill of millet, half a tin of
Kattomeat and two carpets full of brandy, he sang 'A Foggy Day
in London Town'.

It baffled the experts, how *did* he manage it? Maurice
Chevalier, on a time-share pony-trekking holiday in the
Highlands, heard the song and rushed in. 'Quelle magic,' he
said. 'Sacre bleu, voulez-vous chanter encore le song?' he cried
from his time-share pony.

'Un moment, froggie,' said McGonagall. 'Afore ye step one
step forward, are ye insured?'

'Pourquoi?' said Maurice Chevalier and his pony.

'Pourquoi we're starting a fire in this house in a minute.
We've got to make up for lost time,' said McGonagall.

'For the last time I tell you, my pony and I are heavily insured

against fire *and* water, and also against Mlle Mimi le Fromage!'
said Chevalier.

'OK, Georgerge, sing him the sang,' said McGonagall.

'A foggy day in London town . . . ' commenced George
Gershwishin.

'Fermez!' said Chevalier. 'Quelle dommage, I thought I had
heard you sing "a *froggy* day in London town".'

'Are ye off yere head?' said McGonagall. 'There are nae froggy
days in London toon.'

'Ah *that* is what is wrong with it,' said Chevalier. He turned
his time-share pony round and disappeared into the froggy
Highlands leaving the song wide open for Fred Astaire, the
world's worst vocalist, to make famous.

At that very moment, Astaire entered on Ginger Rogers.

'Oh, shucks, I'm sorry, I thought I heard that wonderful
Maurice 'The Frog' Chevrolet, the French tap dancer and mime
artist who is known to have screwed Edith Pilaff in mistake for
Charles Aznavour and collaborated with the Germans in World
War Two and collaborated with the Americans in a film called
High Society pass this way.'

'I thought you'd never finish,' said McGonagall. 'Och, wait a
minute the mackle the noo, are ye the famous Fred Astaire and
Ginger Rogers?'

'Yes, we've just finished *The Gay Divorcee*'.

'So – you're both gay,' said McGonagall.

'Wait,' said Fred Astaire and Ginger Rogers, 'are you the
famous smoke-blackened Scottish figure?'

'Nay,' said McGonagall, 'I'm the bloody awful one that
became David Niven in *Bonnie Prince Charlie*.'

'Then I must be off,' said Ginger Astaire.

'All right,' said McGonagall. 'B off.'

As Ginger Astaire tap-danced gaily out of the room, they got
further away; he went on to become famous as Humphrey
Bogart in *The African Queen*.

'I think it's time you ended this blackened figure period,' said
Gershwin. Bending down he clutched both ankles. 'It's my way
of looking behind,' said Gershwin.

'Would you like me to come round and talk to you?' said
McGonagall.

'If you can find your way,' said Gershwin.

McGonagall tap-dancing, accompanied by Gershwin with Crippen descending

An hour and a half later he found himself on the cliff at Beachy Head.

'Och, he's a long way round,' thought McGonagall.

'Pardon me,' said McGonagall to a passing vicar, 'are you a passing vicar?'

'No,' he said. 'I'm an Irish guardsman on the run.'

'Then why are you walking?'

'I'm in disguise,' said the guardsman.

'I've had the runs myself,' said McGonagall.

'Jesus, watch this,' said the Irish guardsman walking, still on the run. 'I'm going to break the world's long-jump record for the auld country.'

'What old country?' said McGonagall.

'Oh, any old country,' said the Irishman.

'How about Sweden?' said McGonagall.

'OK, I'll do it for the Sweden old country,' said the Irish vicar on the run from a guardsman. Poised at the cliff edge, he cried, 'God bless America'.

'Just a minute,' said McGonagall. 'Have you any loose change I could look after for ye? Ye never know, on the way down you could be mugged.'

'God bless you, my son,' said the reverend Irish guardsman, handing McGonagall a wallet bulging with overdrafts.

With a cry of 'Geronimo', he hurled himself over the cliff.

Halfway down, a coloured gentleman mugged him.

'Ain't you got more dan dis, man?' said the mugger, holding out an empty hand.

'Bejabers and begorra ye spalpeen,' said the Irish vicar. 'Did youse now know that it is a mortal sin to mug a member of the cloth?'

'Oh, dat sta'ement am hittin' me hard,' said the coloured gentleman. 'Me am a Jamaican Catholic.'

'I . . . SPLATT!'

The moment they hit the rocks, they ceased to talk to each other, but they had broken the world long-jump record. They quietly lay side by side with their eyes closed. They were later joined by the English Channel, which floated them out to the Eddystone Lighthouse.

'Och, welcome ashore,' said McGonagall, who had beaten them to it.

'What are you three men doing on my rock?' said a disgruntled lighthouse keeper.

'We haven't done anything on it yet,' said McGonagall, 'but there's always time.'

The lighthouse keeper did give them time. 'It's a quarter past three,' he said. 'It's time for Gloria Hunniford.'

'Is it?' said McGonagall.

'Yes,' said the lighthouse keeper.

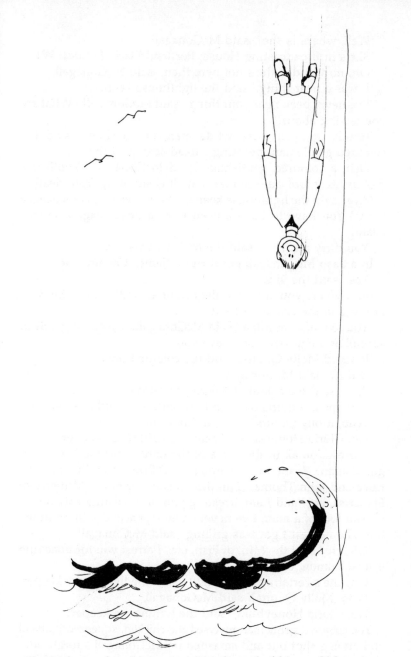

The Irish guardsman/vicar nearing the end of his world long jump record for the old country

'Well, where is she?' said McGonagall.

'She's in Broadcasting House, Portland Place, London W1.'

'Oh, no wonder she's not here then,' said McGonagall.

'It was a near thing,' said the lighthouse keeper.

'I've never been near your thing,' said McGonagall. 'What are you talking about?'

'Hands up, you three white men, or I'll shoot,' said the coloured gentleman, pointing a dead seagull at them.

'Och, a coloured gentleman,' said McGonagall. 'You'll nae fool us. Any fool can see that seagull is suffering from death.'

'Aye,' said the lighthouse keeper. 'And have you got a licence for it? You have to have a licence for a dead seagull on this island.'

'You dirty rat, you,' said the Irish Guards vicar.

In a flash McGonagall got it right. 'James Cagney,' he said.

'Yes,' said the vicar.

'Stay where you are,' said the coloured gentleman. 'One step nearer and the chicken gets it!'

'You fool of a cannibal,' said McGonagall. 'Disguising a dead seagull as a chicken won't save you.'

'It saved Molly Quotts,' said the coloured one.

'Did it?' said McGonagall.

'Aye,' said the coloured Negro gentleman.

'Perhaps the trains delayed her,' said the lighthouse keeper.

'Who, Molly Quotts?' said McGonagall.

'No, Gloria Honeysuckle,' said the lighthouse keeper.

'I arrest you all in the name of the Lord,' said the Irish vicar guardsman. 'I am not Guardsman O'Brien and I'm not the Reverend John Thomas. I am Dick Scratcher of the Ministry of Fisheries, etc., and I am arresting you for poaching salmon.'

'You fool of a man, I've never eaten a poached salmon in ma life. The nearest I got was grilling,' said McGonagall.

'OK, etc.' said the Min. of Fish, etc. 'I arrest you for poaching grilled salmon, etc.'

'Oh, she's certainly late tonight,' said the lighthouse keeper.

'Who, Molly Quotts?' said McGonagall.

'No, Gloria Honeybum,' said the lighthouse keeper.

The coloured gentleman reversed the chicken, squeezed its head and an egg shot out and smashed on McGonagall's forehead.

'You fool of a mugger,' said McGonagall. 'You know I like mine hard-boiled with soldiers.'

'To think,' said the mugger, 'an hour ago I was lying safely unconscious at the foot of Beachy Head having just broken the world's record for Sweden.'

'Look, there's a man rowing a piano ashore and it's not Gloria Honeycombe,' said the lighthouse keeper.

'It's Handel's *Water Music*,' said somebody who up to then had remained silent.

'For God's sake, man,' said McGonagall, 'who are you?'

'I'm somebody who up to now has remained silent,' said the voice.

'Ahoy there,' said the man rowing the piano ashore.

'Ach, there's no Ahoy here,' said McGonagall. 'Are ye sure ye've got the right address?'

'Yes, I've got the right address, it's Carnegie Hall.'

'This is Carnegie Hall?' said the lighthouse keeper.

'According to Gronnicles Streetmap of Sweden it is.'

'Good God, all these light years I've thought it was the Eddystone Lighthouse and now suddenly I'm unemployed. It *can't* be Carnegie Hall. Every night for the past thirty years I've lit the light to stop the ships crashing.'

'I've never heard of a ship crashing into Carnegie Hall,' said McGonagall.

'Ah, that's because I lit the light every night,' said the lighthouse keeper.

'Good God,' said George Gershwin, for it was he. 'All these years I've been giving concerts at the Eddystone Lighthouse, no wonder I stink of fish.'

'How did you find out where I was?' said McGonagall.

'Simple,' said Gershwin. 'I found out where you were.'

'Where was I were?' said McGonagall angrily.

'Allow me,' said somebody that was still somebody who up to then had not spoken. And they allowed him.

There was a loud splashing as a prison warder dragged himself ashore.

'Has anybody seen a Charles Crippen and his string go this way?' he asked.

'Nae,' said McGonagall, and SPLASH went the sea as the prison warder plunged back in.

'There goes a brave man,' said McGonagall.

'Did you notice that one of his arms was eight feet longer than the other?' asked the lighthouse keeper.

'Aye,' said McGonagall. 'I suppose that was the long arm of the law, or as we say in Scotland, the lang orm of the loo.'

'Yours must be a wonderful country,' said the coloured gentleman, who now had the chicken under his arm and was boiling an egg.

'I wonder if he knows where she is,' said the lighthouse keeper, pointing at the retreating prison warder.

'Who? Molly Quotts?' said McGonagall.

'No, Gloria Honeypots,' said the lighthouse keeper.

'Shhh,' said Gershwin and went into the 'Rhapsody in Blue'.

It meant nothing to McGonagall, who was colour-blind. To him it sounded like the 'Rhapsody in Brown'. 'What's it sound like to you, coloured gentleman?' said McGonagall.

'Dat am sounding like a piano,' said the black man.

Thud! A hard-boiled egg hit McGonagall in the middle of his forehead.

'Ach, that's better,' said McGonagall. 'You're getting the range.' He put the boiled egg in his breast pocket. 'I've had a mind to keep that till I find some soldiers.'

'Look at the time,' said the lighthouse keeper.

They all dutifully looked at the time.

'Now what?' said McGonagall.

'I thought it would make a break,' said the lighthouse keeper.

The drenched figure with an eight foot arm dragged itself ashore. 'Are you sure you haven't seen him go this way?' said the warder.

'No, have you seen Gloria Honeybone?'

'Yes, she's at Broadcasting House, Portland Place, London W1.'

'No wonder she's not here again, then,' said McGonagall.

Splash went the figure and dived into the sea. They watched as the flailing figure circled and recircled the lighthouse many times.

'Ach, it's that lang arm that's doing it,' said McGonagall.

> Ooooooh, terrible flailing swimmer in the sea,
> He keeps going round and round, you see.
> It's through that great lang arm that's nearly ten foot three
> That makes him cry, 'Deary, deary, deary me.'
> He would be awful fine

If only he could swim in a *straight* line.
Instead, he keeps going round Carnegie Hall,
Which can't be very good for him at all.
For sure he'll find that Charlie Crippen one day;
Until he does he's only on half pay.

'Feel better?' said the Fishery Inspector, etc.

'Och aye, it's mony a mickle and muckle and y're gannles on yere Grollicks,' said McGonagall.

'It's time to light up,' said the lighthouse keeper, climbing eight hundred stairs to the very top of the top.

The great light crashed out across the sea.

'This ought to bring the crowds in,' said McGonagall, dropping his kilt, and it did.

The staircase was booked out, as were the rocks outside. Even the chicken was booked out.

'Ladies and gentlemen,' said Gershwin as he walked on stage, followed by his piano, 'I'm halfway through "Rhapsody in Blue" – bar 156, to be precise. I won't keep you long, in fact I'll play it at the new reduced rates for matinées and you will all be home by half-past eight in time to see Gloria Hunniford.' So saying, he walked off the stage and they were all home by half-past seven.

CHAPTER TWENTY-THREE

Howarth Parsonage

Upstairs, Bramwell Brontë, naked, was massaging himself with Vaseline, his eyes rolling madly around his head, his ears ablaze with dandruff. 'This is the life,' he screamed as he downed another bottle of laudanum.

Downstairs, the Reverend Patrick Brontë was writing his Sunday address: 'Howarth Parsonage, Howarth, Yorkshire.'

In the music room, Charlotte knelt in silence in front of the upright Broadwood. She worshipped the piano. There was a knock on the door. This could be the Reverend Ian Paisley, but it wasn't. It could be William McGonagall and it was.

'Och, wee lassie, you must be the Reverend Ian Paisley.'

'No,' she said. 'You could be the Reverend Ian Paisley, but you're not, and I'm not the Reverend Ian Paisley as well.'

'Ach, you must be Charlotte Bromley.'

'Not quite,' said Charlotte Brontë.

'So you're not quite Charlotte Bromley,' said McGonagall. 'Charlie Bromley then?'

'Wrong, wrong, wrong,' she said, clapping her hands gaily and pointing to the brass name plate.

McGonagall looked at it. 'Ah, of course I've been a fool of a mon, you are Charlotte Brass Name Plate!'

'I'll make it easy for you,' said Charlotte.

'Oh, great,' said McGonagall. 'I could do with one, which room shall we use?'

'You naughty Scotsman,' she said, hitting him with a stick. 'I am Charlotte Brontë!'

'Then you must have been in the middle of writing *Wuthering Heights*!'

'No, actually I'm in the middle of doing the laundry.'

'Och, my brother did one last week and the police caught him,' said McGonagall. 'They caught him by the cobbler's. That's a fine piano,' he added, then, 'Can ye no give us a fine tune?'

'It had a fine tune this morning,' she said. 'He just left.'

'Can ye no play some colours, for I'm tone deaf you see.'

There came a screaming sound as the naked figure of Bramwell Brontë covered in Vaseline and dog hairs came bounding down the stairs and out the front door, slamming it behind him and catching them.

'He's always doing that,' said Charlotte.

'I wondered why they were so swollen,' said McGonagall.

A further scream came from Bramwell as he extricated them.

'Where's he going?' said McGonagall.

'The tailor's,' she said. 'You see, tonight is one of the hunt balls.'

'Och, I hope he finds a pair,' said McGonagall.

There was a knock at the door. It was the postman. 'Does a William McGonagall live here?' he said.

'Not yet,' said McGonagall, 'but things could improve.'

'There's a parcel for you,' said the postman.

'Ah, I've always wanted a parcel,' said McGonagall, opening it.

It was George Gershwin and his piano.

'Ah, still travelling on the cheap, eh?' said McGonagall.

'Cheap A?' said Gershwin. 'The Cheap A? *That's* it! The Cheap A Train.'

'Is this man Jewish?' asked Charlotte Brontë.

'Yes, aye.'

'How long has he been like that?' she said.

'Oh, right up until now,' said McGonagall. 'Once you're on it's hard to get off.'

'Is this a Kosher house?' said Gershwin.

'Yes,' twittled Charlotte.

'All right, two cheeseburgers,' said Gershwin. 'One with and one without.'

'With and without what?' said Charlotte.

'Without tigers,' said Gershwin.

'You don't like tigers?' she said.

'Surprised?' said Gershwin.

'I think I'll stand inside this cupboard for a while,' said McGonagall, and he did.

'What are you doing in here?' said a man and a woman. 'Can't you see it's occupied.'

'I can see you're both heavily occupied,' said McGonagall. 'I'm taking shelter in here from a cheeseburger without tigers, whichever comes first.'

'Oh,' said Charlotte, 'look, there's a man swimming up the garden path.'

'There must be a shortage of water,' said Gershwin without tigers.

'Has he got one arm longer than the other?' said McGonagall.

She rushed out with a tape measure. She came back flushed, it was all over for her.

'No,' she said. 'All his parts are equal in total length to the other.'

The man with all his parts equal swam through the front door, up the steps, on to the first landing, out of the window, down the wall and across the Yorkshire Moors in the direction of.

'Och! Wet me willie with a window wiper, who was *that* hen?' said William Topaz.

'That was Heathcliffe,' said hen.

'Oh, I'd say he was due for a rest,' said McGonagall.

'Like it?' said Bramwell Brontë, bursting through the door wearing a purple toga, a laurel wreath and a smoking violin.

'You can't go to hunt balls like that,' said Charlotte Brontë.

'Where have they hidden them?' said William Topaz.

'I'm not going to hunt balls,' said Bramwell. 'I'm going up for a kip.' He went up the stairs sinking a bucket of laudanum, shouting 'Rome is Burning' and applying dog hairs.

'I think he's due for a rest as well,' said McGonagall.

'Is there any insanity in the family?' asked Gershwin without tigers.

'Yes,' said Charlotte, 'and it's him.'

'Now, Mr Gershwin, can you play any coloured slave plantation music?' asked Charlotte.

Quickly blacking up, he sat at the piano and sang with a powerful Jewish accent:

Oh Lordy Lordy, I got dose blacked-up blues
From ma head to ma shoes!

'Oh dear,' said Charlotte. 'I'll go and see how your cheeseburgers are getting on.'

She was out there for fourteen minutes three point two seconds. 'You'll be glad to know that the cheeseburgers are getting on fine.'

'There's an old Scottish saying,' said McGonagall.

'Is there?' said Gershwin.

'Yes,' said McGonagall, 'there is.' And apparently there was. It was, 'Man with Phantom on head better off than man with tin leg in thunderstorm'.

'Who's that in a thunderstorm down there?' came the voice of the Reverend P. Brontë.

'It's all right father,' said Charlotte. 'It's a Scotsman and a Kosher.'

The Reverend P. Dodson went back to his room to massage the Old Testament.

'Ach,' said McGonagall, peering out of a window. He liked a good peer. 'It's getting dark.'

'It happens every night round here,' said Charlotte. 'Old customs die hard,' she added.

'I knae a customs officer who died hard,' said McGonagall. 'Dick Bonk. He fell in a trough of cement. He's now one of the

86

supports of the bridge over the M25. Every month his widow lays a bag of flower at the base.'

'Still no tigers,' said Gershwishin with a sigh of relief in C.

'Bag of flower? Surely you mean a wreath of flowers,' said Charlotte.

'Do I?' said McGonagall.

'Yes,' said Charlotte. 'Flour is for making bread.'

'What do flowers make?' said McGonagall.

'They don't make anything,' said Charlotte.

'That's a waste of money,' said McGonagall. 'No, she put a bag of flour in case a passing motorist wanted to make bread.'

'Passing motorists don't make bread,' said Charlotte. 'Passing bakers do.'

'Oh,' said McGonagall. 'Then I stand corrected,' he said, rising from a chair and doing another quick peer out the window.

'You dirty bugger,' said a voice from unconsecrated ground below.

The Reverend P. Brontë came down the stairs with a bald dog. 'Has anyone seen any dog hairs around here?' said the Reverend.

'Yes,' said Charlotte, clapping her hands together and doing a little pirouette. 'They're upstairs asleep under Bramwell's toga.'

The dog gave a baleful howl.

'Don't worry, little doggie,' said McGonagall. 'I'll lend you ma travelling wig.' And so saying, placed a blond parted toupee on the animal's head.

'That toupee's wasted on a dog,' said George Gershwin, grabbing it and putting it on his own head.

'You look lovely,' said Charlotte, clapping her hands and doing a pirouette.

The dog gave another baleful howl.

'There, there, little doggie,' said McGonagall. 'This aught to keep him quiet.' Gently, with great warmth and affection, he picked up the little doggie and threw it out of the window.

'That's no way to treat a wee doggie,' said the Reverend McBrontë.

'That was no treat,' said McGonagall. 'That was a sudden impulse.'

The wee dog landed on the Yorkshire Moors, who were passing at the time.

'Look,' said Mrs Moor. 'A bald wee doggie, it's the first we've seen this year!'

'So it is, dear,' said Mr Moor, and added, 'It's also the last, dear,' and threw it back through the window.

It landed on the sleeping figure of Bramwell Brontë, whose eyes, distended with belladonna, stood out like organ stops.

'This is great stuff,' he said, downing yet another bottle of laudanum. 'Other people see pink elephants, not me! *I* see bald wee doggies, but not for long!' – and hurled it back out of the window.

The wee dog gave a mournful howl and took revenge on tree after tree.

'Now,' said Charlotte, clapping her hands gaily and doing pirouettes, 'now we've settled that, where will you be staying the night?'

'I'm afraid, madam,' said McGonagall, 'I must spend the night here.'

'Why?' said Charlotte, clapping her hands gaily and doing a pirouette.

'For fuck's sake, stop that,' said Gershwin. 'It's driving me insane.'

'Take no notice of him,' said McGonagall, clapping his hands gaily and doing a pirouette.

It was the end of a long day.

CHAPTER 6

Dawn, the sun broke over Howarth Parsonage. Also broke were McGonagall and McGershwin. We find them outside Al Capone's speakeasy in Chicago on Number One Certain-Death-Street, singing, 'Way down on de' levee . . . ' while holding out a begging bowl.

There came a burst of machine-gun fire, a shotgun blasted their suits from their bodies, there were pistol shots which perforated McGonagall's kilt revealing the secret hiding place of Bonnie Prince Charlie. The shotgun blasted the wig from Gershwin's head, a remarkable feat of marksmanship. A silver dollar fell from a window on to the plate.

'T'anks a lot, youse guys, t'anks for the practice,' said Al Capone, opening up again with his tommy gun.

Another silver dollar landed on his plate, together with another burst of gunfire, this time from Lucky Luciano. 'Keep still, you guys, I haven't got all day,' he said.

'*We* could either end up rich or dead,' McGonagall cried as a further shotgun blasted the sporran from his body, showing a gaping hole in his kilt.

'Hey, you there,' said a policeman, 'is that indecent exposure or a Groucho Marx lookalike?'

'Nae,' said McGonagall, 'these are my own wedding tackles.'

'I wouldn't tackle them myself,' said the policeman.

'I should think not,' said McGonagall. 'These are private parts!'

'If I had a part like that,' said the policeman, 'I'd play it on the trombone. Now, move on before I arrest you for being Negroes.'

McGonagall was outraged. 'You mean coloured gentlemen,' he said.

'I'm not a mean coloured gentleman,' said the cop. 'I'm a policeman.'

Gershwin said, 'Now look, this is not helping my career. I'm an outstanding musician.'

'That's right, he's standing out here,' said McGonagall, 'also he has outstanding rent.'

'It must be settled at once,' said Gershwishin.

'Of course,' said McGonagall, pointing to his pocket.

'Twenty-nine dollars sixty,' said Gershwin.

'That will do nicely,' said McGonagall, pocketing the money.

'I had no idea you were my landlord,' said Gershwin.

'Neither did I,' said McGonagall. 'Can I have another three months in advance?'

'Don't pay him,' said the policeman, putting down his trombone, who up till then had been playing 'The Hole in McGonagall's Kilt'. 'For three months you can both live rent free in Alcatraz.'

'Gee, this is great of you,' said Gershwin as they stepped into the boat and were rowed across to the island.

McGonagall gave a little giggle, a little hop, skip and a jump, and disappeared through the bottom of the boat.

'Help!' screamed McGonagall.

'Stay where you are,' said the policeman. 'I'm coming to join you,' he cried as the boat sank.

'Ahoy,' shouted the captain of a passing tramp steamer. 'Are you escaping from Alcatraz?'

'No,' said McGonagall, 'we're trying to get in.'

'That's a new one,' said the captain, and pointed a freshly capped tooth. 'I'll get you aboard,' said the captain. 'I could use some new deck hands. I could also do with some new deck feet and deck chairs.'

'Make up your mind,' said McGonagall. 'We've only got a limited supply down here.'

'Oh, this is a fine ship,' said McGonagall as they were hauled aboard. 'Is this an oil tanker?' he added.

'No,' said the captain. 'It's a tramp.'

'Och, a tramp tanker,' said McGonagall.

'Yes,' said the captain, 'the holds are full of them.'

A great groan went up from the tramps in the hold. 'Bread,' they moaned, 'bread.'

'Here,' said the captain, hurling down six loaves and six fishes. 'If it's good enough for Jesus, it's good enough for you,' he shouted.

'He's not down here,' said the tramps.

'Then there's more for you,' said the captain.

'Don't tell me you've had Jesus on board,' said McGonagall.

'All right,' said the captain, 'I won't tell you.'

'This is not getting my career anywhere,' said Gershwin as he dried off his piano.

'Good heavens,' said the captain, 'are you George Gershwin?'

'Yes, I *am* George Gershwin,' said George Gershwin.

'Are you *the* George Gershwin?' said the captain.

'Yes, I *am the* George Gershwin,' said *the* I *am* George Gershwin.

'Not the George Gershwin who is *the* I *am* George Gershwin?' said the captain.

'Yes,' said *the* George Gershwin. 'I *am the* George Gershwin who is *the* I *am* George Gershwin.'

'Well,' said the captain, 'I hate all of you, especially the one who writes music. Which one is it?'

'It's me,' said George Gershwin. 'I am,' he added.

'I'm going to give you a free trip,' said the captain, hurling him and his piano over the side. 'There, that didn't cost you a penny.'

'You'll pay for this,' screamed Gershwin.

'All right then,' said the captain, 'it's been worth it, how much?'

'For ruining my dress suit and my piano, a thousand dollars.'

'Very well,' said the captain.

'How will you get it to me?' screamed Gershwin with eels now up his trousers.

'Datapost,' said the captain. He stuck the money in McGonagall's hand and threw him over the side.

McGonagall shouted, 'Recorded delivery and Splash' as he struck the water, he struck it.

CHAPTER X

Dawn broke over a beach at Cape Town in the Republic of South Africa and McGonagall in full coon make-up dragged himself out of the sea.

'I don't believe this,' said a white policeman. 'Here's a kaffir trying to get *in*.'

'I'm nae a kaffir,' said McGonagall, wiping off the black.

'He's gone white with fear,' said the disbelieving policeman. 'Now,' said the policeman, 'I'll just set this wee doggie on you for practice' – and released a Dobermann Pinscher.

'But I'm white,' said the speeding McGonagall.

'Don't worry, he's colour-blind and he needs the practice,' shouted the policeman.

'There, there, good doggie,' said McGonagall as the animal took him by the throat and tried to drown him.

'Aha, that's not fair,' said the policeman as McGonagall tried to push the animal's head under the sea. 'Now look what you've done to my poor doggie,' said the white policeman. 'You've filled him up with water.'

The policeman held the dog up by its tail and drained it out.

'I'm going to be frank with you,' said McGonagall. 'Usually I'm William but today I'll be Frank. I dinnae like it here.'

'Well, stand over there then,' said the policeman, hitting him.

'No, it's no better here,' said McGonagall from his position on top of the recumbent dog's head.

'I can't understand,' said the policeman, hitting him. 'He's never let anybody do that before.'

McGonagall in his position atop the Dobermann Pinscher

'He's not likely to let anybody do it again either,' said McGonagall. 'He's dead.'

'He's never done that before either,' said the policeman, hitting him.

'Ach,' said McGonagall, 'there's always a first time.'

The policeman hit him.

'Ahoy there,' cried a Kosher voice from the sea.

'My God, man,' said the policeman, 'there's another kaffir trying to get in on a piano.'

'Nae, he's Jewish,' said McGonagall.

'They all say that,' said the policeman, hitting him. 'That's how they get in.'

'Well, it's time I got *out*,' said McGonagall. He struck out for the nearest Gershwin and piano available. 'We must get away from this place!' he said. 'I've just been attacked by a fierce South African dog.'

'Where is it?' asked Gershwin.

'It's dead,' said McGonagall.

'It's unusual to be attacked by a dead South African dog,' said Gershwin. 'You're lucky it wasn't alive.'

'It was alive,' said McGonagall.

'Oh, what happened?' said Gershwin.

'I killed it with death,' said McGonagall.

'And that's when it attacked you?' said Gershwin.

'Yes,' said McGonagall. 'Anything to keep it quiet.'

'Now,' said Gershwin, 'we'll play a little game. Close your eyes, darling.'

'OK, now what,' said McGonagall.

'Now you have to guess what I'm doing,' said Gershwin.

'Now you're tying my hands behind my back,' said McGonagall.

'Correct,' said Gershwin with granny knots.

'Now you're tying my ankles together,' said McGonagall.

'Right again,' said Gershwin with sheepshanks.

'Now you're tying a rope round my neck with a big heavy rock on the end,' said McGonagall.

'Brilliant,' said Gershwin with more grannies.

'Now you're feeling in ma sporran and taking out the thousand dollars' advance rent,' said McGonagall.

'Getting better all the time,' said Gershwin.

'Who's getting better all the time?' said Topaz.

'Bert Quidge who is in hospital and getting better all the time,' said Gershwin.

'Now you're picking up the big rock and throwing it out to sea and I am following it,' said McGonagall.

'Absolutely right!' said Gershwin, counting the money and watching McGonagall sink.

CHAPTER XIII

'Back again,' said the South African policeman to McGonagall. 'I've got a new doggie for you.'

'Oh no you haven't,' said McGonagall, and swam back to the piano.

'Well done,' said Gershwin, crying, 'You win the game.'

Gershwin went to the keyboard and started to play the piano out to sea. 'A Life on the Ocean Wave', he played.

'Where are we ganging aglae?' asked McGonagall.

'We're ganging aglae to London, I'm due to play at Margaret Thatcher's coming out party.'

'What's she coming out of?'

'She's coming out of a room,' said Gershwin.

'There's wealth for you. Where are they going to put the piano?' said McGonagall.

'Denis has said I can put it on the landing for the time being.'

'And they want you to play the piano just for her coming out of a room?' said McGonagall.

'Just for that,' said Gershwin.

A grizzled Ancient Mariner swam by towing a dead albatross round his neck. From his sea-spumed lips came the immortal words, 'I wandered lonely as a cloud that floats on high o'er dales and hills and into the Valley of Death rode a host of golden daffodils.'

'Och my God, he's in the wrang poem,' cried McGonagall. 'He'll never make it.'

LATER

McGonagall rose at dawn and entered his wallet. He checked his holdings. He was holding his toothbrush; this didn't add up to much. He counted his cash and held his breath. One, two, three, four, five, six, seven, eight, nine, ten – out. McGonagall could hear a fuzzy voice as his head cleared and he rose from the canvas. What a fool he'd been to enter the ring with Frank

Tyson. That swine of a manager, Micky Duff, put on boxing gloves and promised him riches beyond the dreams of avarice.

'What round was it?' he said as the stretcher carried him to the intensive care dressing-room.

'There were no rounds,' said the stretcher-bearer, 'just you hitting the canvas.'

'What's in it for me?' said McGonagall to Micky Duff the manager.

'A week of intensive care at the Betty Ford Clinic,' came the encouraging reply.

'But I'm not an alcoholic,' he said.

He entered the Betty Ford Clinic. On the Third of January he came out a hopeless alcoholic and a life-long friend of Betty Ford.

'Where have you been?' said George Gershwin; who was controlling the traffic at the Neasden crossroads.

'That's no way to write *Porgy and Bechstein*,' said Topaz McGonagall.

'I'm not,' said Gershwin, 'I'm controlling Neasden traffic.'

'Let me take you away from all this,' said William Topaz.

McGonagall grasped Gershwin round the waist and tangoed down Sunset Boulevard, stopping only to post an empty brandy bottle to his mother.

'That's a perfect present for her,' he said.

'Why?' said Gershwin.

'Because she's a teetotaller,' replied the Scot.

'What made her become a teetotaller?' said Gershwin.

'The bill from the Betty Ford Clinic,' said McGonagall, bending Gershwin backwards in a sensuous tango embrace.

'Hey, you two,' shouted a passing patrolman. 'Are you poufs?'

'Nay,' said McGonagall.

'Well, I *am*,' said the patrolman, lowering his trousers and revealing black fishnet stockings with green garterettes.

'Ohh! Just a minute, laddie,' said McGonagall, releasing Gershwin, who thudded back on to the pavement and lay there unconscious. 'Here, laddie,' said McGonagall, pulling the patrolman from his car and clasping him round the waist.

'Darling,' said the patrolman. 'This is my lucky day.'

'Oh nae it's not,' said McGonagall, and drove off in his car.

'Now look what you've done,' said Gershwin. 'You've lost me the finest tango dancer in the world.'

'In the *world*?' said the pouffy patrolman.

'Where else?' said the Kosher Gershwin.

At which moment McGonagall drove up in a cloud of dust, yanked the unconscious Kosher Gershwin and his pavement into the car and was off.

'That's the second time I've been unlucky today,' said the pouffy patrolman, and raised his trousers in salute to the President. 'To Reagan and Nancy,' he said.

A mile later, Gershwin arose from his speeding pavement. 'My God,' said Gershwin. 'What are you doing?'

'Forty miles an hour,' said McGonagall. 'What are *you* doing?'

'I'm only doing thirty,' said Gershwin. 'Pavements aren't as fast as police cars. Now, will you please drive me to Mrs Shiddock's Boarding House for Young Gershwins and Their Pianos. She said I was outstanding,' said Gershwin.

'Outstanding where, Jock?' said McGonagall.

'Outstanding on the pavement,'* said Gershwin. 'That's why I'm here.'

'Och, she'll be glad to see your pavement again,' said McGonagall, pulling up outside Mrs Shiddock's Boarding House for Young Gershwins and Their Pianos. 'Good heavens,' said McGonagall. 'This is the place, this is Mrs Shiddock's Boarding House for Young Gershwins and Their Pianos. Now, there's a thing, Jamie, some of my best friends are Mrs Shiddock's Boarding Houses for Young Gershwins and Their Pianos.'

'So are some of mine,' said Gershwin.

'Some of yours are what?' said McGonagall.

'Some of mine are Mrs Shiddock's Boarding Houses for Young Gershwins and Their Pianos,' said Gershwishin.

'A propos,' said McGonagall, 'have you ever read *Backfire* by Paul Eddington?'

'Yes,' said Gershwin.

'Yes, what?' said McGonagall.

'Yes, Minister,' said Gershwin.

'Who's that out there?' said a female voice.

'Identify yourself,' said McGonagall from the kneeling load position.

---

* Second use of this joke.

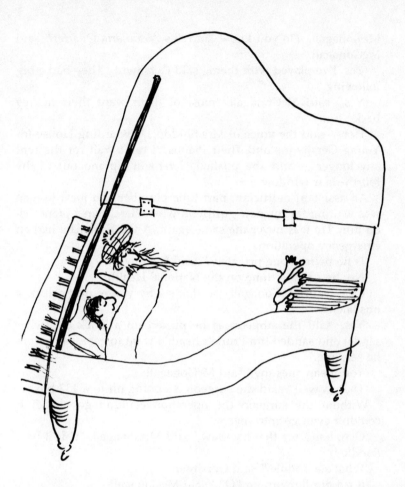

Gershwin and McGonagall resting

'I'm Mrs Shiddock and Her Boarding House for Young Gershwins and Their Pianos.'

'Where's mine?' said Gershwin.

'Where's your what?' said Mrs Shiddock.

'Yes, Minister,' said Gershwishin.

'Thank you, ma'am,' said Paul Eddington and made off in the direction of money.

'Do you think he knows something that we don't know?' said

McGonagall. 'Do you know Durrell's *Alexandria Quartet*?' said McGonagall.

'Yes, I've played with them,' said Gershwin. 'They had a big following.'

'Yes,' said McGonagall, 'most of them want their money back.'

'Here,' said the voice of Mrs Shiddock's Boarding House for Young Gershwins and Their Pianos, 'I can't wait for the rent any longer' – and she pushed Gershwin's piano out of the fourth-floor window.

An assistant mortician, part-time plumber and local Romeo was waiting for his new girlfriend when Gershwin's piano fell on him. He was never the same again. A week later he had an emergency operation.

'Is he being done privately?' said Gershwin.

'No, he's being done on the National Health.'

'Och,' said McGonagall, 'so that's why you're doing it in a bus shelter.'

'Yes,' said the surgeon as he picked up a Black & Decker sander and sanded Jim Prune's head. 'I want to get away before he sees me.'

'You mean sues me,' said McGonagall.

'That as well,' said the surgeon, stepping on to a 137 bus.

Without the surgeon the operation couldn't go ahead, it couldn't even go into reverse.

'Och, hand me that hacksaw,' said McGonagall. 'This'll be a doddle.'

'What's a doddle?' said Gershwin.

'It's a diddle with an "O",' said McGonagall.

'This is getting silly,' said a nurse, and so it was.

'Nurse, put the patient to sleep,' said McGonagall.

'Rock-a-bye baby, on the tree top,' she sang.

CHAPTER TWELVE A

Outside Carnegie Hall the great neon lights flashed out, up, down, sideways, below the waist, then on and off, on and off, again and again. They read:

```
          TONIGHT
      FOR ONE NIGHT ONLY
GEORGE GERSHWIN PLAYS RACHMANINOV'S
         G PIANO CONCERTO
  BY TCHAIKOVSKY WITHOUT A PIANO.
    SEATS IN ALL PARTS EXCEPT.
```

From the stage the acting President, Ronald Reagan, made the announcement. 'Ladies, gentleman, Nancy, and those bastard Arabs/Iranians/Iraqis and Lebanese, etc., tonight we have the pleasure of hearing the very first pianoless concerto. The pianist who will perform without a piano is one of America's greatest pianists, George "Hot Lips" Gershwin. The piano he will not be playing tonight is a Bechstein.'

Said McGonagall to his protégé, 'It's gang tae be a hard nicht braw moolacht bracht the nacht the noo for ye Jamie.'

Gershwin stood clutching a Korean cucumber in his right hand.

'Tell me this,' said McGonagall. 'What good is a Korean cucumber in your right hand?'

'Well, it was getting heavy in the left,' said Gershwin.

'A propos,' said McGonagall. 'Are ye sure you've never read *Backfire* by Paul Eddington?'

'Of course I'm sure,' said Gershwin.

'So! That's *twice* you haven't read it,' said McGonagall. 'What a coincidence, I've only not read it once.'

'Don't read it again tonight and you can catch up with me,' said Gershwin. 'Oh dear,' he added, moving the Korean cucumber to his left hand. 'It's getting heavy again.'

'Give it here,' said McGonagall. 'I'll look after it until it gets lighter again.'

'Then what?' said Gershwin. Gershwin passed the Korean cucumber to the waiting McGonagall. 'I'd no idea you were a waiter,' said Gershwin.

'Aye,' said McGonagall, 'neither did I.'

'For God's sake, don't let anything happen to it,' said Mother Theresa. 'You see, it's only on loan for tonight's concert.'

It was a great coincidence. The entire audience was Korean. They sat in baffled silence as Gershwin sat motionless on a piano stool through the whole of the concerto, holding the cucumber. All was silent, except for the odd shouts from the wings of 'Och, Jamie, slay 'em'. During the last four bars of the concerto he raised the cucumber and was given a Korean standing ovation, primarily because there were no chairs in the hall. It had been a very near thing for Gershwin and his Korean cucumber.

At the end, President Reagan with Nancy Reagan on his back presented him with a White House cucumber-slicer. Reagan, speaking without a script, said, 'Thank you, Yehudi Menuhin and the Third United States Marine Battalion for giving this display of Indian club juggling which has made it a night to remember and you'll be glad to know that as an encore we are going to bomb Libya again tomorrow. Again I would like to thank Mr Gorbachev for not being here tonight. God bless America and its money.'

'Gee up, dear,' said Nancy, and rode the President off the stage.

The curtain came down gradually, McGonagall timed it – Jan, Feb, March, April, May. The first to congratulate Gershwin was Florenz Ziegfeld who had escaped from his window ledge.

'My boy,' said Ziegfeld through the bandages. 'I want you to do this cucumber concerto for me in my big show on Broadway.'

'Give my regards to Broadway,' said McGonagall from the wings.

'Thank you,' said Ziegfeld. Then he screwed up his eyes and unscrewed his legs. 'I remember you,' he said. 'You're the one who made my dreams come true a few moments ago. I remember too a distant shore, the stars fell like rain, etc. Alice Fay, etc.'

'Och, you're a movie buff,' said McGonagall.

'No I'm not,' said Ziegfeld, laughing, 'I'm an envelope buff.'

'Ah, a buff envelope,'* said McGonagall, sticking him down and posting him to China. 'You'll like it there,' he said, putting him on a slow boat to etc.

'You fool of a man,' said Gershwin to McGonagall, the fool of a man. 'There goes my chance of success.'

'No,' said McGonagall. 'There goes Florenz Ziegfeld.'

Through the fallen curtain came a slant-eyed Korean. 'Harro, Geolge Greshwin, Korean Flarmers Corrective Crucumber Farm

---

* Groan. Joke. 3 points to reader.

glive you plesent.' The Oriental bowed furiously at the going rate of fifty a second. From out of the slant-eyed blur appeared a golden cucumber insclibed 'Gleorge Glershwin'.

'You can't eat this,' said Topaz, taking a bite. 'That Korean's a fool,' he said to the blur.

'Thanks for the warning,' said Gershwin to the Korean blur. 'I was about to slice it.'

Picture the scene, dear reader, a blurred Korean, a fine Scotsman in his prime, a George Gershwin and an unsliced golden Korean cucumber.

'Excuse me, sir,' said the upstaged manager. 'Your transport's outside.'

'Och! That's a guid place for it,' said McGonagall. 'But I don't remember ordering a taxi.'

'It's nae a taxi,' said the upstaged manager. 'It's an elephant.'

'I don't remember ordering an elephant,' said McGonagall.

'Well, ye must have, mon,' said the stage manager. 'Elephants never forget.'

'Let's go and have a look at it,' said McGonagall. 'To see if it's there. It might be a mirage.'

'No, it's not a mirage,' said the upstaged manager. 'It's definitely an elephant, didn't you hear me?'

'Well, just this once,' said McGonagall. 'Come, George,' he said. 'It'll take the tae of us to prove that it's there.'

The duo of the Jew and the Scot circled the pachyderm in a passionate tango.

'Wait! Did you nae hear something?' said McGonagall in four-four time, letting go of Gershwin who once again thudded back on to the pavement unconscious. 'Déjà vu,' he said.

McGonagall approached the elephant's trunk. 'Anybody in?' he said, specifically avoiding any jokes about trunk calls, you corny lot of bastards out there.

'Help!' was the reply from inside the elephant.

'What are you doing in there?' shouted McGonagall. 'This is my elephant, get out.'

'No, I'm a squatter here,' said a high-pitched voice.

'My God, you sound like Harry Secombe and I'll Keep a Welcome in the Hillside,' said McGonagall.

Back came the reply. 'I am Harry Secombe and Keep a Welcome in the Hillside,' said the voice of Harry Secombe and Keep a Welcome in the Hillside.

101

'What are you doing in my elephant?' said McGonagall.

'I'm not doing anything at the moment, but if you're not nice to me I will,' threatened the voice. 'Now listen,' went on the voice, 'I need help. The grass is very high in here, and my lawn mower needs sharpening.'

'Just a minute, Sir Harry, how did ye get in there?' said McGonagall.

'I used the ass key,' said the voice.

'You mean the pass key,' said McGonagall.

'No,' said the voice. 'I know what I'm talking about.'

'You'd better come out of there,' said McGonagall, 'or I'll tear up this photograph of Lloyd George.'

'Torn photographs of Lloyd George don't frighten me,' said Sir Secombe.

'I'll have to call the police,' said McGonagall.

'What are you going to call them?' asked the voice.

'Tom, Dick and Harry,' he said, hazarding a guess.

'You can't fool me,' said Secombe through an orifice, 'you're just hazarding a guess.'

That night the Brooklyn Flying Squad surrounded the elephant, their headlights blazing on the pachyderm.

Inspector Elliot Ness called through a bullhorn. 'Come on out, Secombe, we know you're in there and we know we're out here.'

'Come and get me, copper,' snarled Scarface Secombe and Keep a Welcome in the Hillside.

'Come on out,' said Inspector Nescafé, 'with your hands up and your legs down.'

'I'll do a deal,' snarled a Welcome in the Hillside. 'I'll swap my semi-detached house at 12 Piles Road, Neasden for your ivory, marble and gold penthouse at the top of the Empire State Building.'

'That sounds pretty fair to me,' said Elliot Ness.

'He's not well,' said Detective Sergeants Makepeace and Dempsey. 'You'll be all right after this' – and brought their truncheons down on Elliot's head.

'That's funny,' said Elliot. 'I've come over all giddy.'

'Welcome to unconsciousness,' said Gershwin as Ness hit the pavement beside him. 'It's been pretty lonely here without you.'

There was a loud trumpeting as an elephant shot past belching smoke.

'Look out,' said Sergeant Makepeace and Jack Dempsey. 'He's escaping, the bastard's lit a fire in the elephant.'

It was a puzzled Bronx policeman that saw a speeding elephant thunder past trailing smoke and singing, 'We'll Keep a Welcome in the Hillside.'

'Excuse me, puzzled Bronx policeman,' said McGonagall, who took him round the waist and started dancing a passionate tango.

'Excuse me,' said the policeman, 'but weren't you going to ask me something?'

'Aye, it occurred to me that you just might have seen a smoking elephant hurtle past singing "We'll Keep a Welcome in the Hillside".'

'Yes I did,' said the policeman as McGonagall bent him backwards and then upright again.

'Was it nae your duty to stop the creature?' said McGonagall.

'Gee whizz, buddy,' said the 1933 early talking film policeman. 'You sure were right, buddy.' Breaking free, he gave chase, blowing his whistle, whirling his truncheon and shouting, 'Stop that elephant, buddy.'

Behind him, buddy, came a thudding of feet on the pavement as George Gershwin ran past shouting, 'I don't want to be left out of this.' He was followed by Elliot Ness and his pavement shouting, 'Stop that Gershwin trying to stop that policeman trying to stop that elephant, buddy.'

THE NEVADA DESERT

Secombe climbed out of the elephant to find that there was no Welcome in The Hillside.

'There's a fine how do you do,' he said, looking at it.

The scene is an analyst's couch in Swansea, the latest geographical location of Secombe and his elephant.

'How long,' said the psychoanalyst, 'have you and this smoking elephant imagined that you ruled the world?'

'Ever since,' said Secombe.

'Open up,' said a Scottish voice.

There came a thundering on the door.

'Look out!' said the psychoanalyst, diving into the safe. 'It's the Topaz McGonagall. It's worse than AIDS.'

'Open this door,' thundered McGonagall, 'or I'll break my fist down.'

The door shattered and the head of Makepeace and Dempsey splintered through.

'I knew he'd come in handy,' said McGonagall and dropped him.

'The safe!' said Gershwin. 'They're in the safe.'

'Are you in there, Secombe, with that elephant?' said McGonagall.

'No, I am not in here with *that* elephant, I am in here with *this* elephant and a psychoanalyst.'

'So you are in there with *this* elephant and *that* psychoanalyst,' said McGonagall. 'What happened to *that* elephant?'

'I've never had a *that* elephant, only a *this* elephant.'

There came a straining sound.

'Look oot – run fer it, he's going to sing,' said Gershwishin, but too late. There came the sounds of 'If I Ruled the World!'

THE GANGES

Moonlight on the Ganges

It hadn't been an easy journey for McGonagall, George McGershwin and his Kosher piano as they settled by the great Hindu temple on the riverbanks.

'I'm sorry,' said a Pakistani voice. 'It's Thursday and the banks are closed.'

'Oh dear and a half,' said McGershwin in Pakistani. 'You brought me here on a fool's errand.'

'No, I didn't I brought you here on a pavement,' replied McGonagall in Hindu, slipping his Instant-Wog cash card into the riverbank dispenser and collecting a handful of money.

'Are those annas?' said Gershwin.

'Nae,' said McGonagall. 'They're mine! Don't you know the rules?'

'Look, buddy, me and my piano are broke,' said Gershwin. 'Can I have half?'

'Right,' said McGonagall, sawing an anna in half.

'Gee, you're big hearted and big livered,' said Gershwin, looking at McGonagall's X-rays.

'Give me those,' sang McGonagall. 'Those X-rays are secret.'

'What are you two gentlemen doing here with a piano, secret X-ray photographs and a sawn in half anna?' said a Hindu policeman.

'My credentials,' said McGonagall, reaching under his kilt and producing a document. It read: 'This man is a genuine Ganges riverbank inspector. Signed Mahatma Gandhi when I was alive.'

'How do I know this is not a forgery?' said the Hindu policeman.

There was a long pause which contributed handsomely to the silence, broken only by the wailing of the bereaved widows and the splash of the Hindu stiffs hitting the river and floating downstream.

'Och aye,' said McGonagall, 'those stiffs will become a danger to shipping. When the look-out man says, "Slow – Dead Ahead" nobody's going to believe him.'

'You haven't answered my question,' said the policeman. 'Oh, it's *yours* is it, laddie?' said McGonagall. 'I was wondering who the owner was. Do you have a licence for that question?'

A wail went up and came down again. It was Gershwin's. 'Jesus Christ! Some bastard's curried my piano,' he said.

'It's no good telling Jesus Christ, he's been gone for some time,' said McGonagall.

'And,' added Gershwin, 'some swine's poppadomed on my piano stool.'

'Ah, that's what you get when you come to India,' said McGonagall. 'You should have been here last time.'

'I was,' said Gershwin.

'When was that?' said McGonagall.

'*This* was,' said Gershwin.

'Here's something to be getting on with,' said McGonagall, grabbing the Hindu cop round the waist in a passionate curried tango three times round the temple, a quick bout of smallpox and back to George Gershwin.

'Excuse me,' said Gershwin, green with jealousy, purple with anger and Scarlett with O'Hara.

'Who's this woman?' said McGonagall, releasing the Hindu policeman and giving Scarlett's a squeeze.

'I don't know,' said Gershwin. 'She wasn't here two lines ago.'

'Och,' said McGonagall, pulling the policeman up by his turban. 'Arrest that river,' he said.

The curried policeman hurried off with a pair of handcuffs.

'You all, has anyone here seen Rhett Butler?' said Scarlett O'Hahara.

'Nay,' said McG.

'Then,' said Scarlett, 'has anyone here seen Kelly, Kelly from the Isle of Man?'

'Say,' said Gershwin, plunging his fingers into the curry-stained keyboard. 'That's a great tune.'

'Never mind that,' said McGonagall to the curried policeman. 'Have you arrested the Ganges?'

'Yes, sahib, it's under house arrest.'

'Whose house is it under?' said McGonagall.

'It's under mine,' said the policeman.

'Has the damp course gone?' said Topaz.

'Oh yes, sahib, the rat traps are full of fish,' said the policeman. 'Here, here's one for your breakfast,' he said, handing him a salmon.

'That's a great idea for a toon,' said Gershwin. 'Salmon chanted evening,' he sang.*

'Hi there, you all,' said a voice.

'Ach, it's wee Scarlett O'Hara,' said McGonagall.

'Well,' said Gershwin, 'that's better than Scarlett O'Fever.'

'Aye,' said McGonagall. 'Hello, Scarlett, you're back with the wind. How's Rhett Valet?'

'You mean Rhett Butler?' she said.

'Nay, Rhett Valet, did ye no hear he's changed his job.† He's waiting for Lord Longford.'

'Isn't he a peer?' said Scarlett O'Fever.

'Och aye, he does it all over the place,' said McGonagall.

'Pardon, sahib, how long do you want the Ganges under house arrest?' said the policeman.

* Groan 2 points to the reader.
† Groan and 2 points.

106

'Och, about six miles should do,' said McGonagall.

'I've only arrested three,' said the policeman. 'It would have taken two of us to arrest six.'

'Is that within the law?' said McGershwin.

'No, that's within the house,' said the policeman, who opened a large mahogany box reeking of chillies. 'Allow me to introduce you to the Maharajah of Kholapur,' he said.

The rajah rose to his knees, to his shins and finally to his feet. 'Sir, you don't know me.'

'I don't knae ye,' said McGonagall. 'Do ye knae me?'

'I don't knae ye and ye don't knae me either,' said the rajah.

'In that case,' said McGonagall.

'I've just come out of that case,' said the rajah, stepping out of it.

'I was saying that neither of us each knae each other,' said McGonagall.

'I'm glad we agree,' said the rajah, handing McGonagall a pugaree.

'Where's this from?' said McGonagall, wrapping it round his ankle.

'It's from me,' said the maharajah.

'Do I knae ye?' said McGonagall.

'Yes, we met quite recently,' said the maharajah.

'Och,' said McGonagall, doing a little pirouette and tapping his finger on his nose, his kilt flaring out to reveal a massive swing to the left for the Labour Party and a shock for Margaret Thatcher at the size of it. 'It's ma Thursday afternoon amnesia,' said McGonagall. 'I can *never* remember a thing on Thursday afternoons, especially maharajahs. What's today?' said McGonagall.

'It's Thursday,' said the maharajah.

'You see, I couldn't even remember *that*,' said McGonagall. 'And who are you and do I knae ye?'

'I cannot take any more of this, knae ye,' said the maharajah. He threw a rope up, climbed it and disappeared.

'Och, that's a gude trick,' said McGonagall. 'I must take a rope next time I see my bank manager.' (He did, he hung him.) He glanced in a certain direction, screamed and then, with a frenzy of legs and arms, climbed the rope and disappeared.

'Has anyone seen a William McGonagall around here?' said a recently hung Midland bank manager, the rope still intact.

107

'Why, is he overdrawn?' said Gershwin.

'No,' said the bank manager, 'worse than that, he's over here.'

'Follow that rope,' said Gershwin.

'It's a difficult act to follow,' said the bank manager, and ascended the rope and disappeared.

Immediately, McGonagall slid down the rope, followed by the maharajah. They were both overdrawn at the same bank.

'Quick, the rope,' said McGonagall. 'Put it away.'

He gave it a tug. The rope came down with Crippen on the end.

'Still too long,' he said, loosening the noose.

'McGonagall,' came the voice of the bank manager, 'put that rope back at once.'

'We have,' he shouted. 'We've put it back in the box.'

'You can't leave me up here in limbo,' shouted the bank manager, dancing up and down in rage.

'Stop that limbo-dancing,' said a voice. 'Some people down here are trying to get some sleep.'

'Who said that?' said the bank manager from limbo.

'Dick Trollicks,' said a voice, trying to get some sleep down here.

'Have you got an account with the Midland?' said the limbo-dancing bank manager.

'Yes, I've got an account to settle, you bastard,' said Dick Trollicks, trying to get some sleep down here.

'I'll take that into account,' said the limbo-dancing bank manager.

'While you're taking that into a count,' said McGonagall, 'you can take it into the countess as well.'

'I don't know a Countess Aswell,' said the limbo-dancing bank manager.

'Fancy,' said McGonagall. 'Fancy the Midland having a limbo-dancer as a bank manager.'

'Look,' said Gershwin, holding his piano up. 'The Ganges is up to our knees.'

'Oh my God,' said the policeman. 'It must be up to something. I must have left the back door open.'

'It's up to my swonnicles now,' said Gershwin.

'Och, it's always up to something! Ma mither always said, "Son, never trust a Ganges",' said McGonagall.

'We must make for higher ground,' said the maharajah.

'Och,' said McGonagall, 'I don't know of any ground for hire around here.'

'Follow me,' said the maharajah, 'these waters are highly polluted.'

'Polluted with highlies, are they?' said Topaz. 'I should hate to catch them.'

'Oh, they're very hard to catch,' said the maharajah. 'You'll have to use a special bait, like people.'

'Did you hear all that, George?' said McGonagall from high ground.

'Yes, I did,' said Gershwin, from slightly higher ground.

'Me too,' said the maharajamie from a football ground.

A passing coolie struck his wife a glancing blow.

'Do ye not know that it's cruel to strike a woman a glancing blow when there's an "R" in the month?' said McGonagall.

'I thought that was to do with oysters,' said the glancing coolie.

'Aye, you mustn't strike a passing oyster when there's an "R" in the moth either.'

'Moth? You mean month,' said the glancing coolie.

'No, I mean moth, there's no "R" in the month of moth,' said he, glancing a striking coolie.

'Don't you know,' said the coolie, 'that it's wrong to glance a striking coolie when there's a moth in the "R"?'

McGonagall, rather than strike an "R" in the moth, struck a certain pose. 'My lord, my client pleads guilty but insane,' he said.

'Very well,' said Judge Hanging the Jefferys, 'I sentence the "R" in the moth coolie to be hung, drawn and quartered and fined fifty rupees for each quarter; that or his wife will give me relief massage in between cases.'

'I'd rather die than let you hang me,' said the glancing coolie from the gallows.

'Is this hanging day?' said the president of the Royal Academy.

'Nae,' said McGonagall. 'Today is varnishing day' – and applied three coats of it to the glancing coolie, signing it 'William McGonagall, RA'.

'I thought it was vanishing day,' said the coolie, and vanished.

'Does RA stand for Royal Academy?' said the president.

'Nae mon, that stands for Royal Artillery,' said McGonagall.

'I wouldn't stand for that,' said the president.

'I served several years in the Gunners,' said McGonagall.

So saying, he fired a cannon in the general direction of. It fell to earth I know not where.

Mrs Ada Cabbage stood at her front gate saying, 'Where has my bleeding house gone?'

'You'll find this hard to believe,' said her smoke-blackened husband from the ruins, 'but I believe we've just had a direct hit from a man several years in the Artillery.'

'Who ordered it?' she said, swinging backwards and forwards on the gate.

'Not me, my darlin', I would have told you if I'd ordered a direct hit when you weren't here.'

'Who do you think did it?' she said.

'I think it was Princess Margaret,' he said, 'but then, you know I'm never very good at guessing.'

CHAPTER SOMETHING

'One,' said McGonagall, counting his money.

'One what?' said Gershwin astride his piano in G.

'I'm not quite sure till I get the wrapper off,' said McGonagall, removing it.

'That's not one,' said Gershwin astride his piano in A♭. 'That's one toffee.'

'Och, yes,' said McGonagall. 'No wonder the bank wouldn't cash it.'

'I'll swap you this hockey stick,' said Gershwin astride his piano in B♭.

'That sounds a good exchange,' said McGonagall, taking it quickly to the bank.

'We don't cash hockey sticks,' said the teller.

'You tricked me!' said McGonagall, back astride the piano in F with Gershwin. 'Hockey sticks are nae currency any mair.'

'Ah! not *here*,' said McGershwin, astride George McGonagall, 'in *Ghana*.'

'Wait,' said Gershwin, raising the piano lid and sliding McGonagall to the flae. THUD! 'That sounds like a good idea for

110

a song' – and composed himself. 'Thud! Nothing could be *farner* than a hockey stick in *Ghana* in the morning.' Gershwin dismounted. 'I'm stuck for a follow on,' said Gershwin.

'Easy,' said McGonagall. 'You can cash your hockey stick, with any big black Ghana bank on the beautiful bridge over the silvery Tay.'

'Great,' said Gershwin, and telexed the song to an ageing Barbra Streisand.

A year passed away and so did McGonagall's pussy cat Rollo.

'No word from the ageing Barbra Streisand?' said Gershwin from the Finchley labour exchange.

'No, no word from Barbra Streisand,' said McGonagall from the Dundee labour exchange, where he had just been voted UNEMPLOYED MAN OF THE YEAR by Mrs Thatcher.

'We are proud,' said Mrs Thatcher. 'If only we had more dedicated unemployed men like you.'

'This is the Mr Monsieur the French Ambassador,' she said. 'We are having an exchange of unemployed with France, and you have been chosen to be unemployed in France for the next three years, in Marseilles.'

'Adieu,' said the ambassador.

'I am not a Jew,'* said McGonagall, 'I'm a canny Scot.'

'Ah well,' said the Mr Monsieur le French Ambassador. 'It's better than being Selina Scott.'

'I want you to meet ma minder, Mr Jerry Crampton, a Black Belt karate expert,' said McGonagall.

The minder held out his hand.

The Mr Monsieur Ambassador took it and was immediately thrown out of the book.

'There he goes,' said McGonagall, and there he went.

'What a pity Mr Monsieur Ambassador couldn't stay for the ending,' said Mrs Thatcher.

McGonagall hailed a taxi cab. 'Heil! Do you take hockey sticks?' he said to the driver.

'Yes,' said the driver.

'Then take this to Ghana and cash it,' said McGonagall.

'You fool,' said Gershwin. 'There goes our only means of support.'

---

* Yes, used before see page something or other.

'Och, there's many a hockey stick twix a mickle maks a muckle,' said McGonagall, and wondered why Gershwin hit him.

'I'm wondering why you hit me,' said Gershwin.

'There must be some mistake,' said McGonagall. 'I was wondering the same thing about you' – and hit him back.

The taxi cab roared back. 'Did you say Ghana?' said the driver.

'No, I said – there goes our only means of support,' said Gershwin, snatching the hockey stick from the back of the cab, placing a ball on the ground and hitting it up the road. 'Follow that ball,' he said to the driver.

The taxi roared off.

'Stop in the name of the law,' said a policeman. 'This hockey stick is obstructing the pavement. Have you got a licence for it?' said the policeman.

'No, but I have a second-hand umbrella once the property of a Catholic priest with rabies,' said McGonagall.

'Can I see it?' said the policeman.

'If you have good eyesight, yes,' said McGonagall.

'Why?' said the policeman.

'Because it's in Neasden awaiting refurbishment for the London to Brighton Old Car Race,' said McGonagall.

'So, you travel from London to Brighton by umbrella?' said the policeman.

'Yes, it's cheaper than a hockey stick,' said McGonagall.

'Have you any proof of your identity?' said the policeman.

'Yes,' said McGonagall, 'me' – and showed him.

'So, you're claiming to be me,' said the policeman, striking McGonagall rapidly three times on the head with his truncheon. 'I arrest you for impersonating a policeman and resisting a truncheon. Congratulations,' said the policeman, 'you have won three weeks in one of Her Majesty's prisons free of charge.'

'Can you cut me in on this deal?' said Gershwin, folding up his piano.

'Aye,' said the policeman, and belted him three times on the head.

'Well,' said Gershwin, 'that settles our next three weeks' lodgings' – and crashed down to the pavement next to McGonagall.

'I'm going to make an example of you,' said Judge Adolf Balls.

Immediately the judge made an example of him and said, 'There's far too much of this going on.'

'Far too much of what?' said McGonagall.

'Yes,' said the judge, 'far too much of what?'

'What about me?' said Gershwin.

'There's far too much of you,' said the judge pointing at Gershwin. 'You should know better.'

'I *do* know better,' said Gershwin.

'Very well then,' said the judge, and made an example of him.

Gershwin spent the night trying to break into McGonagall's cell. McGonagall lay back in his cell on a Louis Quinze chaise longue. On the floor were sixteenth-century Persian carpets. On the walls hung Degas, Picasso, Turner and Gauguin paintings. From the ceiling hung a hundred thousand pounds' worth of chandelier. A girl with big tits massaged him with Guinness; someone had blundered; mistakenly he'd been sentenced to three weeks at a Cynthia Payne party. He came out three weeks later, four stone lighter, a white wraith on a drip feed wearing fishnet stockings.

'Och,' said McGonagall as the daylight struck his eyes, 'they don't make prisons like that any more.'

'You swine!' said Gershwin, now covered in hoar frost and with stinging nettles on his appendages. 'I've had to sleep rough for three weeks.'

'Thanks for telling me,' said McGonagall, taking off his brassière and girdle and posting them to Billy Cotton Jnr.

'Lucky man,' said Gershwishin.

A huge stretched limousine drove up to a huge stretched halt. Out stepped a huge stretched Negro chauffeur clutching a hockey stick.

'He's from Ghana,' said McGonagall. 'He's holding his pay, we could be in luck here.'

The huge Negro chauffeur opened the huge car door. Out stepped a man in a huge fur coat made out of huge fur. He was smoking a huge cigar and was telling the time from a huge gold watch. 'I,' he said, proffering a huge card, 'am the managing director of Harrods.'

'You lucky bastard,' said McGonagall.

The huge man got back into the car and drove away.

'What's that you were saying about luck?' said Gershwin, now oiling his piano.

113

'Och, look at this,' said McGonagall, pointing to the huge card. 'It says you have just won a holiday for two at the Fort of Siddi bel Abbas in Algeria where a lone company of Foreign Legionnaires are holding out against Sheik the Dripsoff and his Bedouins with only a teaspoonful of water left.'

'Och, an adventure holiday,' said Gershwin.

'Who said that we're nae lucky?' smiled McGonagall, swallowing the card to preserve its identity.

'Let's have a recap on that lucky bit,' said Gershwin, playing it on his piano. 'The holiday fort is surrounded by Bedouins, it's my bet that they're trying to get in.'

'Do you think so?' said McGonagall, easing himself.

'It's my bet,' played Gershwin, 'that those Arabs, if they get into that fort, are going to beat the shit out of those froggie soldiers.'

'D'you think so?' said McGonagall, re-easing himself.

'Now, it says here in the contract,' played Gershwin, 'that they only have a teaspoonful of water. I mean, how many baths could we get out of that?'

'Speaking for myself,' said McGonagall, a dirty bugger, 'ten!'

'Och,' said Gershwin, 'it says here the French defenders are starving to death and have eaten all the cats and dogs.'

'Och, poor devils, so they've nae pets,' said McGonagall. 'That shouldn't spoil ooer holiday.'

'No,' said Gershwin with a cadenza, 'I suspect a trick! Harrods have never been particular friends of mine. I think we should send a duplicate you and me to find out the lay of the land first.'

'I *know* the lay of the land,' said McGonagall. 'It's Miss Rita Whiplash, 33 Westbourne Park Terrace – rubberwear £1 extra.'

'Good, that's that out of the way then,' said Gershwin.

It was a great day for the Foreign Legion as the duplicate Gershwin and McGonagall fell from the helicopter, all four of them. They saw the starving Frenchmen preparing a large baking tray and the voice of their captain came wafting up with the smell of gravy. 'Regardez, mes enfants, il arrive, le lunch.'

After this, the gulf between Gershwin and Harrods grew even wider. It had been a near thing. There were some other near things. A wash hand basin, a small milking stool, half a jar of diced carrots. It wasn't much of a place, but to McGonagall it

114

was home. To the Neasden Council it was a chicken shed on an allotment. 'We've all got to make a start,' said McGonagall, and started.

Back at the real McGonagall and Gershwishin, a taxi arrived. 'Here you are,' said the taxi driver, throwing a ball into the chicken shed. 'I followed that ball like you said and that will be £36.50.'

'Please accept this chicken as a down payment,' said Gershwishin.

The phone rang.

'Prince Philip speaking,' said McGonagall, ever cautious.

'Hello, this is Barbra Streisand.'

'Och, Barbra,' said McGonagall, 'it's great to hear ye. I've seen all your films and I have all your records. Can I have your autograph? It's not for me, it's for my wee daughter.'

'Get off the line, you prick,' she said.

'It's for you, George,' said McGonagall.

'Gee, Barb, did you get the toon?' said Gershwin.

'Yes,' said Streisand. 'And there isn't one.'

'You mean you didn't like "Thud! Nothing could be *farner* than the hockey stick in *Ghana* in the morning"?'

'Yes,' she said. 'I didn't like "Thud! Nothing could be *farner* than a hockey stick in *Ghana* in the morning". Why are you persecuting me like this?' she said.

'Nobody else was available at the time. I've seen all your films.'

'What's the best thing you've seen me in?' said Streisand.

'The nude,' said Gershwin, leaving the right hand free.

'Well, we all have our hang-ups,' said Streisand.

'I know,' said Gershwin. 'But mine's hanging down.'

'How long has it been like that?' said Streisand.

'That's as long as it's ever been,' said Gershwin.

'Here's another hang-up,' said Barbarella Streisand, and hung up and went on to stardom while Gershwin and McGonagall went on to Neasden.

'Is my umbrella ready yet?' said McGonagall.

'No, it had rabies,' said the man.

'You mean you put my umbrella down?' said McGonagall.

'Yes,' said the man.

'Right,' said McGonagall and picked it up again.

'That'll be a pound,' said the man.

'A pound?' said McGonagall. 'It's cheap at half the price,' said the man.

McGonagall gave him half the price* and the man gave him half an umbrella.

'Let's pretend we're rich,' said McGonagall, so they ordered Old English tea with crumpets, scones and tandoori chicken at the Ritz.

'Ooh,' said McGonagall. 'Time for a change.' He whipped off his kilt and donned an inverted hedgehog-skin electric jockstrap.

'Stop that screaming,' said the manager. 'It's very unpopular.'

'Would it help if I accompanied him on the piano?' said Gershwin.

'Oh no,' said the manager. 'You'd get up the resident pianist's nose.'

'Oh no,' said Gershwin, showing his measurements. 'I'm much too big to get up the pianist's nose.'

'Not if it's a piece at a time,' said the manager, producing a carving knife.

It was a very tense moment.

'You're joking,' said Gershwin.

'No, I'm Joe Smith,'† said the manager. 'Why?'

'Well, every dog has its day,' said Gershwin.

'True,' said the manager. 'And there's plenty more fish in the sea.'

'We didn't order any fish,' said McGonagall. 'We ordered tandoori chicken.'

'Very well then, there's plenty more tandoori chicken in the sea,' said the manager.

A quivering joke waiter approached. 'Excuse me,' he said. 'Are you the gentlemen who ordered more tandoori chicken in the sea?'

Gershwin nodded and so did McGonagall, but they did it privately by hiding under the table.

'Is she under the weather?' said the joke waiter.

'No,' said Gershwin. 'She's under the table and, surprise, surprise, would you believe it's a *he*?'

'Of course,' said the joke waiter, 'a she is a he and there is

---

* Yes; again!
† Yes, groan.

116

plenty more tandoori chicken in the sea and would you please settle the bill before they come for you?'

'Very well,' said McGonagall. 'Take it out of this' – and handed him a soup plate.

'This is a soup plate, sir, and is not legal tender in this country.'

'Ah,' said McGonagall. 'It's like the tandoori chicken which was also not very tender in this country.'

'Then take it to another country,' said the joke waiter.

At that point they stopped being rich and left.

'Ghana,' they said to a puzzled taxi driver.

It was a Thursday and a dog had had it.

Ghana by Taxi

'How did you know I was from Ghana?' said the merry taxi driver.

'We saw the film,' said Gershwin.

'Oh dear, dear, dear,' said McGonagall. 'Your piano, you've forgotten it.'

'Oh no I haven't,' said Gershwin. 'I was thinking of it at that very moment and would have gone on doing so had you not interrupted me.'

'Ghana,' said the taxi driver, pulling up outside a collection of mud huts, a pile of hockey sticks and AIDS.

'That must be the bank,' said Gershwin.

'How many hockey sticks is the fare?' said McGonagall.

'Hockey sticks?' said the taxi driver, '£209.50.'

'Bad news,' said McGonagall, 'we're Bankrupts Anonymous.'

'What does that mean?' said the driver.

'It means you sell the cab.'

'What for?'

'£209.50,' said McGonagall.

Gershwin took one pace forward. 'You miserable swine, McGonagall,' he said, taking one pace sideways and two back. 'You mean to let this man go home empty-handed?'

'No,' said McGonagall, and placed a something in the taxi driver's hand.

117

'What's this?' said the merry taxi driver.

'I don't know,' said McGonagall. 'It was dark when I trod in it.'*

'You just wait till I get home,' said the merry taxi driver.

So they waited till he got home.

McGonagall advanced on the Ghanaian bank manager who was eating a neighbour. 'Sorry to break into your lunch, laddie. I'd like to pay this hockey stick into ma account,' said McGonagall.

'But this hockey stick am a counterfeit,' said the bank manager.

'So are these,' said McGonagall, standing on the counter, pointing to his feet.†

'Hoots, mon,' said the bank manager, finishing off his neighbour.

Bow-wow.

Every dog has its day and this dog had just had another.

There was the sound of a bicycle frame. McGonagall, with Gershwin and his piano on the crossbar, screeched to a halt.

'Is that you screeching?' said McGonagall.

'Yes,' said Gershwin. 'I like screeching to a halt.'

McGonagall surveyed the ruins of a house and then gave Mrs Ada Cabbage the bill from the Ritz.

'You don't look like a surveyor,' said Mrs Ada Cabbage.

'Neither do you,' said McGonagall, 'but one of us has to be and it's my turn. You are the owner of a fine building plot.'

'Looks more like the bleeding Gunpowder Plot,' said the husband, poking the fire.

It was the first poke he'd had in about twenty years. McGonagall erected a sign:

BUILDING PLOT
AND SLIGHTLY SCORCHED COUPLE
FOR SALE

it read.

'What's in this for me?' said Mrs Cabbage.

* Yes! Again!
† Groan. 7 points to reader.

'Eviction,' said McGonagall, and moved on to the house next door which he sold to Gershwin.

'What have you done?' said the owner – a circus midget called Nick Sheddells – peering through the letter-box.

'Ach, come on,' said McGonagall, 'this haese is much too big for you now that all the children are married and left.'

'But I'm not married or left,' said Nick.

'Oh dear, I'm sorry to hear that,' said McGonagall. 'I'll fix you up with somebody!' And so saying, he proposed to him on one knee, with the elbows tucked tightly into the waist.

'We'll wait here for a passing vicar,' said McGonagall.

They did wait and, after he'd passed, McGonagall said, 'He appears to have missed us.'

McGonagall and the midget set off in hot pursuit of a marriage. The vicar was appalled. 'I can't marry two men, one a midget and both travelling at thirty miles an hour. That's no way to hold a wedding.'

'All right,' said McGonagall. 'Just marry one of us' – and gave him a soup plate.

When they returned to the midget's house, Gershwin was putting a Bed and Breakfast sign in the window which said 'No Midgets'.

'That's awful hard luck,' said McGonagall, going in and slamming the door.

'You'll be hearing from my solicitors about this,' shouted the midget through the letter-box.

The phone rang.

'Hello, Gershwin Manor,' said the piano player.

'This is the midget's solicitor,' said the caller.

'God, that was quick,' said McGonagall. 'Or is it a coincidence?'

'No, it's not a coincidence,' said Gershwin. 'It's definitely the midget's solicitor.'

'Who's that speaking?' said the midget's solicitor.

'You are,' said Gershwin.

'Who am I addressing?' said the midget's solicitor.

'Me,' said Gershwin.

'Yes, but which me are you?' said the midget's solicitor.

'Which me am I?' said Gershwin.

'No, which me are *you*,' said the midget's solicitor.

'Give me that phone,' said McGonagall, so Gershwin gave

him the phone and he kept it. To this day it stands as a monument to the Jew and the Scot, which was no use to the midget jammed in the letter-box with his solicitor still saying 'Which me are you?'

He was still saying it two days later when they took him away. As the solicitor Reuben Croucher lay on a psychiatrist's couch, McGonagall shouted down the phone, 'Why are you persecuting me and the piano player like this? For three days I've been listening to you saying "Which me are you?" Let me tell you that *I* am the me of you.'

'Give me that phone,' said the psychiatrist, snatching it from the solicitor, who only charged him a pound. 'Listen, whoever the I of me you are, you have caused my patient to have a breakdown.'

'I'll send the AA round and have him towed away right away,' said McGonagall.

'You can't tow him away, he hasn't paid yet and so far he owes me eight million pounds,' said the psychiatrist.

'That makes you a millionaire, I thought you were a psychiatrist,' said McGonagall.

'I was, but now I'm a millionaire.'

'Send me seven million and I'll let you keep the rest,' said McGonagall.

'Do you think I'm mad?' said the psychiatrist.

'Money mad,' said McGonagall. 'You mean swine. You'd no send a poor starving Scottish Poet Laureate a wee seven million pound coin to help him on his way.'

'On his way where?' said the psychiatrist.

'To the bank,' said McGonagall.

By this time George Gershwin and his piano had reached the door of the psychiatrist's consulting room. He burst into the room.

'How dare you burst into this room,'* said the psychiatrist. 'Clean that up.'

'I'm warning you,' said George Gershwin and his piano. 'That phone is bugged.'

'Who's bugging it?' said the psychiatrist.

'Some bugger or other,' said Gershwin.

'Can I get a word in somewhere?' said the solicitor.

* Yes again!

120

'Yes, Iceland,' said the psychiatrist. 'It's very nice there this time of the year. They say that Reykjavik is a must.'

'A must? I thought it was a city,' said the solicitor.

'No, it is a must,' said the psychiatrist.

'Is this him?' said the AA man, backing his breakdown truck up to the couch.

'Yes.'

'We'll soon have him back to his old self,' said the AA man, chaining the solicitor round the legs and hoisting him up by the crane. 'Are you a member of the AA?' said the AA man.

'Yes, I'm on thirty bottles a day,' said the solicitor.

'Ah, that's Alcoholics Anonymous. I meant Automobile Association.'

'I am. I'm a member of the Alcoholics Anonymous Automobile Association.'

'But you're not allowed to drive when you're pissed.'

'I know. That's why I haven't got a car.'

'What have you got?'

'A brewery.'

'Oh, I'll tow you away to the next AA meeting then.'

'Well,' said the drunken solicitor, 'if you can get pissed before we get there, I'll make you a member and you can confess.'

There was a crash as McGonagall burst into the room.

'Oh, not again,' said Gershwin. 'I've just cleaned mine up.'

'Och, do a pal a favour, Jamie,' said McGonagall, and handed him a mop.

'Look, who's going to pay for all this?' said the AA man.

'Let's put it like this,' said McGonagall. 'Not me.'

'Well, how much is it?' said Gershwin.

'Twenty pounds,' said the AA man.

'Well, put it like this,' said Gershwin. 'Not me as well.'

'What about you?' said the AA man, pointing at the rich psychiatrist.

'Let me put it like this,' said the psychiatrist, who had rapidly not become rich. 'He's not paid me yet.'

The drunken solicitor hanging upside down from the mobile crane said, 'I'm no in a position to pay.'

CHRISTMAS

The bells of St Martin's rang out, snow fell, the children sang carols and it was Christmas Day in the workhouse. The poor of the parish were eating a charitable crust with fishbones and applecores recently donated by Mrs Thatcher at the Charing Cross Soup Kitchen.

'Ah, this is the place,' said McGonagall, entering, followed by a snow-covered grand piano, a drunken upside-down solicitor, a pissed AA patrolman, a bankrupt psychiatrist, a scorched married couple and a midget with a letter-box jammed on his head.

At the sight of this, the impoverished soup-slurping poor of the parish gave a great groan. 'Merry Christmas,' they all groaned.

Ooooooooooooh [said McGonagall], 'twas in the year of 1888,
Christmas was approaching at a great rate
And the starving crippled beggars of London's street
Sat awaiting for something to eat.
Some were waiting standing up
And some stood lying down,
Some had come from this country,
The others were coloured brown.
The good city fathers were sending lots of nourishing things:
Fishbones, potato peelings and bits of tasty strings.
And so they all sat down to this great charitable treat
And when they'd finished they all stood up and groaned
   'Now can we have something to eat?'
And the poorhouse manager said, 'You are an ungrateful
   bunch.
What more do you want?' And someone said, 'Lunch.'
They fell to their knees and gave thanks to the rich of the nation
Halfway through which most of them died of starvation!

'Ah, I feel better after that little poem,' said McGonagall.
'Yes, it's a pity they didn't live to hear it,' said Gershwin.
'I couldn't quite hear it,' said the midget.
'Ah, that's because you're further down,' said McGonagall.

'Now we've got to get out of here,' said McGonagall, 'before the next meal arrives, or we'll starve to death.'

'I know how to get out of this,' said McGonagall, leading them to the top table at the Ritz, his favourite café.

'Do you serve crabs?' said McGonagall to the waiter.

'No, sir,' said the waiter.

'That's the wrang answer,' said McGonagall. 'Now then, what's the fare?'

'Sit down, sir,' said the waiter. 'We serve anybody.'

'Did you no hear me, mon, I said what's the fare?'

'There is no fare, sir. This is a restaurant, not a tram.'

'I see, how far do you go?'

'We go as far as the Peach Melba, sir!'

'I see, we'll go as far as that and then we'll get off.'

CHAPTER X

'This looks like a good place for it,' McGonagall said and put it there. He inserted somebody else's credit card in the cash dispenser. The video screen spelt out:

STOP THIEF.

'Here, let me try,' said Gershwin, inserting his piano. Up on the screen came the words:

Embrace me, my sweet embraceable you.

'It must be out of order,' said Gershwin.

'Not only out of order, it's out of money,' said McGonagall.

'Hello, hello, hello,' said the policeman. 'I've been watching you acting suspiciously.'

'Ach, you shouldn't watch people when you are acting suspiciously. State your business and begone, man.'

'Very well, I'm a policeman and begone, man.'

McGonagall and McGershwin being cautioned by a policeman

'What sort of policeman and begone, man?'

'A constable.'

'Really, I thought you were a Gainsborough.'*

Placing his hand on Gershwin's shoulder, he said, 'I must ask you to accompany me to the police station.'

'Very well,' said Gershwin and launched into 'The Laughing Policeman', which he played all the way to the station.

* Groan, groan!

'You've a fine voice for a policeman,' said McGonagall. 'Have you ever thought of taking it up professionally?'

'Yes,' said the policeman.

'Well, I should leave it there,' said McGonagall. 'As a policeman you have a fine voice but as a singer you're bloody awful.'

The policeman burst into tears and, drying his eyes on his truncheon, disappeared into Bow Street police station. From the front came a naked detective sergeant. 'You've made one of our policeman cry and melted his truncheon,' he said.

'Och, you're a fine figure of a man,' said McGonagall, green with envy. McGonagall took a photograph. 'Now, who are you and remember I have the negatives.'

'I'm a plain clothes detective,' said the nude plain clothes detective.

'For the life of me,' said McGonagall, 'I cannae see your plain claes, laddie.'

'Ah, there's a reason for that. You see, it's at the cleaners, I was in a car chase and it's got traffic jam all over it.'

'Well, that's your story,' said McGonagall. 'My story is that you're a pervert seeking employment and living off an illegal clothing allowance.'

'Well, the truth is,' said the perverted plain clothes detective, 'that I've been passed over for promotion and I've been trying to draw attention to myself.'

'Och,' said Gershwin. 'Passed over? Of course, my life! This is the Feast of the Passed Over.' He hastily lit the candles on the menorah and swallowed a metso. 'There, that's over with.'

'Are you a practising Jew?' said the nude detective.

'No, I'm qualified,' said Gershwin, and showed him.

'We'll be on our way now,' said McGonagall.

'All right,' said the perverted detective.

Two shots rang out and his sporran fell off. McGonagall looked at his watch. 'Och, it's the Glorious Twelfth.'

More shots! Two pheasants fell at his feet. 'Ach, they're frae the pot,' said McGonagall, plucking them.

'I see you're a pheasant plucker,' said Gershwin.

'Sit down, sir,' said a voice. 'We serve crabs.'

'Och, it's the waiter from the Ritz,' said McGonagall.

'Yes, sir, thanks to detective work, BO, halitosis and athlete's foot, I've managed to track you down. You didn't settle the bill.' He raised a tray with the bill on it, and by its side a pistol.

'What's the pistol for?' said McGonagall.

'Read the bill,' said the waiter.

'I've nae got ma glasses. Could you read the amount to me? But first wait till I lie down.'

McGonagall remained standing.

'Well?' said McGonagall. 'What are you waiting for?'

'I'm waiting for you to lie down, what are you waiting for?'

'I'm waiting for a 561 bus,' said McGonagall, and caught it.

Gershwin followed on his piano.

'I'm sorry, sir,' said the conductor. 'Pianos and golfers of Jewish origin are not allowed on the 561 bus. You need a 723.'

'That doesn't go where I want to go,' said Gershwin.

'Where did you want to go?' said the conductor.

'I want to go back to my little grass shack in Kalakaliki Hoola in Hawaii,' sang Gershwin.

'No singing on a 561, sir, you need a 483 for that or a 49^B, Albert Hall.'

'What can you do on this bus?' asked Gershwin.

'You can pay bills for meals that have been eaten at the Ritz,' said the conductor, stripping off his disguise and revealing a tray carrying the bill and a pistol.

'Och, you're a hard man to get rid of,' said McGonagall, and threw him off, shouting, 'There are angels dining at the Ritz and a nightingale sang in Berkeley Square.'

The bus stopped and the black driver came round. 'You am not supposing to throw de conductor off de bus,' he said.

'Hold tight,' said McGonagall, ringing the bell.

Gershwin put the bus into gear and they drove off. It was a good day's takings with a total of £210 and the leaving of twenty-three bewildered passengers in a deserted lane in Surrey.

'Does this bus go to Clapham?' said an old lady.

'Not any more,' said McGonagall as he and Gershwin walked off into the night.

CHAPTER VII

'I don't know what we are doing here,' said McGonagall, breaking a rock with a hammer. Pulling his ball and chain with him, McGonagall approached an armed guard. 'Here Jamie,' he said, 'what's the name of this place?'

'It's the Alabama Penitentiary for first-time coloured offenders,' said the guard.

'But I'm nae black,' said McGonagall.

'Not yet,' said the guard, stirring a bucket of tar. 'Just close your eyes buddy,' he said.

By the time McGonagall had opened them again he had become a first-time coloured offender. 'Is this a trick?' said McGonagall.

'No, it's a prison,' said the guard.

'This is a good time to write *Porgy and Bess*,' said George Gershwin, now also black, and chained to his piano. He launched himself into 'Bess, You is Ma Convict Now', while McGonagall tried to sing his way to freedom. The guard ran his finger down McGonagall's face, revealing a white streak.

'These men are imposters,' said the governor. 'Throw them out.'

'You'd no throw us out on a night like this?' said McGonagall.

'You're lucky you didn't get the chair,' said the governor.

'Can we have the table as well?' said McGonagall.

'Shut up,' said the governor, who'd stood for the presidency three times and sat for it five.

Next year he was going to try for it lying down.

'Hey, Governor,' said the guard. 'Why is you all lying down?'

'You'll find this hard to believe,' he said, 'but I'm practising to be President.' Then he looked up the guard's trouser leg. 'You lucky devil,' he said. 'Give my congratulations to your wife.'

Outside, McGonagall and Gershwin had gathered the splintered piano together and were selling it as true relics of the Holy Cross.

'Hey, you're cute,' said Tina Turner. 'How much a bundle is it?'

McGonagall tries to sing his way to freedom

'You can have a bundle free, darling,' said the prison guard from down his trouser leg.

'I wasn't talking to you,' said Tina.

'You can hae a bundle of four relics for a dollar,' said McGonagall.

'Oh, that's very, very cheap,' she said.

'Is it?' said McGonagall. 'Then it's two dollars.'

'That's too expensive,' said Tina, and drove on.

'Och, she must have had a bad year,' said McGonagall.

'I think I'm having one as well,' said Gershwin.

'We can't wait much longer,' said McGonagall, and set fire to the true relics. 'There, George,' he said, 'that's got rid of a liability!'

'Oy vay,' said Gershwin. 'To think all these years I've been playing true relics of the Cross thinking it was a piano. What would my Yiddisha mother say?'

'She would say,' said McGonagall, '"George, if you can write tunes on true relics of the Cross, why buy a piano?"'

'Ah, Jock,' said Gershwin. 'You've got something there.'

'Where?' said McGonagall.

'There,' said the late George Gershwin and pointed to his knee.

'Ach, you're right, I've got a knee there. Aye, I bought them in Japan.'

'So,' said Gershwin (stand by for groan), 'you've got Japa-knees.'*

'Ach, with that kind of wit you should not be a composer.'

'What should I be?' said the late George Gershwin.

'Unconscious,' said McGonagall, bringing a mallet down on his head.

Faithful McGonagall stood guard over the inert figure, faithfully removing Gershwin's last eight dollars. No sooner had Gershwin revived than McGonagall asked him, 'Would you like to borrow eight dollars at sixty per cent interest?'

'What? At sixty per cent I have no interest at all,' he said, and snatched the money back.

A large steamroller drove up. The driver looked down. 'Is this the way to Glasgow?' he asked.

'It is now,' said McGonagall as they both climbed aboard. 'Will you give us a lift?'

'No, I can't give you a lift,' said the driver, 'I've only got a steamroller, otherwise I'd be going up and down all day, wouldn't I?'

'My friend here has got eight dollars,' said McGonagall.

'Ssshhh,' said Gershwin. 'Don't tell everybody.'

'I've nay told everybody, I've only told him,' said McGonagall.

'Allow me to introduce myself,' said the steamroller driver, removing a large meerschaum pipe from his mouth and inserting it into an alternative orifice. 'You'll find this hard to believe, my dear Watson, but I am the late Sherlock Holmes.'

'Were you nay killed by Moriarty?' said McGonagall.

'No,' said Sherlock, 'don't believe everything you read.'

'Ah, you can't argue with evidence like that,' said McGonagall.

'I'm off to solve a crime in Scotland.'

'What, in a steamroller?' said McGonagall.

'I don't like to rush things,' said Sherlock Holmes. 'Now, hold tight, Watson,' said Holmes as the steamroller moved forward.

* Groan.

CHAPTER XXI

'What are these three men and this steamroller doing on the deck of my ship?' said the captain of the *QE2*.

'About two miles an hour, my dear Watson, why?' said Holmes.

'Wait,' said the captain, 'don't I know you from somewhere?'

'From somewhere, yes, from here, no,' said Holmes.

'Your face is very familiar,' said the captain, 'but not your body.'

'I've only got it for the day, dear Watson, it's from Rent-a-face.'

'Your time is up, by the look of it,' said the Captain Nor' by Nor'East.

'Talking about being taken to the cleaners,' said McGonagall, 'ma friend here has got eight dollars.'

'That's it,' said Gershwin. 'Tell everybody.'

'Make up your mind,' said McGonagall.

'Listen here,' said the captain, taking in his spinnaker, 'I want this steamroller off my ship.'

'I'm not going off your ship,' said McGonagall, 'but I'm going off you' – and with a nod and a wink added, 'Will you tell everybody my friend here has got eight dollars?'

'For God's sake,' said Gershwin.

'Yes, for God's sake,' said McGonagall.

'I've read the crew list of names,' said the captain, 'and my advice to you, as captain, is to give me your money for safe keeping.'

Gershwin handed the eight dollars across.

The captain counted the eight dollars. 'One, two, three, four, five, six,' said the captain.

'There's two dollars missing,' said Gershwin.

'I warned you about this crew,' said the captain, lowering a lifeboat and rowing off to Marbella.

'Ach, obviously he keeps the ship's safe somewhere else. Dinna bither, he'll be back in the morning with the interest,' said McGonagall. 'I can tell an honest face when I see one.'

'You nit,' said Holmes, tapping the dottle of his pipe into McGonagall's sporran.

There came ascending castrati screams as McGonagall shot up the mainmast into the crow's nest, smashed the eggs, set fire to the crow, then dived into the ship's swimming pool, which evaporated in a cloud of steam.

'Are you all right down there, Watson?' said Shylock Holmes.

'Ach, all me curlies are gone,' said McGonagall, climbing out.

'Stand on this mirror,' said Gershwin.

'Mein Gott! It looks like Billy Connolly after a dry shave,' said Sherlock Holmes.

'Och, what a pity,' said McGonagall. 'It used to look like Lord Tennyson.' He then started to poem.

> Oh, terrible nicht of the burnt sporran!
> Being set fire to for me was something totally foreign!
> A pubic hair conflagration
> Is something that should only interest a fire station
> And as there are no fire stations at sea
> It was pretty terrible news for the likes of me.
> And standing on that mirror I was appalled,
> For from the waist downwards I was totally bald.

> Signed, William Topaz McGonagall, 1887

'Excuse me, sir, let me show you to my cabin,' said a gay steward in a floral frock.

'Surely you mean mine,' said McGonagall.

'Yes, mine,' said the steward, and showed him to mine cabin.

'Is this mine?' said McGonagall.

'No, it's mine,' said the steward.

'Very nice,' said McGonagall. 'As soon as you move out, I'll move in' – and hung out of the porthole for safety.

While out there he met another passenger, also hanging out.

'What are you doing out there, Jamie?' said McGonagall.

'It's the new economy class,' said the Jamie passenger, 'and I'd be glad if you'd get out of my cabin.'

McGonagall crawled back into mine cabin again.

'Last call for lunch, last call for lunch,' came the voice over the loudspeakers.

'Lunch?' said McGonagall. 'It's nearly midnight.'

'Yes,' said Holmes, 'that's why it's the last call.'

'Hello, I was just dropping off,' said Gershwin, dropping from the top bunk.

131

Sherlock Holmes pulled the blinds on the porthole. 'We don't want people looking in,' he said.

CHAPTER 17

Dawn broke, sailors everywhere were singing 'Yo-ho-ho' and pouring hot tar down the scuppers, hoisting yardarms, lowering spinnakers, swabbing decks, swabbing walls, swabbing ceilings and tying knots in their appendages.

'I've brought up your breakfast, sir,' said a cabin boy.

'Serves you right for eating it,' said McGonagall.

'Ah, Watson,' said Holmes, 'I see you've been swabbed and it's elementary.'

'Where's ma friend the late George Gershwin?' said McGonagall.

'He's practising being sick and it's elementary.'

'My school,' said McGonagall.

'What about your school?' said Holmes.

'That was elementary, too,' said McGonagall.

'Now,' said Holmes, putting a violin under his chin, 'have you ever heard of the Hair on a G String?'

'Aye, I've even seen it!'

'Now,' said Holmes. 'Stand back.'

McGonagall stood back and entered the Atlantic Ocean.

'Man overboard!' shouted a sailor in a frock.

'Help, drop me a line!' shouted McGonagall.

'Very well,' said Holmes. 'What's your address?'

'Number 3, Grot Buildings, The Gorbals, Glasgae Toon. But it'll get to me quicker if you address it c/o the Atlantic Ocean.'

A jolly-boat full of jolly sailors pulled up alongside McGonagall. 'Ahoy there!' shouted one of them.

'Ahoy here!' shouted McGonagall.

'Excuse me, are you Mr William McGonagall c/o the Atlantic Ocean?'

'Yes,' he cried.

'Sorry, no mail for you today,' shouted the jolly sailor.

'Ahoy there!' shouted a swabbing sailor, throwing a ladder over the side. 'If you climb up this you will be taller and, surprise, surprise, you will suddenly become a passenger on the *Queen Elizabeth 2*, all found.'

McGonagall came aboard but didn't find anything, then, with a grin, and a cunning sly wink, said, 'Wait till Prince Philip hears about this.'

So they all waited till Prince Philip heard about it.

'Now,' said McGonagall, adjusting his homing truss, 'now, Jock, about some unspending money.'

'What about it?' said the jolly sailor.

McGonagall went into the foetal position on the deck and then, leaping upright, said, 'I've nae any.'

'You've nae what?' said the jolly sailor.

'That's true, laddie, I've nae what, wait till Prince Philip hears about this.'

'Not again,' said a Jolly Jack Tar. 'I've only got a week to live.'

'Just stay there, I'll run ye up a coffin.' In a frenzy of wood shavings, nails and hammers, McGonagall completed the box, forced the sailor in it, hammered the lid down and threw it over the side. 'You see, you didn't even have to wait a week, after all.'

From inside the floating coffin, a muffled voice said, 'Wait till Prince Philip hears about this.'

'A letter for you,' said a cross-eyed cabin boy, delivering it sideways.

At an angle of forty-five degrees, McGonagall tore open the envelope. 'Just as I thought, it's a letter for me,' he cried, and read:

Dear McGonagall,
You are overdrawn considerably.
Signed,
Midland Bank Manager No. 11

'Och, I wish they'd make up their mind,' said McGonagall. 'Here's a tip,' he said to the cabin boy, breaking off the top of an asparagus. Just then, a drenched head appeared. 'Och, so you've got out of your coffin, you naughty boy. You'll catch your death of cold.'

'Aye, aye,' said the Jolly Jack Tar. 'I don't think that was very funny.'

'Och, you're right, my timing was off,' said McGonagall, and made another coffin. 'Try this and see if it's any funnier,' he said.

The Jolly Jack Tar ran aft – and McGonagall ran after him aft.

'You humourless bastard,' said McGonagall. 'All that comic build-up and now this,' he said, putting up a For Sale sign:

OLD COFFIN GOING CHEAP
WILL SUIT DEAD PERSON DOWN TO THE GROUND
£1.50 o.n.o.

'Ah so,' said a Japanese passenger.

'Ah so to you,' said a rough sailor.

'Ach, a wee Japannee,' said McGonagall, and went into a series of Buckingham Palace photographic poses.

'Thank you,' said the puzzled nip.

'Pity you've nae a camera, ye'd have got it all.'

From the crow's nest, a Jolly Jack Tar did the hornpipe and shouted, 'ENGLAND AHEAD!'

'By how much?' shouted McGonagall.

'TWO GOALS!' came the reply.

'Who were they playing?' said McGonagall.

'NOBODY, THEY STARTED EARLY SO THEY COULDN'T LOSE.'

'Wait until they meet Scotland,' said McGonagall from the poop.

So the Jolly Jack Tar waited till they met Scotland and then came down, by which time the ship was on its return voyage to America and he wondered where McGonagall had gone. He had gone to the Gents but had recovered enough to stand up by himself.

THE DUNDEE MUSICAL MANGLE SHOP

Yes indeed, McGonagall and Gershwin had searched the isles and the Hebrides for early Victorian mangles in a drive to promote Gershwin's music. Why nobody had thought of this before, it is hard to believe.

'Did you hear that, George,' said McGonagall, 'I've decided to promote your music and I've made it a sergeant.'

'Gee whizz,' said George chewing gum Gershwin. 'This morning my music was only a private. "Private Bess, You is Ma Woman Now". Now it's "Sergeant Bess, You is Ma Woman Now".'

McGonagall pivoted on his toe, pivoting 360 degrees and surveying all the mangles in his shop. Outside in gold lettering was:

The William McGonagall
Musical Mangle Shop

'Just wait till the word gets oot,' said McGonagall.

And sure enough the word got oot and in came a heavily upholstered woman in a fur dinghy.

'Gee whizz, buddy, that's a real cute hen,' said George Gershwin, buddy.

'I am nae a hen nor a buddy,' said the lady. 'I am Lady Dalkeith of Dalkeith.'

'We can still be friends,' said McGonagall.

'Now, this is the hundredth anniversary of the battle of Glencoe in which my husband was killed,' said the Dalkeith of Dalkeith.

'Are ye sure you're in the right shop?' said Gershwin. 'We've nae fresh husband replacements the noo. The last one went off this morning, someone left the fridge door open.'

'I know,' said the Lady Dalkeith of Dalkeith. 'If there had only been a fridge at the battle of Glencoe my husband would be alive today.'

'You're wrang,'* said McGonagall. 'There were fridges at the battle of Glencoe, but there was nae electricity. If it had been the other way round it would have been just as bad and your husband would have still been dead today, but I'm digressing.'

* You're wrong.

'Are you?' said Gershwin. 'I'll open a window.'

'Now,' said the Lady Dalkeith of Dalkeith, 'in memory of my husband, can you show me your finest mangle?'

McGonagall mangled a small cat and gave it to her.

'That's no good,' she said.

'No, and it's no good for the cat either, look at the shape of him,' said Gershwin. 'I think you've got it wrong, Jamie, she means one of these' – and of all things Gershwin pointed to a mangle.

'Och, you want of all things,' said McGonagall and stopped there. He sensed now the sale of the century and he said as much. 'As much,' he said.

'You're a very poor salesman,' said the Lady Dalkeith of Dalkeith.

'Aye, lend us a pound or I'll murder ye.'

Rather than get murdered, she gave him a pound. She moved towards the great Rollington Iron Mangle. 'Please demonstrate this,' she said.

'George,' said McGonagall, and snapped his fingers. One fell to the ground and he put the bit in his pocket. 'Play that mangle for the Lady Dalkeith of Dalkeith.'

Gershwin inserted a manuscript between the rollers and started to mangle the song through. The Lady Dalkeith of Dalkeith waited patiently until the music came out the other side. 'Well?' she said.

'WELL what?' said McGonagall.

'Well what what?' said the Lady.

'The what what you said when you first said what,' said McGonagall.

'We're not getting very far,' said the Lady Dalkeith of Dalkeith.

'We're not supposed to. This is not a bus, it is a shop. It's meant to stay where it is in the same place.'

'What I'm saying is,' said Lady Dalkeith, 'that I didn't hear any music issuing from those rollers.'

'Och well, you can't expect music from a mangle,' said McGonagall.

'Well, what can I expect?' said the Lady.

'Laundry,' said McGonagall. 'You see, it's a DIY mangle. George, the upmarket demo, please.'

George inserted a song, started to roll it through all the while singing:

> Embrace me, my sweet embraceable you,
> Embrace me, my irreplaceable you,
> Just one look at you, my heart goes tipsy in me . . .

'That's not the mangle, that's him singing,' said the Lady Dalkeith of Dalkeith.

'That's not hymn singing, that's a tune,' said McGonagall. 'If you want a hymn, what you need is a church, there's one just up the raed.'

'Oh, thank you,' she said, and left, but didn't leave much – just a stain on the carpet.

'We're not going to sell many like this,' said Gershwin.

'Och, this is not a job for the faint-hearted,' said McGonagall, and fainted.

Just to make him comfortable, Gershwin slipped the twisted moggie under his head. When he regained consciousness, every mangle in the shop was gone.

'Ach, ye've had a guid day,' said McGonagall.

'If you call having the bailiffs in good, yes. They've taken all the stock. We were six months behind with the rent. You were out quite a while,' Gershwin said, 'so I've been exhibiting you in the window as a trainee corpse for apprentice morticians to practise embalming on. You were buried three times last week, but it paid off,' said Gershwin, waving a wad of one pound under his nose.

McGonagall sobbed, 'This is nae substitute for the loss of our giant mangle industry which could bring Scotland crashing to its ankles.'

'You mean knees,' said Gershwin.

'You mean bastard,' said McGonagall, snatching the one pound and secreting it in an orifice. 'You'll never touch that again,' said McGonagall.

'You're dead right,' said Gershwin, putting on a pair of gloves.

The door opened and a portly financier came in. 'What are you selling?' said the financier.

'Nothing,' said McGonagall.

'I'll buy it,' said the rich financier. 'How much do you want for it?'

'Would you believe £400, preferably in currency?'

'You mean cash?' said the financier.

'You mean bastard,' said McGonagall.

The financier drew out an item from his safe.

'What's that?' said McGonagall, not well versed in financial affairs. (The last financial affair he'd had was with a lady stockbroker and it left him skint.)

'It's a cheque book,' said the financier as he opened the creaking hinges. 'Who do I make it out to?' said the financier.

'Me,' said Gershwin and McGonagall.

'Which of you mes?' said the financier.

'Me me,' said McGonagall with his hand over Gershwin's mouth.

'Mimi?' said the financier. 'No wonder your tiny white hand is frozen – warm it over this cheque for 50p.'

'50p?' said McGonagall while Gershwin fainted. 'That's a lang way from £400.'

'So is Tipperary,' said the financier.

'Can I have that in writing?' said McGonagall.

'Certainly,' said the financier, and wrote out a cheque for 'It's a Long Way to Tipperary'.

'How do I know this document isn't a forgery?' said McGonagall.

'I give up,' said the financier. 'How do you know this document isn't a forgery?'

Gershwin got to his feet, he reeled forwards, he reeled backwards and finally he reeled upright.

'Is that a Scottish reel?' asked the financier.

'Nae, it's a Jewish one,' said McGonagall. 'They're cheaper.'

'I'll take that one then,' said the financier.

A ruptured bailiff carrying a mangle burst through the door.

'Is that my change?' said the financier.

'No, it's faulty,' said the ruptured bailiff.

'Put it carefully on the flae,' said McGonagall.

Carefully the ruptured bailiff put it on the flae. 'Any more bright ideas?' said the ruptured bailiff.

'Yes,' said McGonagall. 'Why don't you fuck off?'

'That's a good idea,' said the bailiff and left.

'You've forgotten this,' said McGonagall, and threw him a rupture.

'Is this mangle for sale?' said the financier.

'Nae, how many times do I have to tell you, it's for laundry.'

'Three times, then stop,' said the financier.

'My music is now a sergeant,' said Gershwin.

'What? It's in such good condition I thought it was at least a captain. What do you want for it?' said the financier.

'I keep telling you, man, laundry.'

'Ideal,' said the financier, producing from the safe a bag of wet underpants. 'Put these through at speed and there is another 50p in it for you.'

'Stop in the name of the law,' said a Scottish police in a dark blue kilt and a tartan helmet. 'Have ye nae a licence for mangling the underpants?'

'Nae, we have nae licence for mangling underpants,' said McGonagall.

'I knew it,' said the police. 'So you are doing illegal underpants mangling in Dundee. I knew it was going on somewhere, and this happens to be somewhere.'

'I'll plead guilty but insane,' said McGonagall, standing on his head.

'You'll do no such thing,' said Gershwin, and handed the 50p blank cheque to the policeman.

'Well, just this once,' said the policeman, pocketing the cheque, 'and think yourselves lucky that you're not spending the night in a Dundee jail!'

So Gershwin and McGonagall thought themselves lucky that they were not spending the night in a Dundee jail.

'There's a near Miss,' said McGonagall, pointing to an unmarried lady standing close by.

'Am I too late?' said the young lady.

'Not for an out of order mangle you're not. What time did you think it was?'

'Allow me,' said Gershwin.

So McGonagall allowed him.

Undaunted, Gershwin started to demonstrate the faulty musical mangle to the near Miss. 'It's only done 800 illegal underpants with one careful owner.'

'Is that the same one?' said the near Miss.

'The same one what?' asked Gershwin, withdrawing the song sheet from the rollers.

'The same one wot was one careful owner,' said the near Miss.

'Oh yes,' said Gershwin, patting the mangle. 'With every mangle you get 800 pounds of wet laundry free.'

'Free of what?' she said.

'Rabies,' said Gershwin. 'They've all been through quarantine.'

'I thought they went through the mangle,' she said.

'And just as a final closing-down generous offer I'll throw these in free,' said Gershwin. So saying, he ripped off his underpants through the flies of his trousers.

'That must have hurt,' said the near Miss.

'It didn't do me any good and it's acted as a powerful stimulant. Would you mind looking the other way?'

'I can't see much from here,' she said.

'Use your driving mirror,' he said.

'Now tell me how much does all this cost?' said the near Miss.

'A pound,' interrupted McGonagall. 'That or 100p cash.'

'I prefer the former,' she said, and gave him a pound of former.

'Wait,' said McGonagall, holding it up to the light. 'This looks like a former pound.'

'Why, would you rather have the latter pound?' said the near Miss.

'Yes, if you don't mind,' said McGonagall. 'I would prefer the latter pound.'

The exchange was duly made. Gershwin wrapped up the mangle in Christmas wrapping paper.

'How did you know it was to be a Christmas present?' said the near Miss.

'I saw the film,' said Gershwin with a nod and a wink.

'Och, you're no Greta Garbo yourself,' said McGonagall.

She smiled. 'How observant of you to know I'm not Greta Garbo.'

'I'll tell you who else you're not.' He proceeded to reel off the names of a hundred people she wasn't, including Lord Longford, and she was well pleased.

'Here,' said McGonagall, 'let me help you' – and lowered the mangle into the pram. 'Is that your wee bairn I've just killed?' he said. 'Oh well, never mind, you can have another go tonight.

Here, read the book of instructions,' he said, handing her a copy of the *Kama Sutra*.

'What's the *Kama Sutra*?' she said.

'It's a sort of curried copulation,' said McGonagall.

It has been a long hard day and what was to be the end of the mangle industry in Scotland.

BY THE SEA CHAPTER

It was the high holiday season in Scunthorpe in Mrs Hatch's boarding house. Eric Sykes was appearing at the end of the pier. It wasn't a show, he was just appearing at the end of the pier.

'Och, that's a funny act you've got,' said McGonagall.

'I'm not acting,' said Sykes, 'I'm fishing.'

'Fishing?' queried George Gershwin, the American pianist and composer who wrote 'Rhapsody in Blue' that was performed by Paul Whiteman and his Orchestra at the Carnegie Hall for its world première.

'I know you,' said Eric Sykes. 'You are the American pianist and composer who wrote "Rhapsody in Blue" that was performed by Paul Whiteman and his Orchestra at the Carnegie Hall for its world première?'

'Och,' said McGonagall, 'how do you know ken this is George McGershwin the American pianist and composer who wrote "Rhapsody in Blue" that was performed by Paul McWhiteman and his McOrchestra at the Carnegie Hall for its world première?'

'It was just a shot in the dark,' said Eric Sykes, who had once fired a pistol in a blacked-out room.

'Och, mon,' said the McGonagall, 'what are ye fishing for?'

'Fish mainly,' said the wily Sykes.

'Och, mon, you're a fool, the shops are full of them,' said McGonagall.

'I know,' said the wily Sykes. 'Where do you think I got these from?'

'Billingsgate?' said McGonagall.

'That's right,' said the wily Sykes. 'They call me Eric "Billingsgate" Sykes,' said Eric 'Billingsgate' Sykes.

'All of it?' said McGonagall.

'All of what?' said Eric 'Billingsgate' Sykes.

'All of Billingsgate?' said McGonagall.

'Yes, I wouldn't have it any other way,' said Sykes, hauling up a smoked slamon.

'Isn't that a spelling mistake?' said Gershwin.

'No, it's a smoked slamon,' said McGonagall.

'There goes another one,' said Gersh.

'Excuse me,' said Sykes. 'I feel an act coming on' – and left.

Gershwin looked at his watch on McGonagall's wrist. 'It's time to find a residence for the nicht,' he said.

It was evening as Gershwin and McGonagall rang the bell at Mrs Retch's fine boarding house for refined gentlemen.

'Are you refined gentlemen?' said Mrs Retch, gobbing into a nearby spittoon. 'I miss the old-style spittoons,' said Mrs Retch.

'Aye, and you've just missed a new-style one as well,'* said McGonagall, wiping it off.

'In answer to your enquiry,' said Gershwin. 'We are not refined gentlemen,' said Gershwin. 'But we'll bear it in mind and if it happens we'll give you first choice of the negatives.'

'Now,' said McGonagall. 'We'd like a single door with adjoining rooms,' said McGonagall.

'That,' she said, gobbing again, 'will be thirty shillings.'

Thirty shillings for a gob, that was expensive. 'Would you like an advance?' said McGonagall.

'Yes,' she said.

So McGonagall took one pace forward. 'Och, about the rent, can we no come to some arrangement?' said McGonagall.

'Yes, we can no come to some arrangement,' said Mrs Retch. 'You pay it or follow the dotted line back to the street.'

Gershwin and McGonagall unchained their cheque books.

'Why are you two gentlemen so distressed?' said Mrs Retch.

'Och, ma'am,' said McGonagall, 'you see, we are yuppies anonymous.' He slumped over his cheque book.

'Are you overdrawn?' said Mrs Retch.

'No, I'm over here,' said McGonagall, leaping the counter and robbing the till.

'Quick, into this taxi,' cried Gershwin, grabbing Mrs Retch and riding off with her.

* OK, OK.

'There's been an awful mistake,' said McGonagall. 'If ever a mon needed glasses, it's him.'

In the taxi, Mrs Retch confronted Gershwin. 'What are you playing at?' said Mrs Retch.

'I'm playing at the local seamen's mission hall and you're the audience.'

'All right, just this once,' said Mrs Retch. 'You never know, I might meet a Hello Sailor, I could do with the smell of the salt sea and air and an ounce of shag.'

'That won't last you long,' said Gershwin.

'I'll tell him when to stop,' she said.

In the back of the dining-room, McGonagall had ordered a smoked slamon. It was served by a waiter called Eric Sykes.

'I thought you were supposed to be on stage?' said McGonagall.

'I am,' said the wily Eric Sykes. 'This is part of my act and you are the audience.'

'Then do you serve crabs?' said McGonagall.

'Serve them?' said Sykes. 'I've *got* them!' he said, scratching a few.

'Aye,' said McGonagall. 'I dinnae see your act on the menu.'

'No, I'm on the à la carte,' said Sykes.

'I do not care if you're in the D'Oyly Carte,' said McGonagall. 'I've come here to eat a langoustine.'

'I'm sorry, the langoustine is off,' said wily Sykes.

'It's the hot weather,' said McGonagall. 'So I'm off.'

'No, wait! Why does Prince Philip wear red, white and blue braces?' said Eric Sykes as part of his à la carte act.

'Say that again,' said McGonagall.

Sykes coughed, struck a pose, stuck on a Billy Bennet moustache, a scarlet nose, a ginger wig and a revolving bow tie, then, rapidly elevating his eyebrows up and down at speed, quite clearly said, 'Why does Prince Philip wear red, white and blue braces?'

The whole restaurant was enthralled. All eating stopped. The spotlight fell on McGonagall. Standing upright, McGonagall pointed an accusative finger at the wily Sykes. 'You're nae a waiter, you are a comic. No wonder the people are all laughing instead of eating. I demand to see the manager.'

Sykes handed him a telescope. 'There,' he pointed. 'He's up at that window there.'

Through the telescope, McGonagall could see Mrs Retch escaping through the window of the seamen's mission hut accompanied by George Gershwin playing 'Rhapsody in Blue' by Paul Whiteman.

'Wait! She won't be long,' said Sykes, doing a buck and wing. 'A 137 bus should see her here in no time.'

'Och,' said McGonagall. 'There's no time like a 137 bus' – and stole the soup spoon.

'Stop thief!' said Eric Sykes through a false ginger beard. 'Stop thief or order some soup,' he said.

'I have ordered some soup to fit this spoon,' said McGonagall.

'Let go of that spoon or I'll call a cutlery squad policeman,' said Sykes.

'Oh? What are you going to call him?' said McGonagall.

'I'll call him Irene,' said Sykes.

'He won't be very happy,' said McGonagall.

A 137 bus drew up at the side of the table and Mrs Retch leapt off. 'Arrest that man for stealing my best silver soup spoon,' she said to the bus conductor.

'Oh man,' said de bus conductor. 'Dere am some mistake, I am not a policeman.'

'Just this once,' pleaded Mrs Retch. 'It will make a break from what has up to now been a very dull life.'

'Just dis once, den,' said the conductor. 'You, Scottish man, hand over de silver soup spoon to alleviate what has up to now been a very dull life.'

McGonagall leapt up on to a chair and went through it. Pulling the chair up round his waist, he sat down. He addressed the room:

To the diners at Mrs Retch's dining-rooms, The Retch Hotel, Scunthorpe:

Dear friends,
You are totally mistaken. I am holding this solid silver EPNS soup spoon in an attempt to break the world's record.

Yours sincerely
William McGonagall

Mrs Retch immediately addressed McGonagall:

William T. McGonagall
c/o the broken chair
The Dining-Room
The Retch Hotel
Scunthorpe

Pay for the damage.

McGonagall replied thus:

Not known at this address – gone away.

So he leapt out of the window on to the pavement, where he slipped on a bit of it.

'Upsadaisy,' said a kindly Mr Guinness.

'Och,' said McGonagall, 'this is a coincidence.'

'I thought it was dog shit,' said the kindly Mr Guinness.

'You see this silver soup spoon of the River Tay?' said McGonagall. 'I'm about to attempt the world record on it.'

'The hundred metres?' queried the kindly Mr Guinness.

'Nae, it's not long enough for that. You see here,' he whispered, 'I'm gaeing for a world alternative record. It's for the world record for holding a soup spoon, starting now.' He took a firm grasp on the soup spoon and switched on the chronometer.

'What is the time by the chronometer?' said the kindly Mr Guinness.

'Eighteen seconds,' said McGonagall.

'Oh, I'd better be going,' said the kindly Mr Guinness.

'I hope you're going better than this watch,' said McGonagall. 'It's stopped.'

'Let me know when you've broken the record,' said the kindly Mr Guinness, climbing into a Rolls-Royce and out the other side, trying to give an impression of wealth. The Rolls-Royce drove off, leaving him in a squatting position on the pavement.

'No, no,' said McGonagall, 'you're no allowed to do it there, laddie.'

'Blast! Oh dear!' said the embarrassed Guinness. 'I keep misjudging the width of Rolls-Royces and exceeding them by three feet.'

'*Three* feet,' said McGonagall. 'And here's me with only tae. Still, from now on you'll be able to enter three-legged races alone.'

Clutching the silver soup spoon over the River Tay in his left hand and the chronometer in his right hand, he headed west towards Mrs Retch's hotel.

'Hello and goodbye,' said Mrs Retch as he reached the counter, and before he could stop her she swallowed the till.

'Och, lassie. Have you seen ma composing friend?' said McGonagall.

'Do you mean the Hungarian explorer with six Roman Catholic sledge dogs trying to reach the Pole and Captain Scott's bank manager?'

'No,' said McGonagall. 'I mean the composer who wrote "Rhapsody in Blue" with six sledge dogs and Captain Scott's bank manager at Carnegie Hall with Paul Whiteman's sledge dogs.'

'Oh *him*!' she said, adjusting a solid goldfish. 'He is in the kitchen washing dishes.'

'Why?' said the horrified McGonagall.

'Because they're dirty,' said Mrs Retch.

'Is that because we've nae paid the rent?' said McGonagall.

'No,' she repeated. 'It's because the dishes are dirty.'

McGonagall had now been clutching the silver EPNS soup spoon for three and a quarter hours and was on course for a world record. No man in the history of man had ever clutched one for so long. The only parallel to this was Derek Squirts who had sung 'Ave Maria' in the kneeling load position for a fortnight in Iceland. To this day he remains a cripple.

Gershwin arrived with his piano and wearing an apron. 'The water's off,' he said.

'That's a coincidence,' said McGonagall. 'So was the langoustine, Eric Sykes said so. It was part of his act on the à la carte,' said McGonagall.

'À la carte?' said Gershwin. 'That's funny, I just saw him go past in his à la carte, he must be having a bad season.'

'Oh,' said McGonagall, 'was he smoking a slamon?'

'No,' said Gershwin. 'It was a spelling mistake.'

'So,' said McGonagall, 'he must have run out.'

'Yes,' said Gershwin. 'I saw him run out to get into his à la carte, it was going pretty fast, too.'

'Four hours,' said McGonagall, holding up the silver spoon.

'Four hours?' said Gershwin. 'That looks like a silver soup spoon to me.'

'You dinnae ken,' said McGonagall. 'I'm breaking the world record for soup-spoon-holding.'

'How far is that going to get you?' said Gershwin. 'It stays where it is.'

'Look,' said Mrs Retch, gobbing. 'Do you want this single door with adjoining rooms or not?'

'Ach, I've changed our mind,' said McGonagall. 'All right, can we have a single room with adjoining doors?' said McGonagall.

'We only do half board,' she said.

'OK,' said McGonagall, 'if the beds are uncomfortable we'll have half a board.'

'Mr Modo,' she said to the hunchbacked porter, 'will you show these gentlemen to their adjoining doors?'

'Have you any luggage?' said the porter.

'Nae,' said McGonagall.

'Would you like some?' said the porter.

'Sure would,' said Gershwin. 'Got any in crocodile leather, Gucci, etc.?'

Gershwin and McGonagall on half board at Mrs Retch's

'No, we haven't got any crocodile leather, Gucci, etcs,' said Quasimodo. 'There's only these,' he said, holding up two pairs of army boots.

'Och,' said the horrified McGonagall from the recoiled position. 'That's nae luggage, any fool can see that,' said McGonagall. 'Those are army boots. I mean, what would people say?'

'They'd say,' said Quasimodo, 'look at those men with two pairs of army boots.'

'Och, it doesn't sound too bad,' said McGonagall from the upright recoil position. 'It's better than them saying, "Look at those men with those dead elephants."'

A price was agreed and Quasimodo wheeled the boots on the luggage trolley into the lift. They went to the fifth, the sixth and the seventh floor, the eighteenth, the nineteenth, the basement, the car park, the kitchen, the laundry, the karzi, the tenth floor, the twelfth, the roof, the pavement, No. 23 Shaggers Lane, there seemed to be some doubt about where the rooms were. To make matters worse, a passer-by said, 'Look at those fools with those dead elephants.'

'Oy vay,' said Gershwin. 'I told you it wouldn't work.'

'You swine of a porter,' said McGonagall. 'You'll pay for this.'

So Quasimodo gave them a pound.

'My life, this is not enough,' said George Gershwin.

McGonagall took his revenge on the porter. He straightened him out.

'You've ruined my act,' shouted Quasimodo. 'I'll never be able to do "Sanctuary, sanctuary" hanging on the bell ever again.'

'Oh, laddie, I didnae ken you were a bell hop,' said McGonagall and bent him double again. 'It's double or quits,' said McGonagall.

'Ah,' said Quasimodo. 'This key fits this door, this must be your room.'

They opened the door. McGonagall switched on the light.

There before him stood a voluptuous, six foot tall, scarlet-haired, naked lady. 'Good heavens, I didn't order a Scotsman, a Jew and a hunchback,' she said. 'I ordered two boiled eggs and toast. What do you want?'

'Well, I didn't want anything,' said McGonagall, 'but now I've seen you.'

'Put those binoculars down at once,' she said. 'And why are you all staring at me like that?'

'We don't know any other way,' said McGonagall.

Gershwin pushed forward with his piano. 'Sorry, madam,' he sang, 'but there appears to have been a double booking and they both appear to be you.'

They apologised again and again and again. It was several hours before they took their leave and a number of photographs of her which were on sale at Ronnie Scott's Jazz Club within the hour. They left the room bent double in a certain condition.

'Quick,' said McGongall, 'where is the nearest relief massage parlour?'

'We've just left it,' said Quasimodo.

It had been a long hard day when they finally reached their room in the basement. They were only disturbed once in the early hours by a fall of coal from the circular hole in the ceiling.

'Ach, central heating,' said McGonagall as the coal dust settled on both of them.

The next morning, Mrs Retch was surprised when two coloured men turned up to pay the bill. 'I don't remember booking any black men in,' she said.

'Well, you'll remember booking us out,' they said, running out of the door without paying. 'Give us a lift,' they said as Eric Sykes galloped past in his à la carte.

'My word, you've caught the sun,' said Eric Sykes to the two coloured gentlemen.

McGonagall explained how they had been tricked into sleeping in a coal cellar, covered in coal dust and unable to wash it off as the langoustine and the water were off.

'Cheer up,' said Sykes, offering them a smoked slamon and a spelling mistake.

'Ooooooooooooooh,' said McGonagall in a sudden fit of poeming.

OOOOOOOOOOOOOOOhhhh, wonderful gift of smoked salmon,
You are better than fowl, veal or gammon
And given to us without costing a penny
Which is just as well as we ha' nae any.
It's great tae have a lift in Sykes' à la carte
In spite of being in the back end of a horse's part,
For if he decided to let one go

It would be something about which I would not wish to know.
It was good to escape from Mrs Retch's clutch,
And for my part I would rather have been living in a rabbit
   hutch,
Except for the naked redhead in Room 13
Which was one of the nicest places in which I've ever been.
And a new place to find we must,
Preferably one without a shower of coal dust.
The public baths we soon must find
To leave all this terrible blackness behind.
It's amazing what can be achieved with a towel and carbolic
   soap,
It can turn a man white and fill him with hope
And, whether you would like to agree or not,
We'd even be accepted by the late Ronnie Scott,
And if we find a refuge soon
I can go on practising the world record holding of the silver
   EPNS soup spoon!

'What do you think of that, laddies?' said Gershwin to Eric
Sykes.

'I'll never think of that,' said Sykes.

'Quick,' said McGonagall. 'Play a Scottish reel. Here comes a
lively customer.' He placed his inverted Scottish hat on the
pavement and went into a vigorous Highland fling with
screams of 'Och aye'.

The American thundered at ye piano and called out to unsuspecting pedestrians, 'A penny for the guy.'

'What guy?' said the unsuspecting pedestrian.

'That guy over there,' shouted Gershwin, pointing to the
frenzied dancing McGonagall.

'But it's not November the Fifth,' said the unsuspecting
pedestrian.

'No, it's December the Twenty-fourth,' said the thundering
pianist. 'If you haven't got a penny for the guy, how about one
for Jesus Christ?'

'He doesn't look like Jesus Christ to me,' said the unsuspecting
pedestrian.

'All right then,' said Gershwin. 'How about a penny for the
man who *doesn't* look like Jesus Christ?'

'For God's sake, hurry up,' said McGonagall. 'I'm running out
of steam.'

*McGonagall, George Gershwin and his piano begging, with a
suspicion of Dr Crippen*

'I've never seen a steam-driven Scotsman before,' said the
pedestrian, and threw a bright copper penny into the upturned
hat.

'Great,' gasped McGonagall. 'A few more like that and we'll
be on our way.' So saying, he grasped the pedestrian by the
throat and, by manipulating it, managed to force the unsuspecting pedestrian to empty his wallet, his pockets and a

quarter of Bassett's Liquorice Allsorts in mint condition into the upturned bonnet.

'I've never been so insulted in my life,' said the pedestrian, readjusting his throat.

'Och, there's always a first time,' said McGonagall, slowing his reel down to a gentle trot.

'I'm going to report you to the Highland Fling Police Squad,' said the pedestrian. Hardly had the words fallen from his lips than a Highland Fling Police Squad car screamed to a halt at the side of Gershwin's steaming, thundering piano.

The Highland Fling police leapt out. 'Stop everything at once immediately and hurry,' cried an inspector rattling a bag of truncheons. 'You're all under arrest for a performance of illegal Highland flinging in a restricted foxtrot and tango area.' So saying, he manacled McGonagall's wrists to his ankles and McGonagall's ankles to the pedestrian's knee and the pedestrian's throat. 'It's this,' said the inspector, 'or a spot fine of a quarter of Bassett's Liquorice Allsorts in mint condition.'

'Och, Bobby, you've picked the right spot,' said McGonagall, counting out the liquorice allsorts one by one along the inspector's truncheon. 'And for good measure, cop this,' he said, and handed him a voluptuous blow-up rubber sex doll and several vibrators. 'Smile, please,' said McGonagall as he took an incriminating photograph of the Highland Fling Police Squad, all with their hands on various parts.

'Och, oh dear,' said the inspector. 'We've been incriminated and he's got the negatives.'

'Och, I've got the negatives and it's much better than having herpes. Now hand me back the mint conditions and we'll say nae mair about it.'

They all stood and said, 'Nae mair about it.'

'This is a truly awful way to spend Christmas,' said the pedestrian. 'Can you release my knees from the police bondage?'

'A Merry Christmas to all our customers,' said the inspector as he removed the manacles. 'And God Rest Ye Merry Gentlemen,' sang the inspector as he continued to remove the manacles. 'And the Holly and the Ivy,' continued the inspector, 'and good King Wenceslas looked out.' Almost immediately, 'Adeste Fideles,' he gaily sang, 'and a partridge in a tree and, would you believe, I'm Dreaming of a White Christmas?'

By this time McGonagall had donned his hat, counted the allsorts, pocketed the pedestrian's money, folded up the piano and was on top of a number 74 seafront tram heading for Mrs Scrowell's Home for Starving Tramps.

'No smoking pianos allowed on top,' said the officious tram conductor.

'I'm not smoking it, buddy,' said the witty American pianist.

'In that case, why are you striking that match? What harm has it ever done you?' said the conductor.

'I'm just igniting it to bring a glow of Christmas cheer to this tram,' said Gershwin.

'Oh,' said the officious conductor. 'Adeste Fideles and, would you believe, I'm Dreaming of a White Christmas,' he said.

'Just a minute,' said McGonagall. 'You've only got one leg, mon.'

'Yes,' said the officious conductor. 'It's an economy cut. It's cut my expenditure on footwear by half and my wife is well pleased.'

'Why?' said McGonagall.

'Because I left her a year ago,' said the conductor.

'Oh, what else did you leave her?' said McGonagall.

'Fuck all, she told me to hop it – so I did.'

'Where's the other leg?' said McGonagall sympathetically.

McGonagall and Gershwin with his folded piano waiting for a bus

'Oh, that,' said the officious conductor. 'It's in a glass case in the Bank of England to show the economy what can be achieved under Mrs Thatcher's government.'

'Och! But she's got two legs and, counting Denis Thatcher's, it's a grand total of four, that puts her three ahead of you.'

'Och, but mon,' said the officious McConductor. 'She can afford more legs than me.'

'Is it insured?' said the wily Gershwin.

'Och, yes,' said the even wilier conductor of the 74 seafront tram now rapidly approaching Mrs Scrowell's Home for Starving Tramps. 'It's been quoted at Ladbrokes at 40 to 1 on.'

Despite all this, the conductor continued along the 74 seafront tram which was rapidly approaching Mrs Scrowell's Home for Starving Tramps, none of whom had won the Grand National. 'It's registered as an oil tanker in Panama,' he said. 'Under a flag of inconvenience. It's amazing what you can get at Lloyd's of London for a pound,' he added.

'You're insured with Lloyd's of London?' said Gershwin.

'No, they're insured with me,' said the conductor. 'That way it's cheaper.'

'How often does your leg sail?' asked the Gershwin.

'Oh, it's not for sale,' said the conductor. 'I mean, who could mistake my leg for a million-pound oil tanker?'

'Alfred Throck,' said the Gershwin.

'What about Alfred Throck?' said the conductor.

'He's a man who has often mistaken a leg for an oil tanker and as a result he's very, very poor.'

'What do you mean?' said the perplexed tram conductor.

'He is now the owner of a fleet of legs that just won't carry oil.'

'Six hours,' said McGonagall, leaping to his feet. 'Six hours and ten seconds,' he added.

'What is?' said the tram conductor and Gershwin, now holding hands.

'This,' said McGonagall, pointing to the silver EPNS soup spoon. Then, with a sly nod and a wink, he added, 'I'm on course for the record.'

'You must be mad,' said a passenger who up to then had remained silent due to careful writing by the authors. 'Who would want to buy a record of a silver EPNS soup spoon? I mean, it doesn't give off any sound.'

154

'Och, that's where you're wrong. This record will be done with the spoon being used to drink soup noisily by Lyndsey de Paul and Placido Domingo. Does that answer your question?'

There came a distant groaning and a rattling of non EPNS spoons on empty plates.

'Och, list,' said the tram conductor, leaning forward on one leg, his ear cupped in one hand. 'That's the sound of the starving tramps at Mrs Scrowell's Home for Starving Tramps.'

'We must be getting near then,' said McGonagall.

'Yes, we are quite near,' said the conductor. 'Look, I can touch you from here' – and straight away touched McGonagall for a fiver.

'You fool,' said the wily Scot. 'You'll have to touch me in a better place than that to get a fiver from me.'

'Mayfair,' said the tram conductor, leaning backwards on one leg.

'What about Mayfair?' said McGonagall.

'Well, it's a better place,' said the conductor, moving uneasily from the one leg back to the one leg.

McGonagall grinned, but the answer was drowned out by the now overpowering groans of starving tramps and rattling spoons on empty plates. 'So we're here,' said McGonagall in Braille.

Clutching the spoon and the folded grand piano, they descended the steps of the tram. As they entered the cacophonous portals of Mrs Scrowell's Boarding House for Starving Tramps, she turned down the volume.

'I'm sorry about the noise,' she said. 'Are you starving?' she added.

'No,' they said.

'Well, you will be if you stay here,' she said.

'Och, a wee minute, lassie,' said McGonagall, producing a hatful of coins. 'We're nae your average starving tramp, we're a well-nourished piano player and a Scottish poem writer' – and he pointed at the heap of pennies.

'Oh, this can make all the difference between life and death,' she said, producing a revolver from her skirts.

'Is this a stick-up?' said McGonagall.

'No, it's a pistol,' she said. 'Stand and deliver,' she said, dismounting from her horse.

'Och, you're a very strange landlady,' said McGonagall. 'I've never met a mounted one before.'

155

'I always like to make an impression on my customers,' she said, and did an impression of Vera Lynn. 'This is my horse, Coloured Bess.'

'You mean Black Bess?' said McGonagall.

'No, not in the Borough of Brent,' she said.

'Och, lassie,' said the Scot with a gay twirl on one leg which hurt considerably as witness his 'Och, ma focking knee.'

'What was it you intended to say?' said the dismounted landlady. 'Hurry up, my horse is getting hungry. He's training to be a tramp! Look, he's fallen down already,' she said, pointing to the hapless creature lying starving in the gutter and wearing a ragged overcoat and cap.

'I was going to say nae in the Borough o' Brent,' said McGonagall.

'But you didn't,' she said. 'You said, "Oh, my focking knee", which is not in the Borough of Brent.'

'Och, we all make mistakes,' said McGonagall, making one and carefully donning the hat with the money in it.

'Gee,' said Gershwin. 'How's *this* for an exit?'

Her bullets whistled over their heads as they ran for dear life out of the door.

'This is a dear life,' said McGonagall, counting his money.

'Don't you dare darken my doorstep again,' she shouted after

George Gershwin and McGonagall leaving Mrs Scrowell's boarding establishment

them. And they promised very faithfully that they would abide by her decision as being final.

It was the end of another long hard page for both of them, for both McGonagall and both Gershwin, in fact for both boths, not to mention the conductor.

'Conductor?' said Gershwin.

'I told you not to mention that old joke,' said McGonagall.

'Old joke?' said Gershwin.

'I told you not to mention that conductor,' said McGonagall.

'What conductor?' said Gershwin.

'*That* one,' said McGonagall.

'Oh, *that* one,' said Gershwin. 'I thought you meant *this* one.'

'There never was a *this* one,' said McGonagall. 'There's only ever been a *that* one.'

At that one moment the Highland Fling Police Squad car screeched to a halt. The inspector leaned out of the window. 'You're lucky you weren't doing an armed Highland fling,' he said, and drove off.

'Was that a *this* inspector or was this a *that* inspector?' said the Gershwin.

McGonagall gave him a long meaningful stare. 'Och, ye'll never learn, laddie, will you?' he said, and he never learned.

It was a long hard day for our merry pair.

'Och,' said McGonagall, and came to a grinding halt. 'I'm ready for ma bed,' he said as the sun settled over Scunthorpe.

'Try this for size,' said Gershwin, generously pointing to the pavement.

'Och, that's dead right for me! It's flat as all good beds should be,' said McGonagall. He stepped over the sleeping body of Gershwin on to the pavement and lay back in the municipal flower bed. 'Oh, it's roses all the way for me,' he said, picking the thorns out of his arse.

At dawn they were awakened by the council gardener spraying them with paraquat. 'Ah! I've got rid of this greenfly,' said the jolly gardener running his spray up McGonagall's legs and under the darkest regions of his kilt.

'Look here,' said McGonagall. 'You may be a good gardener, but you're a pain in the arse to me,' he said, removing the syringe.

'I thought you were a bit big for a greenfly,' said the suspicious gardener, and went on thinking it all day until 1800 hours.

CHAPTER 18

The Court Case Case

Justice Ongat Twilight banged his gavel on the court desk. 'Next case,' he said.

A constable placed a leather suitcase in the dock.

'Six months,' he said. 'Next case.'*

The constable took it away and replaced it with a William McGonagall case.

'What is the charge?' said the judge.

'Impersonating greenfly without a licence and furthermore removing the syringe at a critical moment in the career of Dick Head the Gardener.'

'What does the accused wish to say?' said Justice Ongat Twilight.

'I don't know,' said the dreary constable. 'He hasn't said it yet.'

A considerable pause ensued.

'I still don't think he's said anything,' said the dreary constable. 'I haven't heard nothing, have you, My Lord?'

'Yes,' said My Lord. 'I heard a 74 seafront tram go by on its way to the dismounted landlady, but that's not enough evidence to put this man away for life, and you know I won't settle for less.'

At this point McGonagall rose to his feet, held up a silver soup spoon over the Tay bridge and a chronometer. 'Nine days, six hours, four minutes and two seconds.'

'Oh, very well,' said the judge. 'If that's what you want, I sentence you to nine days, six hours, four minutes and two seconds for life.'

A devout Jewish pianist rose from his piano in the press box. 'My Lord,' he said, 'my friend is innocent of being a greenfly. He would never stoop so low. It's a case of mistaken identity.'

The constable opened the case and Gershwin was right, the case was full of mistaken identity.

* OK, OK, we know.

'Och,' said McGonagall as he stepped from the dock into the suitcase. 'It's the worst nine days, six hours, four minutes and two seconds I've had this month.'

'Never mind,' said Gershwin, gently closing the suitcase and carrying him out.

'Excuse me,' said McGonagall through the keyhole. 'Where's the light switch in the karzi?'

'As long as you stay in the foetus position, you are safe,' said Gershwin.

'Safe from what?' said McGonagall through the keyhole, sending out clouds of spittle.

'Well, tigers for a start,' said Gershwin.

'Tigers for a start,' shouted McGonagall through a spit-shattered keyhole. 'Why should I want to start a tiger?' said McGonagall.

'Well,' said Gershwin back through the spittle-covered keyhole. 'Someone has to start them, otherwise they wouldn't get anywhere.'

'Och, mon,' said McGonagall. 'So *that's* what I'm safe from.'

The suitcase weighed heavily on Gershwin's right piano arm, now a foot longer than the other one. 'Can I leave this case here for ever?' said Gershwin, putting it on a railway lost property desk.

'Sorry,' said the lost property man, 'we only accept lost property lost for ever and this doesn't look as if it has been lost for ever.'

'Let me out,' said McGonagall, 'or I'll push something nasty through the keyhole.'

'Good heavens,' said the amazed lost property man. 'A talking suitcase. That must be worth a fortune.'

'Not so,' said the now pressurised Gershwin.

He slid the lock and raised the lid. The lost property man gazed at the doubled-up figure of the grinning McGonagall with his head protruding behind his legs.

'Does that look like a fortune to you?' said Gershwin hopefully.

'No, it's a misfortune,' said the lost property man. 'It looks like a worthless Scottish cripple, worth two pounds at the outside.'

'Ah, but he's inside,' said Gershwin, easing McGonagall out with the EPNS silver soup spoon.

159

'Och, that's better,' said McGonagall, easing his legs and stretching his limbs. 'Och, laddie,' he said, shaking him warmly by the hand, knee, foot and elbow. 'Thanks to your intervention, you've saved my life.'

'Ah, we all make mistakes,' said the lost property man. 'It's my lunch break now. Would you like to take over? There's a pound in it for you.'

Immediately McGonagall took over for a pound in it for him while Gershwin assembled his piano downwind.

'Ach, here comes a merry customer,' said Gershwin, putting on a porter's hat.

'Oh dear,' said a little bearded man. 'I've left my tools on a Northern Line train.'

'Thanks for telling me,' said McGonagall, making a note of it in his diary while Gershwin played it on his piano. 'Where were you going at the time?' said McGonagall.

'Camden Town,' said the man's beard.

'This is nae Camden Town,' said McGonagall as Gershwin played it on the piano. 'This is Mornington Crescent,' said McMornington and Gershwin played it on the piano. 'What I'm saying is your tools are not lost, *you* are' – so saying, McGonagall put a label on the man and slid him on to the lost property rack along with Michael Foot who had lost at the last election, David Steele, who also lost, and David Owen, who was lost as well.

'I wonder what my tools are doing without me?' said the bearded man to Michael Foot.

'I was wondering the same thing about the Labour Party,' said Michael Foot. 'How did Neil do in the last election?' he added.

'I'm up here on the next shelf,' came the voice of the leader of the lost Labour Party.

'Ach,' said McGonagall, putting a lost label on his foot. 'Mrs Thatcher's got a lot to answer for.'

A large portly man with the label saying Robert Maxwell approached McGonagall. 'I've just lost some money on my last takeover. Has anybody handed it in?' he said.

'How much was it then, Mr Muckwell?'

'It was in the neighbourhood of forty million,' said the stout Czech.

'Well, you're in the wrong neighbourhood,' said McGonagall.

160

'Do you think you could edit the *Scottish Daily Express*?' said Robert Maxwell, holding up 50p on elastic.

McGonagall snatched the coin and cut the elastic. 'Och, mon, I could do it standing on ma heed,' said McGonagall.

'That's no use to me,' said Maxwell. 'I want somebody the other way round' – during which time McGonagall dived deep into Maxwell's pocket and reappeared with another 50p.

'The interest,' said McGonagall with a wink.

'I'm not interested,' said Maxwell. He snatched the coin, climbed into a Rolls-Royce, drove to a bigger one and then drove off. He paused only at the piano to toss a Queen Victoria penny into the lap of a pianist a long way from the lap of luxury. The coin lodged in a private crevice causing him acute pain. Mind you, Gershwin didn't think it was cute.

'Could *you* edit the *Scottish Daily Express*?' said Maxwell.

'Not at the moment,' said Gershwin, clutching his acute pain.

'Here, here's my card,' said Maxwell. 'If ever you change your mind, tear it up.'

The two Rolls-Royces drove off at speed. Gershwin changed his mind and tore it up.

'Well, that's that,' said the lost property man, returning from lunch.

'Och, you've promised me a poond,' said McGonagall, holding out his hand.

True to his word, the railway man gave him sixteen ounces which came to exactly one pound.

Waving goodbye to the lost politicians on the shelves and with a last feel of Barbara Castle's battlements, McGonagall bid them a fond Scottish farewell while Gershwin folded his Bechstein into seven-foot planks and draped the keys round his neck. It was a touching picture, the underworld had never known such a spectacle.

As a final tribute to the muse of music, Gershwin sang, 'Mind the doors' as the once-monthly train to High Barnet made off with a full head of steam.

We move now to the queue for auditions at the Palace Theatre.

'Next, please,' said Andrew Lloyd-Webber from the middle of forty million pounds.

Gershwin launched into 'Happy Days are Here Again'.

McGonagall tapped on a top hat with a magic stick. In cod

Chinese, he said, 'Mee makee whitee rabbittee comee outee of toppee hattee', dressed as the late Kaiser.

These words came strangely to Andrew Lloyd-Webber's ears. 'Stop,' he said, holding up his cheque book. 'What are you supposed to be?'

'The Phlantom of the Operla' was the witty cod Chinese reply.

Again, the German-speaking Chinese tapped the top hat with the magic stick. 'Mee makee whitee rabbittee comee outee of toppee hattee.'

Andrew Lloyd-Webber waited with his money to see 'whitee rabbittee comee outee of hattee'. While he waited, the interest alone came to a million.

Meanwhile, Gershwin, oblivious of time, was now halfway through the Chinese national anthem played in a fiendish key. After half an hour's rapid tapping on the hat and German-Chinese comic patter, nothing happened.

Andrew Lloyd-Webber's money said, 'Where's this rabbit?'

'I'm sorry about the delay, och,' said McGonagall, reverting to Glaswegian vernacular. 'It's on the way from Harrods Pet Department marked urgent.'

'It should have been marked rabbits,' said Gershwin in G sharp.

'Look,' said Andrew Lloyd-Webber's money, which was now much higher. 'If this urgent rabbit does arrivee, I can't see what partee it can play in *The Phantom of the Opera*.'

'Och, Mr Lloyd von Weber,' said the Chinese German, 'there'll only have to be a wee change in the billing. It'll read *The Phlantom White Rabbit of the Operla flom Harrods*. I tell ye, it'll be a smash hit, expecially with Mrs Mona Dongle of Bromwich.'

'Why her?' said the money.

'Well, she breeds white rabbits, you see.'

As Gershwin, his piano and McGonagall and their accoutrements were hurled through the stage door, they knew they were on course for the pavement.

'Here it comes again,' warned Gershwin.

'By God, you're right,' warned McGonagall as he contacted the pavement at the going speed of twenty-eight miles an hour, crushing his where-with-alls. 'I'll sue Harrods for this,' he said. 'I'll bring them crashing down, you see.' This was a great

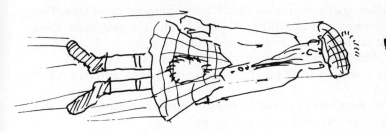

McGonagall being hurled out from somewhere

prediction, as he crashed down himself.

'Sue Harrods? Who's she?' said Gershwin, clutching his where-with-alls.

'It's nae a she, it's a he,' said McGonagall.

'Sue Harrods a he?' said Gershwin, reclutching them. 'How does he get away with it?'

'Och, look,' said McGonagall, pointing at the silver EPNS soup spoon. 'Twelve days, six hours and four minutes! Ye see, laddie, Sue Harrods is an Arab and they can get away with diplomatic immunity.'

'Look,' said Gershwin, pointing to an Arab with diplomatic immunity who at that very moment was getting away with a whole rail of ladies' diplomatic immunity see-through yashmaks.

'Och, did ye no see that?' said McGonagall.

'Yes, I did no see that,' said Gershwin. 'Now what?'

McGonagall cast his eyes over the *Exchange and Mart*. 'Look here,' he said. 'Wanted, top hat, stick and white rabbit, will exchange for gallon of fish oil, umbrella and wooden leg or part in *The Phantom of the Opera*, apply Lionel Blair, Bermondsey labour exchange, Monday to Fridays or weekdays, Saturdays, and Name *That* Tune.'

'Oh, what a bit of luck,' said Gershwin.

'Yes, I wonder which bit it is,' said McGonagall. 'Listen,' he said. 'If we don't eat soon, we'll get hungry. We'd better busk here for a few coppers.'

Gershwin adjusted his piano stool and played the introduction to 'Poor Black Joe' while McGonagall tap-danced on a small rubber mat so as not to disturb the neighbours.

163

McGonagall's prediction about 'a few coppers' came true. Two policemen arrested them. Constable Mullins cautioned them that silent tap-dancing was forbidden in Soho.

'What about Greenwich?' said McGonagall.

'Greenwich? Ah,' said the policeman, 'that's a different cup of tea.'

So they went to Fred's carmen's pull-up in Greenwich and asked for two different cups of tea.

'How do you like your tea?' said Fred.

'We like it different,' said McGonagall.

'Right,' said Fred. 'Is this different enough?' – and gave them two cups of Horlicks. 'That's 50p.'

'Look, laddie,' said McGonagall, with a sly wink, and handed Fred a brown paper parcel. 'This is a twenty-one million pounds' worth of Van Gogh painting of sunflowers.'

A look of disgust came across Fred's disgusting face. 'You're not palming me off with this twenty-one-million-pound painting, I want 50p,' he said. 'Or the Horlicks goes into yon cat.'

'Stop,' said McGonagall, raising a hand. 'Please, sir, we are starving and near to death. If we give you three choruses of "I Belong to Glasgow", will you give us a sandwich?'

'I'll think about it,' said disgusting Fred.

There and then McGonagall and Gershwin gave the finest performance ever, before a packed carmen's pull-up.

As they sang, played, danced and starved, Fred thought about it and said, 'I've thought about it. Now bugger off,' he said.

'Have pity,' they said.

So he had pity and told them to bugger off again. But too late. Mad with hunger, McGonagall and Gershwin ate him. Soon the sign above the café read:

MCGONAGALL AND GERSHWIN
Twice Nightly, Music and Munches

and below it a sign which read:

For Sale, One Horlicks-filled Cat.

'Och,' said McGonagall. 'There has been a great change in our fortunes.'

They ate the last of the bread, cheese, ham and sausages and put up a sign saying:

SOLD OUT – Closing Sale, November 5th

Charrington Noggles, chief auctioneer for Sotheby's, hit his desk with his gavel, heaven knows why. Like striking an innocent match, it had done him no harm.

'Lot number 12B,' he said.

'That's your lot,' said Gershwin to McGonagall.

'What,' continued Noggles, 'am I bid for this car men's pull-up complete with Horlicks-filled cat? The reserve is £100, now. What do I hear?'

'You can hear the traffic outside,' said a voice.

'Any advance on the traffic outside?' said Noggles.

'I can hear the traffic in Bermondsey,' came another offer.

'Any advance on the traffic in Bermondsey?' said the auctioneer, striking his hapless desk yet another blow.

'I can hear the traffic in Lewisham,' came another bid.

'The traffic in Lewisham, going once; the traffic in Lewisham, going twice; the traffic in Lewisham, going thrice. Do I hear the traffic in Mayfair? No? – then sold to I hear the traffic in Lewisham.'

Again, the gavel thudded down on the hapless desk, rendering it uncosnius (sic) for the rest of the auction. The auctioneer's accountant made out a cheque as follows: Pay Messers McGonagall and Gershwin the Traffic in Lewisham less ten per cent commission, being the traffic outside. Signed Tom Sotheby.

'Look here, Tom. What's this messers bit?' said McGon to Sotheby. 'We've never made a mess in our lives.'

'Don't come near me,' said Tom Sotheby, backing away. 'I don't want to catch it, it was bad enough having to handle that Horlicks-filled cat.'

'We're awful sorry, we thought the cork fitted perfectly.'

'Well, he's empty now. I filled him with anti-freeze for the winter.'

165

'Sold to the traffic in Lewisham,' said the auctioneer

The manager of the Lloyds Bank in Lewisham examined the cheque. 'I see, the Traffic of Lewisham,' he repeated. 'This is an unusual type of cheque,' he said, tearing it up and consigning it to the rubbish bin. 'Good day, gentlemen,' he said. 'Here's the address of the psychiatrist I was telling you about.'

'What's this, Screaming Lord Sutch?' said McGonagall. 'He's nae a psychiatrist, he's a singer.'

'Very well,' said the bank manager. 'Get him to sing to you. It'll be cheaper than a psychiatrist and more pleasant.'

'Wait,' said Gershwin, the musical one of the two. 'I am the musical one of the two, and I want very much to know if Screaming Lord Sutch can sing, "I Can Hear the Traffic of Lewisham Outside".'

The bank manager arose from his seat and walked up and down, pondering a reply. He circumnavigated the entire room as Gershwin and McGonagall followed him with their gaze. Revolving ever so slowly, he returned to his chair and stopped pondering.

Emptying the contents of his dustbin into a Tesco bag, he handed it to them. 'I'm sorry, gentlemen, you've got me there. Will you take this small present as a token of my esteem for you?' He then showed them the door, then the window, the ceiling, the floor and finally the door again. He then stepped into the safe, slamming the door after him.

McGonagall looked at Gershwin. 'I'm withdrawing my business from this bank at once,' he said. 'Follow me and I will show you a secret route to the outer world.'

'What's this?' said McGershwin as they reached the street.

'This, my son,' said McGonagall with a munificent gesture, 'is the outer world. My secret route has proved infallible! Let's try this pawn shop.'

'What can I do for you gentlemen?' said one Solly Black.

'Well,' said one McGonagall, emptying the contents of the Tesco bag. 'What will you give us for this?' he said.

'A match,' said Solly, and set fire to it.

'Do you realise you have just ruined the contents of my bank manager's dustbin including a cheque for "I Can Hear the Traffic in Lewisham",' said an infuriated McGonagall.

'Oh, you should have told me in time,' said Solly.

'There wasn't any time,' said McGonagall. 'By the time I had time you had time to burn them. You'll be hearing from my dentist about this,' he said.

'Surely you mean your solicitor,' said Solly.

'No,' said McGonagall, 'I dinnae have a solicitor, only a dentist.'

'Oh,' said Solly, swallowing an unredeemed watch, 'what harm can he do me?'

'Oho,' said the wily McGonagall, 'I'll hae some of ma teeth taken oot and send ye the bill.'

'Stop all this,' said Gershwin. 'What can you give me on this piano?'

'A tap dance,' said the quick-witted pawn merchant, leaping on to the piano and doing a furious buck and wing.

'Stop that,' said Gershwin. 'Don't you know it's Sabbath? You're a disgrace to the Jewish race.'

'Who's the jockey?' said McGonagall.

'Look,' added McGonagall, 'I know a better pawn shop than this.'

With the furiously tap-dancing pawn broker on the top, they wheeled the piano down the high street.

'Don't stop now,' said McGonagall to Solly. 'We're just start-

George Gershwishin pushing the tap-dancing pawn broker on his piano to a better pawn broker

ing to enjoy it. My, you're talented, if you go on like this you won't have to go on swallowing unredeemed watches.'

'Don't let him go,' shouted Ziegfeld, hanging from a seventh-storey window. 'He's a great act. I can see it now – Solly Black, the tap-dancing pawn broker and his famous watch-swallowing act. He's just what the show needs.'

'But when, but when,' groaned the spectators.

'Here we are,' said McGonagall. 'Levy's Electronic Pawn Shop.'

'Nothing Too Big or Too Small,' said the sign.

'That's too big,' said Levy, pointing to the piano. 'And he's too small,' he said, pointing to the tap-dancing Solly.

'Aw, gee, come on,' said Gershwin.

So he came on.

'Now what?' said Levy.

'Well,' said McGonagall, 'what will you give us for it as a going concern?'

'A push,' said Levy, heaving the piano back out into the street again.

'Stop,' said a policeman, grabbing hold of Solly Black as the piano gathered momentum down a slight incline.

'It's not me,' said Solly, 'it's the piano that's moving. I'm standing still. Don't you know it's Sabbath?'

'Blow into this bag,' said the policeman, running alongside.

'Blow into the bag?' said Solly. 'Why me, why can't you do it?'

'I haven't had enough to drink,' said the policeman.

'Well, here you are,' said Solly, giving him a bottle of whisky.

'Is this a bribe?' said the policeman.

'No,' said Solly, 'it's a bottle. Can't you tell the difference between a bribe and a bottle? No wonder you never get promotion.'

The piano was now gathering further momentum. It was a great sight for the spectators to witness the piano travelling downhill at forty miles an hour (Allegro ma non troppo) with a frenzied tap-dancing pawn broker on top pausing now and then to swallow another unredeemed watch, while galloping alongside was the faithful policeman alternately taking swigs from a bottle and breathalising himself.

'You know,' said Gershwin, 'this is definitely no way to write *Porgy and Policeman.*'

'You'll never get promotion like this,' said McGonagall from a stationary position on top of the piano.

'Oh dear, look, buddy,' said Gershwin, buddy, furiously playing at an ever-increasing speed and crashing through the traffic lights. 'This is no way to write *Porgy and Policeman*.'

'Do you know you've just been through a red light?' said the policeman.

'So have you,' said McGonagall. 'We're all in this together.'

'You know,' said the policeman, now down to the last drop and staggering at forty miles an hour, 'you know that green is the most popular light for going through in England?'

'Och, it's also very popular on the Continent,' said McGonagall as the piano ground to a halt at the bottom of the hill.

'I'm sorry, this is as far as I go,' said Gershwin. 'Everybody off.'

'I suppose you know,' said the policeman, 'that you've put my career back.'

'Of course, mon,' said McGonagall. 'We always return everything to its original owner. Mind you, you don't look very original to me. You look like a fake Van Gogh.'

'I knew you'd say that,' said the policeman, now inside the bottle. 'It's only having one ear that does it.'

'You've had more than one here,' said McGonagall. 'You've had twenty doubles to my knowledge. Was that Teacher's whisky?'

'No, it was the Chief Superintendent's,' said the policeman.

'That's right,' said Solly. 'He pawned it on a very bad day. He managed to redeem the cork, but that was about all.'

'I can hear a telephone ringing,' said the policeman.

'And I can hear the wind blowing through the trees,' said McGonagall. 'But I should answer the phone first, the trees can wait.'

'If you're a tree, that's all you can do,' said Gershwin. 'I know a forest in Epping that's full of trees and they're all waiting.'

'What are they waiting for?' said McGonagall.

'They're waiting for the chop,' said Gershwin.

'The chop?' said McGonagall, releasing one. 'I thought trees were vegetarians.'

It had been another long hard day.

CHAPTER ONE

They spent the night. That's all they could afford to spend. McGonagall rose from the grass of the park in fine style.

'I think I'll apply for sick benefit this morning,' said McGonagall.

'But you're nae sick,' said McGershwin.

'That will follow as soon as the money arrives,' said McGonagall. 'Now, unless my eyes deceive me, that's a funfair over there.' And then, taking careful aim, he pointed.

Gershwin looked carefully along McGonagall's arm and pointing finger and, sure enough, there at the end of it was a fair.

MADAME ZONG –
Have your fortune told

read a legend above a tent.

McGonagall was in and out in thirty seconds.

'I haven't got one,' he said to Gershwin.

When Gershwin went in, she was disinfecting the place.

'I didn't want to catch it,' said Madame Zong. 'Scotsmen are very contagious. My late husband caught Scotsman off one of them. Now, let me see your palm,' she said.

'Ah,' she said, 'I can tell you haven't had a wash this morning and that'll be a pound.'

'No,' said Gershwin, 'that'll be I haven't had a wash this morning and goodbye.'

Gershwin landed in a heap at the feet of McGonagall.

'What are ye doing down there?' said the wily Scot.

'Getting up,' said Gershwin. He stood upright. 'Now do you believe me?'

'It's a whole new world out there,' said McGonagall.

'Yes,' said McGershwin, straightening his piano. 'Yes, the world's our oyster.'

'Only when there's an "R" in the month,' said McGonagall.

'There's no month in "R",' said Gershwin. 'What are you talking about?'

'I'm talking about eighteen words a minute,' said McGonagall, 'which is the going rate for Scotsmen at the moment.'

'And what's this about an oyster in the month?'

'There's no "R" in oyster,' said Gershwin.

'Yes there is,' said McGonagall, 'O-Y-S-T-E-R.'

'Ah, so you spell yours with an "R"?' said Gershwin.

'Yes, if there's one in the month I do. Look at that sign,' said McGonagall, again taking aim and pointing in the direction of Look at That Sign.

Gershwin cast his eye along the line of McGonagall's arm and finger and, sure enough, there was a Look at That Sign.

'Five pounds for any man who can stay one round with the Fred the Fighting Fijian from Lewisham.'

'Och, this is going to be a pushover,' said McGonagall, pushing somebody over.

'That's not very nice,' said the pushed-over person from the supine position. 'I'm going to teach you a lesson. Two and two is four, C-A-T spells cat. There, let that be a lesson to you.'

Our heroes entered the Fighting Fred tent pushing through a crowd of insensate bodies fresh from the ring.

'Right, who's next?' said Fighting Fred's manager from inside his safety cage.

'Look nae further,' said McGonagall, pushing Gershwin forward.

'But, buddy,' said Gershwin, 'I can't box.'

'You don't have to, Fighting Fred will do all that, all you have to do is avoid him.'

The fight started with Gershwin cowering behind a stool.

'Now, I want a fair fight,' said the referee, pointing to the twenty-three stone Fighting Fred. 'In case of a knock-down you will go to a neutral corner.'

'I'd rather go to a neutral country,' said Gershwin.

The gong went, and with it went Gershwin. It took McGonagall twenty-three miles across country to catch up with him.

'You only had to stay there three minutes to win five pounds,' said McGonagall.

'OK,' said Gershwin. 'You've talked me into it,' – and ran twenty-three miles back into the ring just in time to receive a head-crushing blow from Fiji Fred which sent him hurtling to the canvas.

'Look out, here comes the flae,' advised McGonagall, in an attempt to soften the blow.

He failed – too late – Gershwin's unconscious body hit the canvas again and again and again. It went on like that for three minutes.

'I'm very disappointed in you,' said McGonagall as Gershwin regained consciousness in the hospital. 'All you had to do was to keep upright for three minutes.'

'He was too strong for me,' said Gershwin.

'Don't give me that,' said McGonagall.

'I'm not giving you that, he gave me that,' said Gershwin, pointing to broken teeth in a glass.

'I'll wait here,' said McGonagall.

'Wait here for what?' said Gershwin.

'Wait for you to get better,' said McGonagall. 'Can't you discharge yourself?'

'I think I already have,' said Gershwin.

'Nurse, the screens,' screamed McGonagall. Too late.

It was a week later that McGonagall took Gershwin to meet Fiji Fred's manager.

'We want compensation,' said McGonagall to the manager. 'Your client grievously injured my client.'

'Is that so?' said the manager, massaging his giant charge.

'Och, that's the worst charge since the Light Brigade,' said McGonagall.

'Yes, I was saying when the gong went that your client attacked my client for no reason at all. I mean, it said nae a thing about fighting outside on the wall. It just said – and I have a copy of it here – that my client had to stay in the ring with your client for a period of three minutes, after which he would receive a payment of five pounds.'

'I see no point in giving five pounds to an unconscious man,' said the manager, massaging his giant Charge of the Light Brigade.

'You see,' said McGonagall to Gershwin, 'you see what you've done? By going unconscious you've lost us what was a cert five pounds.'

'I wasn't, I wasn't unconscious,' said Gershwin. 'I just had my eyes closed.'

'Why?' said McGonagall.

'I just thought it was safer that way,' said Gershwin.

'Aye, but nae as remunerative.'

'If you'll excuse me,' said the manager, 'I have things to do.'

So McGonagall excused him because he had things to do. The manager went into a corner and started to do things.

'I'm glad my five-year-old niece is not here to see this.'

'Why?' said Gershwin.

'Because I could not afford the fare,' said McGonagall.

'And I'm glad my entire family of eighteen are not here to see this either, which is a bigger saving,' said Gershwin.

'It's amazing the things that make you glad these days,' said McGonagall. 'I mean, my five-year-old niece and your family of eighteen are making us glad just by not being here.'

'Do you mind going away, I'm doing things,' said the manager, while the giant charge on the massage table just lay there and groaned as the Light Brigade charged over him.

'I didn't know you liked horses,' said McGonagall to the giant charge.

'Thank you very much for telling my giant charge that you didn't know he liked horses,' said the manager. 'Up until then he was apparently unaware of this fact. But in future when he sees you he will immediately know that you didn't know that he liked horses.'

'Look out,' said Gershwin, 'they're coming back.'

'Och, ye're right,' said McGonagall, flattening against the wall as the Light Brigade thundered past for lunch.

'Oh,' groaned the giant charge from under the massage table, 'have they gone yet?'

'No, I don't think they've gone yet, but you can see where they've been,' said McGonagall.

'The roses, the roses,' groaned the spectators.

'Don't talk to me about roses,' said Ziegfeld from the seventeenth-storey window ledge. 'Jack Rose and his family all owe me money.'

'Excuse me,' said a thin ragged man from somewhere in the region of Deptford and the Bermuda Triangle, 'but how long would you be occupying this window ledge?'

'I'm coming in any minute now,' said Ziegfeld.

'Would you be more specific and tell me which of those any minutes?'

'I'm sorry, I can't go into detail,' said Ziegfeld. 'Why?'

'Well, you see,' said the man, 'Dick Quonck wants to commit suicide from here on the recommendation of his bank manager.'

'So where do you come in?' said Ziegfeldski, trying to shake them free.

'I came in through the door, I thought it was the decent thing to do,' said the thin ragged man from Deptford and the Bermuda Triangle.

'I see from that last line,' said Flo Ziegfeld, 'that you are from the Bermuda Triangle.'

'Well, actually no,' said the thin ragged man. 'I have a travel agency which books holidays for mothers-in-law in the Bermuda Triangle. Unfortunately, one of the mothers-in-law came back and ruined the business. Since then I have been registered in Panama as a thin ragged man from Deptford only.'

'I see, I've never been to Deptford only,' said Ziegfeld. 'What's it like in Deptford only?'

'I don't know,' said the Registered in Panama man.

'Can you hear horses?' said Ziegfeld.

'Yes, but take no notice,' said the thin Panamanian registered in Deptford. 'They come through every night about this time.'

'It makes a change from Crippen,' said Ziegfeld. 'Now state your business.'

'Well, Dick Quonck asked me to come and save this space on this window ledge until such time as his bank manager allows him to commit suicide.'

'Is that the listening bank?' said Ziegfeld.

'No, this one just watches,' said the man. 'It watches as you jump off.'

'Don't you know this window ledge is mine?' said Ziegfeld.

'Yes,' said the man. 'I don't know that this window ledge is mine.'

He trod on one and exploded.

'Yes, he's going to feel that in the morning,' said Ziegfeld. Little did he know that the man felt it every morning and was well pleased with the arrangement.

'The show, the show,' groaned the spectators. 'What about the show?'

FRESH CHAPTER

McGonagall and Gershwin dismounted from the piano by a cactus. They looked at the notice:

REWARD

ONE DOLLAR DEAD OR ALIVE o.n.o.
WILLIAM TOPAZ MCGONAGALL
WANTED FOR POETRY
AND OTHER CRIMES

'You're a wanted man,' said Gershwin.

'I wonder who it is who wants me?' said McGonagall, patting the piano lightheartedly with overtones of liver and kidney.

'Search me,' said Gershwin, so McGonagall searched him and found the following items:

> Six army blankets
> A quarter of an ounce of margarine
> A photograph of Neville Chamberlain
> An oil slick
> A tin of Kattomeat
> and a dead canary

'Why are you carrying all this?' said McGonagall.

'Well, it's a free country,' said Gershwin.

'Is it?' said McGonagall, startled out of his life. 'To think I put two pounds away in case it wasn't.' So saying, he carefully restored the items to the place where they originated. In this case to George Gershwin.

'Och, that's a funny place for a dead canary,' said McGonagall. 'A jockstrap.'

'Oh, it's a great comfort in the winter,' said Gershwin. He gave a sickly grin and was sick.

'Hands up and don't move,' said a stern American voice from the rear.

So they put their hands up and they didn't move, so they adhered to the instructions perfectly, but eighteen hours was a bit much.

'Can we put them down now?' said McGonagall to the stern American voice from the rear.

'OK,' said the stern American voice from the rear eighteen hours later. 'Turn around.'

They turned around and found themselves back where they started.

'You should have stopped halfway,' said the stern American voice, etc.

They turned to face the voice, etc., and there before them in *High Noon* was Billy the Yid.

'Och,' said McGonagall, 'Billy the Yid, they say you're the fastest gun in the West.'

'Yes,' said Billy. 'And they say you're the fastest gun in the East.'

'Aye,' said McGonagall, 'I also happen to know that you're the fastest gun in SW2.'

'Och,' said Billystein the Kid. 'And I know that you're the fastest gun in NW11.'

'Ochstein,' said McGonagall. 'And I hear you're the fastest gun in SE6, Zipcode 3X1 529.'

'And I hear, Abie Gershwin,' said Billy the Kidstein, 'that you're the fastest pianist in E11, so go for your piano.'

Gershwin went for his piano, but it was already there.

'You're too quick for me,' said Billy the Kidstein.

'I hear he's too quick for you,' said McGonagall.

'And I hear music and there's no one there,' said Gershwin.

'Listen,' said Billy the Kidstein. 'Do you know there's a price on your head?'

'No, it's not,' said McGonagall, 'it's a hat.'

'Are you calling me a liar?' said the Kid.

'No,' said the McGonagall, 'I'm calling it a hat.'

'Well, perhaps I've got it wrong,' said the Billy. 'Perhaps there's a price on your knee.'

'Well, I'm not selling it,' said the William. 'Who wants to go around with one knee?'

'I'll go around with it,' said Gershwin. 'Anything to help out,'

'Go for your guns,' said Billy the Yid

he said, pouring oil on troubled waters.

'That's a terrible mess,' said McGonagall as he watched Gershwin mixing the two ingredients together.

'Wait,' said Billy the Eckstein, 'I hear music and there's still nobody there.'

That night, what sounded like an exhausted McGonagall and Gershwin drew up their piano and hitched it to the rail outside the Mamloot Saloon. The guy at the piano was playing a ragtime tune.

'What'll it be?' said the barman.

'What'll what'll be?' said McGonagall.

'What are you drinking?' said the barman.

'I'm not drinking anything, man,' said McGonagall. 'Can't you see? What's the matter, have you been drinking?'

'No, I'm not drinking,' said the barman.

'That makes two of us,' said McGonagall, 'and with Gershwin that makes three and with Mrs Elizabeth Brains of Lewisham that makes four of us not drinking up to date, and if you add Alcoholics Anonymous you could go bankrupt any minute.'

'I'm not standing here arguing,' said the barman.

'All right then, have a chair,' said Gershwin.

'I thought I told you guys to get out of town,' said a *High Noon* cowboy.

'Oh, so that's what you thought,' said McGonagall. 'Thanks for telling us. Two glasses of milk,' he said to the barman.

'We don't sell that crap here,' said the barman.

'All right then, sell it to us over there,' said McGonagall, pointing in a certain direction.

'I'm sorry that direction is not licensed,' said the barman. 'I tell you what I'll do,' said the barman and told them what he would do, which was throw them out.

'This appears to be the main exit,' said McGonagall to Gershwin as they were hurled through the swinging doors. They crashed at the feet of *High Noon* Cowboy II.

'I thought I told you two to get out of town,' he said.

'We are, and this is the first instalment,' said McGonagall.

A shot rang out and the *High Noon* Cowboy II crashed to the ground. 'I've been shot,' he gasped, he was shot.

McGonagall tenderly leaned over the cowboy and gently removed his wallet. 'Shall I call a doctor?' said McGonagall.

'No,' groaned the *High Noon* Cowboy II. 'Call a policeman.'

'Leave him, boys,' said a voice.

They turned to see Jesse James with a gun in each hand and one in each orifice. 'He had it coming to him,' he said.

'I don't know about coming,' said McGonagall, 'I think it's arrived.'

'Never mind about him, I can use you boys. Have you ever robbed a bank?'

McGonagall thumbed through his diary. 'As far as I can see, the answer is no,' he said.

'How about you, Gersh?'

And Gersh said, 'I hear music but there's no one there.'

'That doesn't sound much like a bank robbery to me,' said McGonagall.

'OK,' said Jesse James, 'you're both innocent but we'll soon fix that, now hold these horses. No, no, not up in the air, just by the reins will do. These are the getaway horses.'

'Get away?' said Gershwin in surprise.

'I wonder if these are the right men,' said Jesse James under his breath.

'I wonder why these men are holding us,' said the horses under their breath.

'I wonder why everyone is speaking under their breath?' said Gershwin under his breath.

'Where has everybody gone?' said McGonagall under his house.

'They're hiding under their breath,' said a complete horse.

'Now I'll take these sticks of dynamite,' said Jesse James. 'They never fail.' He crept stealthily towards the bank, which was closed due to early closing.

'This looks like daylight robbery to me,' said McGonagall.

'Why are we doing it at night-time, then?' said Gershwin.

'Because everybody does it at night,' said McGonagall.

'Oh, is that why I can never get any sleep?' said Gershwin.

'I thought I told you guys to get out of town,' said *High Noon* Cowboy No. III.

'We can't leave town without the permission of these horses,' said McGonagall.

'I'm gonna count up to three,' said the *High Noon* Cowboy No. III. So he counted up to three and left.

At that moment there came what appeared to be a very loud explosion. The front of the bank blew out and through it came ace gunman and master bank robber Jesse James.

'Did you see who that was?' said Gershwin to McGonagall as he passed them.

'Aye, that was ace gunman and master bank robber Jesse James,' said McGonagall. 'I wonder where he's going, he seems to be in an awfu' hurry.'

'He didn't seem to be in anything to me, except a state,' said Gershwin.

In a moment, a ragged charred smoking figure drew nigh. It

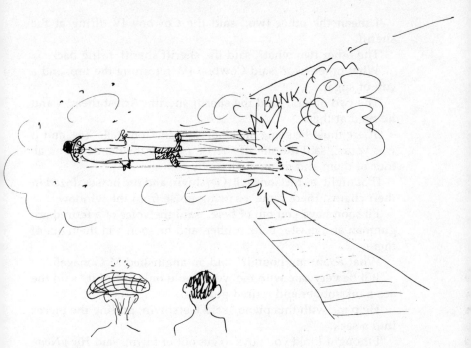

Departure of ace gunman and master bank robber Jesse James

was the ace gunman master bank robber Jesse James.

'Have you seen any money coming this way?' he said. 'I thought I saw some come out with me.'

'Oh dear, oh dear, oh dear, oh dear,' said McGonagall. 'What happened, Mr James?'

'If you didn't see, I'm not going to do it again,' said Jesse James. 'And I'll tell you something else, never buy dynamite from a Chinaman.'

'Is the robbery over?' said McGonagall.

'Yes,' said Jesse James. 'It's all over the street, didn't you see?' Quickly borrowing a pound from McGonagall, the ace gunman and bank robber rode out of town.

'Those are the men, sheriff,' said the *High Noon* Cowboy IV to the sheriff firing a pistol at McGonagall, Gershwin and the horses.

'Make up your mind,' said the sheriff sheriff, firing back at the cowboy. 'Two of those men are horses.'

'I mean the other two,' said the Cowboy IV, firing at the sheriff.

'The other two what?' said the sheriff sheriff, firing back.

'What other two?' said Cowboy IV, returning the fire, and a cup of sugar.

'The two others,' said the sheriff sheriff. 'Arrest them' – and he fired at them.

'There must be some mistake,' said McGonagall. 'Yes, and it was yours,' said the sheriff sheriff, putting the handcuffs on all four of them and firing at anybody.

That night, as McGonagall, Gershwin and the horses dozed in their chains, there came a sawing noise from the window.

'I'll soon have you out of here,' said the voice of a retired ace gunman and master bank robber, and he soon had them out of there.

'What about my pound?' said an anguished McGonagall.

'It'll be very safe with me, you would only spend it,' said the ace bank robber and retired gunman.

'Help me with this piano,' said Gershwin, putting the pieces into a sack.

'I thought I told you guys to get out of town,' said *High Noon* Cowboy V.

'For God's sake, shut up,' said McGonagall I.

'Do you think there'll be a world war?' said Gershwin.

Before McGonagall could answer, the chapter came to an end and cut him short.

NEW CHAPTER II

'Let me see,' said Gershwishin inspecting. 'Buddy, that's a nasty cut you've got, buddy.'

'Here, let me suck the blood out,' said Count Dracula, stepping out of a Transylvanian coach tour.

'Don't let him near you,' warned Gershwin.

'Well, it's the only way he can do it,' said McGonagall.

'He'll bleed you dry,' said Ziegfeld from a window ledge.

'You must be mistaking him for my bank manager.'

'No, I'm mistaking him for a Count Dracula,' said McGonagall.

'But I am a Count Dracula,' said Count Dracula the Count. 'There must be some mistake about you mistaking him for me, and hurry up, the sun is rising, and I'm not so good after dark.' So saying, he flew away.

'That was a close shave,' said Gershwin, coming out from behind the piano.

'What were you doing behind there?' queried the McGonagall.

'Didn't you hear me, I was having a close shave,' said Gershwin.

'Och, dear, you don't know what you missed back there, you missed a mistaken Count Dracula on a Transylvanian coach tour who are now one Dracula short.'

'What have you got in that box?' said Gershwin, pointing to a long coffin-like structure.

'I'll show ye,' said McGonagall, flipping the lid open.

'What's that?' said Gershwin.

'Och, that, my laddie, believe it or not, is a Fijian phallic shield,' said McGonagall. 'And a wooden leg,' he added.

'Hello, Jock,' said a one-legged Fijian without a phallic shield and minus a wood leg.

'Och, Jamie, is this your lucky day,' said the McGonagall, holding his hand out for some money.

The Fijian shook his hand warmly.

'Ach, luke, here is your long-lost phallic shield and your long-lost Fijian wooden leg,' said McGonagall.

'There must be some mistake,' said the one-legged Fijian, hopping forward. 'They must be someone else's.'

And sure enough someone else came along and it was theirs.

'You know when I last saw these?' said someone else.

'Do I?' said McGonagall. 'Don't worry, I'll no tell anybody, your secret is safe with me.' So saying, he thrust someone else into the box, nailed it down and pushed it over a cliff. 'Och, there he goes, you won't get a cheaper packaged tour than that these days.'

(Jack Hobbs will have it known that he has a record by Bill Evans called 'California Here I Come' and Spike Milligan hasn't.)

CHAPTER LE FIRST

'I've always loved Montmartre,' said McGonagall.

'I've always loved ici Paris,' said Gershwin.

'Thank heaven for little girls,' said a passing Maurice Chevalier.

'Thank heaven for little boys,' said a passing curate.

'Thanks for the memory,' said a passing Bob Hope.

'Thanks for the mammary,' said a passing Dolly Parton.

'No, thank *you*,' said a passing groper.

The west light shone through his studio window as McGonagall stood there, palette in hand, brush poised, about to cook breakfast.

'That's no way to cook breakfast,' said Gershwin, standing nude on a plinth.

'Och, it's the best I can do without money,' said McGonagall, painting eggs and bacon twice, bread and butter and a pot of tea for two.

'You know, I've never posed for breakfast before,' said Gershwin.

'Oh, nonsense, you're just about the right shape for breakfast,' said McGonagall. 'There,' he said, tearing it in half, 'breakfast is served' – and collapsed to the floor faint with hunger.

'Ah, goody-goody,' said Gershwin, 'more for me' – eating his half and putting McGonagall in the oven on a low gas.

'Stop zat,' said ze landlady, 'I will not have you cooking my lodgeurs in zis 'ouse. And why are you naked?'

'I am posing for an eggs and bacon,' said Gershwin.

'You could have fooled me,' she said. 'You look more like ball curry or sausage toad in the hole.'

'I'm sorry I've disappointed you,' said Gershwin. 'I'll try and do better next time.' And he did it next time and it was better.

'Ahhhh,' she complimented him. 'Quelle belle tackle de mariage.'

'Madame,' he said tenderly, kissing her wallet. 'Can you please lend us a few francs so we can buy a dinner at Maxim's?'

'Very well, just this once,' she said. 'But remember, I have ze negatives.'

A stunned waiter at the head table at Maxim's or the headwaiter at the stunned table in Maxim's listened to McGonagall's order.

'Listen, Jamie, eggs and bacon twice, four slices of bread and butter and a pot of tea for two.'

'We don't serve that crap here,' said the waiter.

'Weren't you the barman at the Manaloot Saloon?' asked McGonagall.

'Yes, wasn't I the barman at the Mamaloot Saloon?' said the stunned barman waiter head.

McGonagall waved several francs under the waiter's nose. He waved three more behind his ear, a few more under his armpits, six in the pit of his stomach and several behind his knee. He then replaced them in his sporran.

'Och, mon Dieu,' said the head barman waiter, 'ze millionaire. Zis way, messieurs.'

In a few moments, they were out in the street again.

'Oh, this is no way to eat breakfast,' said Gershwin.

'Aye, laddie, isn't it time you dressed?' said McGonagall. 'The posing is over. People are going round thinking you are a ball curry or ze sausage toad in ze hole.'

'Well, it's not a bad thing to be on a rainy day,' said Gershwin.

'A propos of that, do you think there's going to be a world war?' said Gershwin.

'Well, where else?' said McGonagall.

Gershwin thought hard, but he couldn't think of anywhere else, so he put on a raincoat.

'Ah, that's better,' said McGonagall. 'You're looking more like the raincoat I used to know.'

'Stop in ze name of ze lair,' said a French gendarme.

Our heroes stopped in the name of the lair.

'Are you loitering with intent?' said the gendarme.

'No, we're loitering without it,' said McGonagall. 'Why?'

'Good question,' said the French Frenchman. 'You will receive my reply on a postcard.'

'That's a good question,' said McGonagall. 'And you'll receive our reply by return. Have you ever received mail by carrier pigeon before?'

'Yes,' said the gendarme. 'And it was delicious. And what are you hiding under that mackintosh?' said the policeman.

'I'm hiding a Gershwin,' said McGonagall.

'Open up, we know you're in there, Gershwin,' said the French cop. 'Come out with your hands up.'

McGonagall threw open the raincoat, revealing –

'Mon Dieu, sacre bleu,' said the French frog gendarme. 'Un ball curry avec un toad in ze hole.'

'Ach, di' ye hear that?' said McGonagall. 'Did you hear the bad name you're getting us? For God's sake, pull yourself together, mon.'

Gershwin pulled himself together, mon.

'Stop that,' said the gendarme, 'or I'll go blind.'

'Don't take it that hard, officer,' said McGonagall.

So the French gendarme frog didn't take it that hard.

'Would it be criminals you're looking for, Officer Froggie?!' asked McGonagall.

'Och,' said the McFrenchman, 'you've discovered my secret.'

'Well, I can put work your way,' said McGonagall.

'That's not exactly where I want it,' said the wily frog.

'All right somewhere else, then,' said McGonagall.

'Billy the Kid, arrest him tout suite,' said McGonagall.

'But sacre-bleu-Billy-ze-Kid-tout-suite is mort,' said the froggie.

'All right, then,' said McGonagall, 'arrest sacre-bleu-Billy-ze-Kid-tout-suite-is-mort's corpse.'

'What, do you want me to become ze laughing stock of ze gendarmerie?' said the frog.

'No,' said McGonagall.

'Ah, so you 'ave changed ze mind,' said the Frenchman frog. 'In zat case I arrest you for the mort of Billy ze Kid tout suite.'

'But I thought his name was sacre-bleu-Billy-ze-Kid-is-mort-tout-suite,' said McGonagall.

'Not any longer,' said the frog.

'He can't be getting any longer,' said McGonagall. 'He's been dead ninety years, and I would think that by now the death certificate is much more valuable.'

'I'll cash it in the morning,' said the Frenchman, and put it in his truncheon. He blew his whistle and ran away shouting, 'Stop thief.' He returned and asked them, 'How did that sound to you, messieurs?'

'Well, to our messieurs,' said McGonagall, 'it sounded very good. We would like you to accept this Fijian phallic shield and this wooden leg as a going away present.'

186

'But I'm not going away,' said the gendarme.

'Then you're not getting it,' said McGonagall.

'You're right, I've not been getting it for quite a while now,' said the demoralised Frenchman. 'Have you got any addresses?'

'Aye,' said McGonagall, and gave him the address of Count Dracula and a blood bank.

'Ah, wunderbar,' said the schizophrenic gendarme. 'Will I get it there?'

'Well, it's up to you get it there,' said McGonagall. 'There are trains every half hour.'

'You'll be well looked after. You'll be met at the station by a saline drip.'

'What's his name?' said the gendarme.

'What's whose name?' said McGonagall, temporarily at the mercy of the Frenchman's powerful intellectual questioning.

'The name of the drip,' said the frog.

'For all I know his name is Eric,' said McGonagall.

'For all you know his name is Eric?' said the Frenchman.

'For all I know his name is Tom,' said McGonagall.

'For all you know his name is Tom?' queried the Frenchman. 'Quelle happened to Dick and Harry?'

McGonagall admitted he didn't know what had happened to Dick and Harry, for all he knew they could be dead. And that was all they knew.

'For all ye know,' said Gershwin, 'I'm freezing to death in this raincoat.'

'Aaach, buddy, if that raincoat is freezing you to death, take it off.'

In one bound Gershwin removed it.

'Mon Dieu, encore le ball curry avec le toad in ze hole,' cried the gendarme, who for all he knew was a policeman.

That night Gershwin sat at his piano in a French attic composing a dinner.

'How does this sound?' he said to McGonagall, playing egg and chips twice, four slices of bread and butter, rice pudding with jam and a pot of tea for two at Maxim's.

'Seems to me I've heard that song before,' said McGonagall. 'Now can you play me the following:

Smoked salmon on a bed of farm fresh lettuce
with cayenne pepper, a slice of lemon,

187

a glass of Sancerre, some thinly sliced organically
grown brown bread with unsalted Normandy butter

followed by

New season's grouse stuffed with pâté de fois gras and
    walnuts
nouvelle potatoes,
spinach cooked in vermouth,
with a bottle of Château La Tour, 1947

then

Strawberry sorbet with a half bottle of Château d'Yquem

and finally

Crêpes Suzette flambé
with a 1940 Barsac

to conclude

A fine stilton accompanied by Taylors 1909 vintage port
and a good fuck.

The landlady burst into the room. It went all over the place.*
'You are three months behind with your rent,' she said.
'Och, thanks for telling us,' said McGonagall, and threw her
down the stairs.
'You shouldn't have done that,' said Gershwin. 'You know
she doesn't like it.'
'How long have I been without food?' said McGonagall.
Gershwin ran a tape measure over him. 'About five feet nine
and a half,' said Gershwin.
'Och, that's too long,' said McGonagall. He took his shoes off,
reducing himself to five foot eight and a half. 'Ach, laddie, I'll be
able tae last another inch now before I eat.'
'What about me?' said Gershwin. 'I've not eaten since five
feet eleven and a half.'

* Yes, again.

188

A diplomat entered. 'Gentlemen,' he said, mistaking them for them. 'The fame of your hunger has reached the ears of the Diplomatic Corps. It's also reached the neck, the shoulders and the waist and, in some parts of London, the teeth.' He opened the diplomatic bag and took out a ball curry and a sausage toad in the hole. 'Now, which is which?' said Sir Dull, the diplomat.

'Never mind silly questions,' said McGonagall, saliva pouring like Niagara from his mouth. 'Put it on the table.'

'You can thank the Queen for this,' said the Dull diplomat, putting them on the table.

So they thanked the Queen.

'Well, what are you waiting for?' said McGonagall as he ravaged the food.

'Well, we're waiting for the plates,' said the diplomatic Dull.

'Too late,' said McGonagall, who had already eaten his.

'Oh dear, the embassy dog will have to eat off the floor,' said the diplomatic Dull.

'Och, can you no get him any food?' said McGonagall. 'I mean, when the wee doggie has finished the flae, what are ye diplomats going to be walking on?'

'What we've always been walking on – air,' said the retreating Dull diplomat Sir Richard. 'Do you know there's a dead land-lady on your stairs?' he said.

'Och, they're not our stairs,' said McGonagall. 'They're hers, so it's perfectly legal.'

'Is that how you feel?' said Richard Dull the Diplomatic Dull.

'I've not felt anything yet, but then it's early days, and this is our first dinner in quite a few early days,' said McGonagall.

'Tell me,' said Gershwin, licking the pattern off the plate. 'Is yon sausage toad in the hole made of pork?'

McGonagall crouched low and gave an evil sideways grin. 'Och, do not tell me – you're in trouble with the rabbi, aren't you?'

'Yes,' said Gershwin, also from the crouching and evil grinning sideways position.

'Here comes one now,' said McGonagall as a rabbi's face appeared in the attic window. 'God, he's a tall man, I will say that for him.'

'It's got about that you've been eating pork disguised as a sausage-shaped toad in a hole. Tell me it's a lie,' said the rabbi.

Gershwin drew himself up from the crouching evil grinning

189

sideways position. 'I tell you, a sausage toad in the hole could never lie.'

'What are you talking about? I saw it lying on your plate,' said the rabbi.

'Does this mean I'm no longer Jewish?'

By now the rabbi had lifted the sash and, with Zionist groans at considerable decibels, had squeezed through the gap and squirmed across the floor holding out a begging bowl.

'Sorry, but I'm skint,' said Gershwin.

'So am I,' said the rabbi. 'That's why I'm selling the bowl. What am I bid, do I hear five pounds?'

'No, you can hear the traffic in the Champs Elysées,' said McGonagall.

'Any advance on the traffic in the Champs Elysées?' said the rabbi.

'Yes, I can hear the traffic on the cross-Channel ferry going from Calais to Dover,' said McGonagall.

'Any advance on the cross-Channel ferry to Dover?' asked the rabbi.

'Yes,' said Gershwin. 'I can hear William McGonagall.'

'Going once, twice, three times – sold to the man who can hear William McGonagall,' said the rabbi, diving out of the window and taking the bowl with him.

'Och, that's a very strange religion you're into there,' said McGonagall.

There came a distant Zionist groan as the rabbi and his bowl hit the pavement. As hits go, it should have been one of the top ten rabbis.

'Are you loitering with intent?' said a gendarme.

'No, I'm loitering with a bowl,' he said, holding it up.

'Quelle handy,' said the gendarme, filling it to the brim.

Now upstairs in the attic, McGonagall started to poem:

Oooooooh, wonderful gift of food from the Queen.
It was the finest ball curry I have ever seen.
Lying there steaming on that diplomatic plate,
If I remember correctly it's the last thing I ate.
I'm not particularly fond of curry
It always goes through you in such a hurry.
However, the dinner was totally free
And that's why most of it is now inside me.

190

The very next day unexpectedly McGonagall and Gershwin had a windfall. A tree fell on them.

'What are you doing under there?' said a forestry inspector from a log.

'We're stopping this tree from hitting the ground,' said McGonagall, acting as spokesman for both of them.

The forestry inspector replied, speaking for both of them: 'Have you got a licence for stopping trees from hitting the ground? Otherwise it's illegal,' he said.

'If only we had known that earlier,' said McGonagall. 'By the way, Jock, have you got a licence for standing on that log?'

'Oh yes,' said the forestry man. 'I'd be a fool to do it otherwise.'

'Can you do it otherwise?' said McGonagall, speaking for both himself and one.

'Not without a licence,' said the forestry inspector from a log. 'Well, I'm off for dinner, have you any last requests?' he said.

'Yes, could you introduce us to a good crane driver to get this tree off us?'

So he introduced them to a good crane driver to get the tree off them. 'Stay there, we'll have it off in a jiffy.'

'Oh God, he's gonna screw both of us,' said McGonagall, dragging them clear of the tree, neutralising the crane and running for some distant hills, at the same time running for Parliament. Not all people run for Parliament. Some walk and some take taxis.

'It must have been something I said,' said the crane driver. 'Who'd have thought that lifting a fallen tree off two recumbent figures could have led to a seat in Parliament.'

He was mistaken. Neither McGonagall nor Gershwin had a seat in Parliament. They couldn't even get a seat on the train, so they were standing for Parliament via a 127 bus to Ealing, a minicab to Shepherd's Bush and the Tube from there to the Isle of Dogs. 'Isn't it time you gave that plate back?' said McGonagall to Gershwin, still trying to squeeze some extra dinner out of it.

'It's part of a dinner service,' said Gershwin.

'No it isn't,' said McGonagall. 'It's part of the Diplomatic Service.'

'Whatever happened to the distant hills we were running for?' said Gershwin.

'Och, we lost our deposit,' said McGonagall. 'This looks like a good place for it,' said McGonagall, pointing at one.

'Good place for what it?' said Gershwin.

'It's a saxophone factory for Rastafarians,' said McGonagall, opening the door.

'What a lucky break for us it was here,' said Gershwin, pointing. 'Another two paces and we'd have gone past it.'

McGonagall groaned. He'd been past it for years. 'Look,' he said to Gershwin, showing him a photograph of it all shrivelled up.

'You could do with a trim,' said Gershwin. 'It looks like Groucho Marx.'

Suddenly there came a Gentille knocking on the factory door and in came a Gentile woman with one "L" short. 'I'm looking for a Bechstein,' she said.

'I'm sorry, we only sell Rastafarian saxophones,' said McGonagall.

'But it says outside pianos for sale,' said the Gentile.

'Oh yes, outside they're selling pianos,' said McGonagall. 'But inside it's Rastafarian saxophones.'

'But, man, there are no pianos outside,' said the Gentille Gentile woman.

'Och, then we've sold out,' said McGonagall. 'I tell you what, the 74 tram goes right past the door.'

As he spoke, a 74 tram went right past the door, bearing out his prophecy.

'Good heavens, can you tell the future?' said the Gentile woman.

'Yes,' said McGonagall. 'What would you like me to tell it?'

'I'd like you to tell my husband that I won't be in till eight this evening.'

McGonagall turned and faced the future, and said to it, 'Your wife won't be home until eight o'clock tonight.' He then turned and faced the present and said, 'That'll be a pound.'

'I haven't got a pound,' she said. 'I've only got a fiver. Can you change it?'

McGonagall took it and tried to change it, but it stayed exactly as it was. He then turned and faced the future and said to the woman, 'I owe you four pounds. Can you come back tomorrow?'

'I can't come back tomorrow,' said the woman.

'Well, that's all right by me,' said McGonagall.

Two days passed with not a single Rastafarian in sight.

'If a single Rastafarian doesn't turn up soon, he won't,' said McGonagall. 'I'd better go outside and tout for Rastafarians.' He went outside and touted. He touted all that day, and into the night. He started touting early in bed. There was a knock at the door and in came a touted Rastafarian. 'Hello dere?' he said.

'Hello where?' said Gershwin. 'Make up your mind.'

'Have you the price of a saxophone?' said McGonagall.

'No, but I'm having de price of two eggs and chips.'

'Business is business,' said McGonagall, and in a flash cooked two eggs and chips and placed them before the steaming Rastafarian and chips.

'What about saxophones?' said the worried Gershwin.

'Oh, it's goin' to be a bad year for them,' said McGonagall, posting off a bankruptcy notice to the Gentille Gentile woman, who was in for a nasty shock the following morning.

The following morning, she came into her husband's room with a nasty shock.

'What's all this about you and saxophones?' said the husband.

'I was trying to buy one for you,' she said, 'hoping you'd become a Rastafarian with a big one.'

'But,' said the husband, hopping around, 'I'm the wrong colour for one of them.'

'Yes,' she said, 'but you're the right height for that colour.'

A mile away, Gershwin and McGonagall had decided to have a lunch break. They broke into a pub. 'Look here,' said the bucolic North Country landlord with pronounced sideboards.

'Och, how do you pronounce sideboards?' said McGonagall, pocketing a scotch egg.

'I pronounce them mine,' said the landlord, making sure they were there. And they were there. 'Listen, lad,' said the North Country landlord. 'I'll spin thee a riddle.' Which went like this: 'Put that scotch egg back.'

So McGonagall put the scotch egg further back. 'Are ye satisfied now?' he said.

'Take no notice of him,' said Gershwin. 'He's mad.'

So the North Country sideboarded landlord took no notice of him because he was mad.

'Do you know what this is?' said McGonagall, holding up the Gentille Gentile lady's five-pound note, whose husband at that moment was hopping around the room in the wrong colour.

The sideboarded North Country landlord raised his finger. 'Five pounds, that's the going rate,' he said.

'Good,' said McGonagall, 'give us five pounds and we'll go.'

The landlord with the sideboards and cupboards handed the currency across.

Scotching a pocket egg, our two heroes along with McGonagall and Gershwin backed out of the door where they were run over by a 69 bus.

'What are you doing under there?' said a cross-eyed Irish conductor, looking both ways at once.

'We're having an accident,' said McGonagall.

'Begorra and Bejabers and Stage Irish and you're not having it under my bus' – and drove off in two directions.

'Did you hear that, he thought we were having it under his bus?' said Gershwin.

'That's the last place I'd have it,' said McGonagall.

'You're right,' said Gershwin. 'That was the last place you had it. I remember her well, I pushed her down it.'

'What are you two men doing lying in the road?' said a constable.

'We're not quite sure,' said McGonagall. 'We were an accident, but it seems to have passed off.'

'Yea,' said Gershwin, 'you've caught us on the hop, very much like the husband of the Gentille Gentile lady.'

'Do you mean Dick Squandle the Rastafarian?' said the policeman.

'No, I mean the husband of that Gentille Gentile lady,' said Gershwin.

'We'd better get up,' said McGonagall. 'There'll be another bus along in a minute.'

So they got up and another bus came along in a minute.

'What did I tell you?' said McGonagall.

'You told me to get up because another bus would come along in a minute, and it did. I don't know how you do it.'

'How do I do what?' said McGonagall.

'How do you tell when a bus is coming along in a minute?' said Gershwin.

'Have you both finished?' said the policeman.

'I have both finished,' said McGonagall.

'And so have I both finished,' said Gershwin.

'If you're not careful, I'll run all four of you in,' said the policeman.

194

'The four of me or the four of him?' said McGonagall.

'All eight of you,' said the policeman.

'Will we be up before the beak?' said McGonagall.

'There are no chickens in the police,' said the constable. 'What are you talking about?'

'I was talking about thirty seconds,' said McGonagall, 'but I didn't have a stop-watch on it.'

'That's enough of your lip,' said the policeman. 'It's also enough of your nose, ears and teeth.'

'If you must know,' said McGonagall, 'I've had enough of them as well and you're lucky, you can walk away from them. I can't.'

'I see. Just as a matter of interest,' the policeman said, displaying his truncheon, 'do you pick your nose?'

'No, if I did, I'd have picked a better one than this.'

'No hard feelings?' said the policeman.

'No, not for quite a few years now,' said McGonagall sadly.

'Let this be a lesson to you,' said the policeman, poking McGonagall in the chest with his displaying truncheon.

It was the end of a long friendship with the police.

The phone rang.

'My God, it's the phone,' said McGonagall, running four miles to answer it. 'It could be work.'

'No, no, it's the phone,' said Gershwin. 'If it was work it would sound entirely different.'

McGonagall picked up the handset. 'Hello, this is William Topaz McGonagall, poet and tragedian, actor, holder of the Burmese Order of the White Elephant.'

'Sorry, wrong number,' said a voice.

'It's not a wrong number,' said McGonagall. 'I've had this number for years and it's always been right.'

'Well, that's funny,' said the voice. 'I was dialling the Bromley Maternity Hospital.'

'Ah,' said McGonagall, 'then *you* have the wrong number and *I* haven't.'

'Are you sure that's not the Bromley Maternity Hospital?' said the voice.

So McGonagall made sure that it wasn't the Bromley Maternity Hospital.

'Are you expecting a child?' said McGonagall.

'No,' said the voice, 'I was expecting the Bromley Maternity Hospital.'

195

'This is no way to write *Porgy and Bess*,' said Gershwishin, removing one shoe and lying on the floor in the phoetal position.

'Do you mean foetal with an "F" or phoetal with a "P"?' said McGonagall.

'Neither,' said Gershwin. 'I mean *Porgy and Bess* with a "P" and a "B".'

'Look, George,' said William Topaz McGonagall, poet and tragedian, actor and holder of the Burmese Order of the White Elephant and Bromley Maternity Hospital.

So Gershwin looked, and saw William Topaz McGonagall, poet, tragedian, actor and holder of the Burmese Order of the White Elephant and Bromley Maternity Hospital and occasionally the White-eared Elephant.

'Very good,' said Gershwin, who had never seen it done before.

'Och, George,' said McGonagall, 'Gie us a tune on your old piano, lad.'

'All right,' said Gershwin, and sat down to his old piano, lad. 'What would you like to hear?' said Gersh.

'I'd like to hear the traffic in Lewisham.'

So Gershwin plunged into the keyboard filling the room with sound of traffic while McGonagall plunged into a wild Highland fling. There was a knock at the door. It opened to reveal the landlady.

'You're disturbing the neighbours,' she cried, and threw a rock at them.

'Thank you for telling us,' cried McGonagall and with great Scottish gallantry he bowed low and butted her in the guts.

'Sacre bleu,' she said, 'vous avez 'urled moi down les stairs encore.'

It must surely baffle the reader as to why Mrs Windust the Cockney landlady should lapse into the French linguidge.

After about half an hour her husband appeared. 'Excusez-moi,' he said in fluent Cockney. 'Are you ze man who 'urled my femme down ze apples and stairs?'

'McOui, McOui,' said the Scot.

'Thank you very much,' said the landlord, shaking McGonagall by the hand. 'Thank you,' he said again, the tears rolling down his cheeks on to his shirt, then disappearing inside to lodge in his underpants and then escaping as steam through his pockets. 'You have my everlasting gratitude, your rent will be reduced, but I will be sending her up again tomorrow.'

'Don't worry,' said McGonagall. 'I've been sent up quite a few times myself.'

'Oh, so that's how you got here. I knew it wasn't the stairs,' said the landlord.

Gershwin thundered on at the piano. Music filled the room among other things, some too terrible to mention.

'What's that he's playing?' said the landlord.

'It's a piano, can ye no recognise it?' said McGonagall.

'I recognise it,' said the landlord, and recognised it.

Just then the phone rang. McGonagall picked up the receiver in complete confidence. 'Hello,' he said. 'Congratulations, your wife's just given birth to an eight-pound baby boy.'

'Good heavens,' said a surprised voice, 'is that the Bromley Maternity Hospital?'

'No, I used to be but now I'm just a wrong number,' he said, and hung up with confidence.

'There,' said George McGershwishin, finishing his traffic in Lewisham and other things too terrible to mention. 'What did you think of it?' said Gersh.

'At my age I never think of it,' said McGonagall, making a certain gesture and yet again the White-eared Elephant.

Gershwin was aghast with aghastness. 'I don't believe it,' he said, staggering back. 'You told me you were brought up by the nuns.'

'Och aye,' said the Scot, 'I was brought up by the nuns and brought down by Mrs Doris Shaggs when I was sixteen.'

'Ah, but you don't look a day over seventy,' said Gershwin.

'Och, it's no the days, it's the nights,' said McGonagall.

'I see, so you're on nights now,' said Gershwin.

'There's been a change of government and a revolution in the Middle East and I am forced to increase your rent,' said the landlord.

'Who's forcing you?' said McGonagall. 'It can't be us, we're the ones trying to force it down.'

So the afternoon was spent with the landlord forcing the rent up while McGonagall forced it down. By teatime, it went from £110 a week to 50p in one direction and from 50p to £110 in the other direction. Suddenly when the rent was at its lowest,

McGonagall called a halt and threatened the landlord.

'Remember, we've got the negatives,' he said.

The landlord blanched white. 'Oh my God, if ever my wife saw them.'

'We've got to get rid of him,' said McGonagall, and got rid of him.

The phone rang. McGonagall answered it. A voice spoke to him.

'Congratulations,' it said, 'your wife has just given birth to an eight-pound baby boy.'

'Eight-pound baby boy?' said McGonagall. 'There must be some mistake.'

'Just a minute,' said the voice. 'No, there's no mistake, we've weighed him again and it definitely is an eight-pound baby boy.'

'Just a minute,' said McGonagall. 'Who do you think you're speaking to,' said the wily Scot.

'I think I'm speaking to you,' said the wily voice. 'Who do you think I'm speaking to?'

'I think you're speaking to me,' said McGonagall. 'Why?'

'We're trying to ascertain the parentage of this child,' said the voice.

'Well, good luck with your search and a Merry Christmas,' said McGonagall.

'A Merry Christmas?' said the voice. 'But this is only July.'

'Och, I never wait till the last minute, and a Happy New Year as well. And while I'm on the phone, a Happy Easter and Hogmanay and goodbye' – and hung up.

'Och, we all have our hang-ups,' said McGonagall, hanging it up.

'Oh, this is no way to write *Porgy and Bess*,' said George Gershwishin, putting on his pyjamas.

'Och, you can shoot an elephant in those,' said McGonagall. 'And furthermore, a gude night's sleep will do ye a power of gude.'

'Oy vay,' said George Gershwin. 'The trouble with that is when you're asleep you don't know that.'

'Och, then try sleeping awake,' said McGonagall, 'and see how that goes down.'

After half an hour, Gershwin said, 'It's not going down very well with me.'

'Ah, George, laddie, come here,' said McGonagall. 'And let me rock you to sleep,' he said, dropping a rock on his head.

It was the end of another hard Rastafarian saxophone day with brown music and things too terrible to mention.

Morning came.

'Are you still asleep?' said McGonagall to Gershwin.

'Are you mad?' countered Gershwin. 'Do you think I'd be sitting here eating eggs, bacon, two slices of toast, lightly done, spread with Olio margarine and a cup of coffee if I was still asleep?'

'Then why have ye got yer pyjamas on?' countered McGonagall as he started to transfer Gershwin's breakfast to his own plate during the pause.

'Well, I was going out shooting elephants,' said Gershwin, scooping his breakfast back again.

'Good God,' said McGonagall, looking at the empty plate, 'I appear to have finished.'

'Yes, you have a fine finish,' said Gershwin. 'I thought it was french polish' – and french polished off the breakfast.

'I'd no idea you could eat in Parisian,' said McGonagall. 'Eight weeks, four days, three hours, twenty seconds,' said McGonagall holding up his EPNS soup spoon and checking his watch on Gershwin's wrist. 'I must be nearing a record,' he said. 'Hello,' he said down the phone, 'is that the *Guinness Book of Records*?'

'No, actually it's the *Dx Record Book of Guinnesses*,' said a drunken Irish voice. 'Have you heard about the Irishman and the sack of unripe tomatoes?' said the voice.

'No,' said McGonagall enthusiastically.

'Well, that makes two of us,' said the Irish voice and was sick.

'What are you doing for Christmas?' said McGonagall enthusiastically.

'I'm doing Arctic Queen in the St Leger, what are you doing?' said the voice.

'I'm doing Mrs Ethel Terrible in the back room at 10 to 1,' said McGonagall.

'Is that a race?' said the voice.

'No,' said McGonagall, 'but you have to be quick, her husband's due back at ten past.'

Gershwin came in with a smoking elephant gun in his pyjamas. 'Yow,' he screamed as it burnt his balls. 'I've just shot an elephant,' he added.

'You fool of a pianist,' said McGonagall. 'There are nae elephants in England.'

'Not any more, there aren't,' said Gershwin, pouring cold water on them and giving a sigh of relief as they hissed and steamed.

McGonagall looked at his notebook. 'Just as I thought,' he said. 'I've got a boil coming.'

'Well, let me know when it arrives,' said Gershwin. 'I'll get the polaroid ready.'

'Och,' said McGonagall, 'are ye going to take a photograph?'

'No,' said Gershwin, 'I'm just getting the polaroid ready. I'm not going to shoot any more elephants, I'm just going to photograph them – they stay alive longer that way.'

'Ach, I think ma boil's going to start on ma knee,' said McGonagall.

'Well, they've got to start somewhere,' said Gershwin, going out to photograph an elephant in his pyjamas.

He came back. 'Look at this,' he said proudly, handing a photograph to McGonagall.

'There's nothing here,' said McGonagall, scrutinising the photograph with an intense scrute.

'Oh, he must have escaped,' said Gershwin. 'You see, you can never trust an elephant unless you shoot him.' He exited with his elephant gun and there was a loud explosion.

'Och, did you shoot another wee elephant in your pyjamas?' said McGonagall.

'No, I shot a bus conductor,' said Gershwin.

'Och, mon, bus conductors are nothing like elephants,' said McGonagall.

'Of course not,' said Gershwin in his pyjamas. 'They wouldn't have them on the buses if they were.'

There was a knock at the door. McGonagall opened it to reveal a magnificent postman, possibly the finest postman going at that time.

'Ah, Mr McGonagall,' said the magnificent postman.

'That's me,' said McGonagall, speaking from memory.

'Mr William McGonagall?' said the magnificent postman.

'Aye,' said McGonagall, referring to his birth certificate.

The magnificent postman continued. 'Mr William Topaz McGonagall?' he said. 'Of the Grand Order of the White Elephant?'

'Aye,' said McGonagall.

'Then there's fuck-all mail for you,' said the most magnificent postman in the world.

'I didn't know you had the Order of the White Elephant,' said Gershwin, taking aim.

'True. I didn't want you to go around shooting it in your pyjamas,' said McGonagall.

'There's a black-edged letter for you, Mr Gershwin,' said the magnificent postman.

'It must be bad news,' said Gershwin, hiding under the bed and colliding with a chambre de nuit. 'Will you read it for me?'

McGonagall refused to read the chambre de nuit, but opened the letter. 'It says: You swine of a man,' said McGonagall.

'Who's it from, Jamie?' said Gershwin.

'It's signed Elephant's Mother,' said McGonagall.

'Any answer?' said the magnificent postman.

'Yes, any answer,' said McGonagall, and slammed the door. On second thoughts he opened it to let the magnificent postman out.

'You could have timed that better,' said the departing magnificent postman. He was back in a second. 'My God,' he said, 'there's an angry elephant's mother outside.'

It was a tricky situation. Let us recap on the scene.

McGonagall is leaning well forward on the balls of his feet peering through the letter-box. The magnificent postman stands behind him, back on his heels with a sack of Christmas goodies pulling heavily on his energies. Gershwin is in the supine position adjacent to the chambre de nuit and getting the full benefit of it in his pyjamas. It is a picture that must be etched in the reader's mind, while the two authors wrack their minds as to how to get out of this situation.

CHAPTER 64

Artistic gentlemen need nude model to assist in their work.
Apply 36 Grotters Terrace, Lewisham

A Miss Muriel Body read and reread the article in the news-agent's window. An hour later she was knocking on their door. She was very good with knockers. Their knocker was out of order, but hers were in perfect condition.

'There's a cheque in the post,' hissed a Scottish voice through the letter-box and directly at her groins. The hot haggis breath agitated her vacant areas.

Miss Body blushed. 'Are you a squatter?' she enquired.

'Nay, I do it standing up,' replied McGonagall.

'Thank God for that,' said Miss Body with a sigh of relief.

'My, you're a fine-looking woman,' said the pair of red Scottish eyes through the letter-box again at her groins. 'What have you come about?' said the Scottish letter-box.

'I've come about six miles,' said Miss Body.

'Who are you?' said the red-eyed Scottish letter-box.

'I'm the model lassie,' she said.

'Och, lassie, but ye've got your claes on,' said the Scottish voice now at the keyhole, a distinct improvement in social relations.

'Yes, but I'm nude underneath,' said Miss Body.

'Then the job is yours, lassie,' said McGonagall, opening the door. 'Now come in and take your claes off. The moment you're nude we'll start talking terms.'

'Now,' said the naked Miss Body, 'I want six pounds an hour.'

'That's not what I want,' said McGonagall, reloading the camera. 'What I want is for you to want 50p an hour.'

'That's not much,' said Miss Body.

'I know. That's why I want it,' said McGonagall on the verge of doing the White-eared Elephant.

'For God's sake, don't,' said Gershwin, appearing from under the bed and knocking it over.

McGonagall carefully posed Miss Body on a rostrum. He spent the rest of the afternoon adjusting her and it. Then, without taking his eyes off her, he wrote to his bank manager. Then, without taking his eyes off her, he wrote to his dear old mother in Scotland. He then readjusted her nose and, without taking his eyes off her, wrote to his cousin Macbeth in Glenfiddich. Some of it he wrote in English. And, without taking his eyes off her, he cooked dinner and then, without taking his eyes off her, he went to bed.

'Well, that's all for today. Same time tomorrow, Miss Body,' said McGonagall, not taking his eyes off her.

'I didn't notice you doing any drawing or painting,' said Miss Body.

'No,' said McGonagall from beneath the blankets. 'I always spend the first two or three days concentrating on the outlines and the shapes. It's the same technique as used by Michelangelo.'

'Who's he?' said Miss Body, putting on her knickers.

'He's Michelangelo,' said McGonagall.

'Oh,' she said, ladling them both in. 'They're both the same person, how interesting.'

'Yes,' said McGonagall. 'Both yours are interesting, too. Do you need any help?'

'No, I have a help, she comes every Monday morning,' she said. Now fully dressed, she enquired, 'Are you going to settle up?'

'No,' said McGonagall, pulling the blankets round him. 'I'm going to settle down. And it's good night.'

At that very moment on the Majuba Hill in Africa, 30,000 Zulus under Shaka Zulu stormed the gates of the British square of eight men.

'Keep firing, men,' said the sergeant. 'Under the circumstances there is little else we can do.'

'Biya tye,' said 31,000 Zulus now charging down Majuba Hill towards the eight British soldiers who were firing in the general direction.

McGonagall slept on. Another 34,000,000 Zulus came round the back and attacked the square from the rear. 'Rapid fire,' said the sergeant. Another 10,000,000 Zulus came down the west flank. 'Death to the white man,' shouted Shaka Zulu from a tree.

McGonagall slept on as another 10,000,000 Zulus charged the

east side of the square. The British rifles spat fire. 'Fix bayonets,' shouted the sergeant at the little British square. Time and again the billions of Zulus charged the little British square. And like Harley Street doctors they went on charging. So rapid was the rapid fire from the British square that the Zulus were thrown back. 'Cease fire,' said the sergeant as the 10,000,000,000,000 Zulus reformed for another attack. The noise was deafening, but despite it McGonagall in Lewisham didn't hear a single sound.

'I think you'd better go,' said Gershwin to Miss Body. 'Your employer is in a deep, deep sleep.'

'I'm waiting for the money,' said Miss Body.

'That's what he's waiting for as well,' said Gershwin.

'Here they come again,' said the sergeant as thirty billion Zulus thundered down on them. 'Don't waste a bullet, lads,' said the sergeant, giving them one round each. 'Come back when you want some more.'

'I don't see how he could sleep through all that,' said Miss Body. 'How can you stand by and see all those British soldiers get massacred in Africa?'

A million assegais flew through the sky, some of them landing close to McGonagall's bed.

'I'm not staying here,' said Miss Body. 'It's bloody dangerous.' So saying, she fought her way out through a mass of screaming Zulus to a number 9 bus.

'Cor, struth,' said the conductor, pulling her from the jaws of death. 'It's almost as bad as Brixton' – pulling the spears out of the bodywork. 'I don't know what this country's coming to,' he said as they were chased down the street by 10,000 Zulus.

The little British square had now been condensed into a cube as another ten billion Zulus parachuted in on top of them.

'Who's making that noise?' said McGonagall, still half asleep.

'Don't bother,' said Gershwin, 'it's only ten billion Zulus attacking a British cube at Rovark's Drift.'

But the ten billion Zulus were no match for the eight British soldiers who drove them back to Brixton and they in turn drove buses.

McGonagall slept through all this and dreamt that the book was finished. So until then the book is finished. God save the Queen and her money.